TIT

MW01233729

Book 1 of the Tennessee Tinys series

By Gary E. Reavis, Sr.

TO: BREE

I Hope You Like my Tinys

Gary E. Reavis Sr.

2024

Special Thanks:
To my Lord and Savior who guides me daily.

To my wonderful family and friends for their support, help and encouragement.

Herb Hamilton my brother whose talent at painting pictures with words helped smooth out some of the rough spots.

Artist Ariel Caceres - For Drawing the five Tiny scenes.

Artist and my son Bryan Reavis - Drawing of the Tiny's Village.

Graphic Designer Nate Saenz - Help with Cover Design.

Advance Imaging - Jamestown, TN. - Final Cover Design.

Ariel and Danielle Thompson - two wonderful young ladies, for reading and editing suggestions.

Editor Diane Lee - An answer to my prayers! I cannot thank you enough for your time and extreme effort in not only edit but teaching me as well.

1

Tinys
Chapter 1
Grandfather's Trouble

Mrs. Morris's history class at Warren White Academy is packed with restless juniors not the least bit interested in world history. Conor O'Brien is one such junior. As Mrs. Morris lectures on and on about the Huns or the Romans or some other ancient civilization, Conor wishes his life was more exciting.

He is busy daydreaming about being a secret spy when his best friend, Brittany, kicks the back of his chair. Conor looks up to find his teacher glaring at him!

"It is evident, Conor, that Alexander the Great does not hold your attention. It appears you're needed in the office. I'll deal with you on Monday." Since Mrs. Morris never jokes around about history, Conor is glad to have an excuse to leave.

Just as he stands to leave, the bell rings, and the rest of the class files out behind him. Brittany runs to catch up to him. "Boy, you're in for it Monday," she teases. "Where were you, anyway? You didn't even hear them call you over the intercom."

Conor just shrugs. "Daydreaming, I guess; that class is so boring."

"Well, I like history. I think it's interesting," she says.

"Yeah, you would -- you're such a bookworm," he says, giving her a friendly shove. She heads to her next class and he starts down the stairs to the office.

* * * * *

When Conor transferred from his public school in Tennessee to the Warren White Academy, a private boarding school in Los Angeles, he felt everyone thought he was a hick or hillbilly. Brittany was the only student who talked to him – maybe because she, too, had come from Tennessee. They have a few classes together, and over the past months had become good friends.

Brittany is 17 years old, 5 feet 2 inches tall. She liked to wear many layers of colorful apparel. Her long, dark brown hair is always worn in a ponytail that swings from side to side when she walks, and she wears stylish wide-rimmed glasses to match

3

the color of her hair. She's very smart and among the top of her class; her positive attitude about things is different from many kids her age. Brittany's dad was a Marine captain who died while fighting in the hills of Afghanistan and she misses him terribly. The school in Los Angeles is one of the best schools in the country, and she finds it challenging. Brittany likes the school, but she and her mom miss each other terribly. Being an only child and with her mother working all the time, they both had agreed a private school would be best.

Changing schools in the middle of the year had been hard for Conor, especially since he didn't understand why his grandfather had insisted he go to a school across the country in California. He really misses Tennessee and his friends back home.

His grandparents had become extremely protective of him after he lost both of his parents in a plane crash. Conor is their grandchild and only-living relative. He loves his grandma and grandpa very much, so he didn't put up much of a fuss over the move. His grandpa told him getting a scholarship to Warren White is quite rare. Conor is pleased he had received one, but he is also required to work. At first he didn't understand why he needed to work after school, but he soon realized it must be to help pay for his room and meals; besides, cleaning the cafeteria when other students are not around, really isn't all that bad. It has taken awhile, but now he is settling in and has made a few friends.

At 17, just shy of 6 feet tall with a movie-star smile, bright blue eyes, and dark-red wavy hair, Conor has grown into a handsome young man. His favorite form of dress is blue jeans, T-shirts, and Keds. He keeps his hair short and combed, at least some of the time.

Even though he likes most sports, he never seems to find time for them. When he's not doing homework or working in the cafeteria, he spends his spare time playing on his computer, watching spy movies, or dreaming up new computer games and high tech gadgets.

* * * * *

Reaching the first floor, he walks down the hall to the

4

principal's office. As he approaches the receptionist's desk, he notices her talking to one of the students. The student on desk duty today is a cute blonde, 5-foot-4, and one look at her beautiful smile would brighten anyone's day. But when she sees Conor, the smile that was there a moment before disappears.

"Hi, Conor. A messenger just brought this message for you." As she hands him the envelope, she asks, "Why didn't they just call or text you?"

"My grandparents are not really tech savvy; they're a bit old-fashioned."

"I hope it's not bad news," she said, biting her lower lip.

Conor opens the envelope slowly, hoping the same thing. Worry etches his face as he reads the few words: *"Family emergency -- come home right away! Grandpa."*

Feeling like his heart is in his throat, he reads the words again. Turning to the receptionist, he says, "I need to see Mr. Dougherty right now!"

She points to the principal's door. "Knock; he's by himself." Conor knocks.

"Come in" is the reply from the other side of the door.

He opens the door and steps into the lavish office he's only been in once before in the months he has attended the school. Crossing the room, he stands in front of the principal's desk. Dougherty, who is reading some papers, looks up; "Well, what is it?" he says with a scowl. Dougherty is well over 50, short, with a receding hairline that leaves the top of his head completely bald except for a little tuft of hair just above his forehead. When he scowls, the jowls on each side of his face puff out; it always reminds Conor of a bulldog. Conor clears his throat, "Sir, a messenger just brought this --"

"A messenger? Who uses messengers these days?" Dougherty interrupts. "Who's it from?"

"It's from my grandpa, um...my grandfather," Conor corrects himself and continues. "The message says there's been a family emergency and for me to come home right away."

"Home? Where is this again?" Dougherty asks.

"Tennessee," Conor answers.

Dougherty raises his voice angrily, "Is this some kind of a joke? Why didn't he just call?"

5

"They live off-the-beaten-path, in a secluded area, and they're not up on new things," Conor says, trying to control his own temper. "That's why the messenger."

Dougherty stares at him, the muscles in his jaw twitching, "This better not be some kind of prank just to get out of school for a day or two."

"No, sir," Conor answers. As he leaves the office, he wants to slam the door. *"What a jerk,"* he thinks to himself. Then his mind goes back to the telegram, wondering what can be so wrong that he needs to rush home?

6

Chapter 2
Graybeard

Conor is able to catch a late flight from Las Angles (LA) to Nashville. As the 757 heads for Tennessee, he sits looking out the window, wondering and worrying what this is all about. His grandfather would never ask him to leave school and rush home like this unless he or Grandma was very sick or dying. This might be anything; he just doesn't know.

"I hope and pray they're all right; they're all I have, now that Mom and Dad are gone."

Thinking back, he remembers the only other time he had received an urgent message at school. The small plane his dad owned had disappeared from radar somewhere over Nevada. His parents were on their way out to California to visit some friends. The search had taken two days, ending when the wreckage was found, with no survivors. His heart feels heavy as he thinks of that day and how much he misses them. Now, only a year later, something is wrong with his grandparents! The tears run down his face as he sits alone, looking out into a dark and empty sky.

"God, please take care of Grandpa and Grandma!"

* * * * *

As the plane lands in Nashville at 6:00 in the morning, Conor rechecks the note in his travel packet that was waiting for him at the ticket counter in LA. The note said a car and driver would be waiting for him at baggage pickup. To be safe, Conor is to ask the driver how long he had been waiting. The correct answer would be "Since around 5:15."

When Conor finally gets his luggage, someone calls his name.

Turning around, Conor sees a man coming over to him. "Mr. O'Brien, my name is Ed Barns; your grandfather sent me. I will be your driver. I've been instructed to drive you to your grandparents' house and wait."

Conor, remembering his grandpa's instructions, "Oh, hi, Mr., eh.. ?"

"Barns, Ed Barns," the stranger repeats.

7

"Mr. Barns, have you been waiting long?"

"Not very long, I got here a little early -- I think it was around 5:15."

Hearing the correct answer and considering it safe, they start to the car. Along the way, Mr. Barns explains, "Conor, I work for your grandfather."

"My grandfather? Doing what?"

"Let's just say I've been assigned to assist your grandfather and you."

"Assist? I don't understand."

"I believe it best if your grandfather does the explaining."

Reaching the car, Conor yawns as he climbs into the back seat ready for the long ride to his grandparents' house.

As they merge onto Highway 40 out of Nashville, Ed checks in the rearview mirror to find a very tired young man fast asleep.

One hour and 45 minutes later, the car pulls into the driveway.

Ed announces, "Mr. O'Brien, we have arrived."

As they stop in front of the house, Conor sees Grandpa standing on the front porch.

He leaps out of the car, only to find his grandpa smiling at him.

"Hey, Conor -- sure is good to see you. How was your trip?"

Conor is the spitting image of his grandfather. Just tag on 50 years, turn his dark-red hair to white, and add a mustache and beard. Grandfather stands tall and straight for a man in his early 70s, and has a smile that's contagious. He is wearing what he almost always wears, a flannel shirt and bib overalls that always look clean and pressed.

"Grandpa, are you okay?" Conor asks, jumping up the steps. "Where's Grandma? Is she okay? I got here as quick as I could. What's happened? You said emergency! Is she sick?"

"Whoa, easy there, Grandson!" Grandpa says, putting his hand on his grandson's shoulder. "We're all okay."

"Where's Grandma?"

"She's in the kitchen, cooking up breakfast; bacon, eggs, homemade biscuits, and gravy. All the things you like."

"Breakfast!" Conor half yells, "Your message said this was an emergency! My principal thinks this is an emergency!"

8

"Well, this is an emergency, a life-changing emergency, and your principal can think whatever he wants. You can finish school here."

Conor is totally confused. "You're both okay, and I need to change schools again? Grandpa, what's going on?"

His grandfather pulls him to his side and hugs him, then turns him to the front door, "Let's go to the kitchen, and we will explain everything." Before going inside, Grandpa nods to Mr. Barns. "Come on in, Ed, and get some breakfast. This is going to take a while."

Entering the kitchen, Conor's nose is overcome by the heavenly smells of the morning feast being prepared. Upon seeing Conor, Grandma wipes her hands on her apron and wraps her arms around his neck, giving him a hug and kiss on the cheek.

"Honey, I'm so glad you're here," she whispers. The past 66 years have been kind to his grandmother. Oh, she has gained a little weight, and her once-blond hair has turned silver, but she carries herself well, and the twinkle in her eyes is still there. She always makes him feel like this is home.

Grandpa, Ed, and Conor take a seat at the breakfast nook. Before Conor can say a word, Grandma hands Ed a cup of coffee and Conor hot coco. "Thanks," he manages to get out before Grandpa starts talking.

"Well, Conor, it's like this. We were hoping to wait a little longer to give you more time, but the accident with your folks has changed things."

"Changed things? What things?"

Grandpa frowns as he looks at him, "It's just..." he pauses with a sigh. "Well, we're getting too old to take care of the Tinys anymore."

Conor sits silently for a moment and then asks, "The little what?"

"No, not the little what -- the Tinys!" replies Grandpa.

"What?" Conor is still puzzled.

"Huh?"

"Okay. What small things?" Conor asks his grandfather.

"Small things?"

"Well, you said you're getting too old to take care of a small

9

something or other."

"I didn't say small, I said Tinys!" Grandpa responds.

"Okay, and I said a tiny what?"

"Well, you know, the Wee Folk," Grandpa tries to explain.

"The wee folk? What are wee folk?"

"The Tinys."

"Huh?"

Grandma, shaking her head, sits down next to Conor and takes his hand. She looks over at her husband of 47 years, "Let me try and explain it to him, Dear. You see, Conor, our family, going back four generations, has had a secret task to perform: to watch over some very special friends. Your grandpa and I have been the guardians now for more than 40 years, and your father was to take over this year. But now that he's gone, it...well, it has fallen to you to take charge."

With the last few words, tears form in her eyes, and she starts to weep.

Conor put his arm around her, "Grandma, it's going be okay. I don't know what you two are talking about, but I'm sure it will be all right."

Just then a small voice is heard coming from the counter top just behind Grandpa's head.

"Maybe I should explain things to him."

Conor looks from Grandpa to Grandma, then back to Grandpa, wondering where the voice is coming from. Then, from behind the cookie jar, comes the smallest man Conor has ever seen: a tiny, little man no more than 12 inches tall, with shoulder-length, wavy gray hair, and a beard flowing down to his chest. He has dark-green eyes and a friendly smile and is wearing a forest-green jacket, brown pants, and a floppy hat.

10

Conor sits there stunned, as the tiny man walks across the counter to the edge, leans on Grandpa's shoulder, crosses his legs, and stands there smiling. He looks at Grandpa, and they exchange winks!

"Conor," Grandpa announces, "I would like to introduce you to my old and dear friend, Mr. Daniel O' Doul, known to all as Graybeard."

Mouth and eyes wide open, Conor continues to stare, wordlessly. Grandma nudges Conor with her elbow, "Mind your manners, Dear."

Looking at her, then to Grandpa, then to Graybeard, Conor tries to speak, "Whoa...you said...I mean...whoa...tiny...I thought..."

"Conor, calm down and say hi." His Grandma instructs.

Conor looks again at Grandpa and then Graybeard, "I'm so sorry. Hi. I mean it's just so...weird. Wow!"

Graybeard chuckles, "That's okay, Lad; we do take a bit of getting used to, I suppose."

Then the little man turns and points at Grandpa's shoulder, "Grandpa, if I may?"

"Be my guest," Grandpa replies with a smile as he watches Conor's face.

The tiny man climbs up on Grandpa's shoulder and slides

11

down his arm to the tabletop, walks over to look up at Conor, and extends his hand. "I'm very glad to meet you, Conor O'Brien, the Fifth."

Conor reaches across the table and takes the little hand between his thumb and forefinger and gently shakes it.

"I'm glad to meet you, Sir. This is really something. You've got to be the smallest man in the world! Oh! Sorry. I meant no offense by calling you small."

"None taken, Lad. Actually, I'm quite tall among my people," Graybeard replies.

"Your **people**! How many of you are there?"

"First things first, my young friend. I'm not offended when you refer to us as small or little. We call ourselves Tinys, and we call you folks Bigs. Now to answer your question, there are 402 of us here in Tennessee. About 45 are children; they, of course, are smaller than me." Graybeard says as he chuckles at his remark.

Conor thinks for a moment, and then says, "You said in Tennessee -- there are more of you somewhere else?"

Graybeard looks up at Grandpa, who nods his head. "Yes, we assume there are about 200 or so still in Ireland."

"Ireland!" exclaims Conor. Then he slowly asks, "You're not.... leprechauns, are you?"

"Well, no. No, we are not leprechauns, everyone knows there's no such thing as a leprechaun," he remarks with a twinkle in his eye.

Conor shakes his head. "I can't believe I asked that. But how is this possible? Where did you come from? How and where do you live? I have so many questions."

Graybeard smiles, takes his hat off, reaches up, and scratches his head, "The **how** we came to be will be told at the Telling tomorrow. As for **where** we live, it's not far from here, in the woods. We survive by growing some of our own food, but your grandparents supply most of our needs. You see, Conor, we cannot live in your world as you do. We would be put on display or become the attraction of the media or scientists or the government. In the past, unscrupulous people have mistreated our people, and so we must not be exposed to the world outside. After all, we are just plain, God-fearing folks, like you, with a

12

few small drawbacks." He chuckles at his play on words.

Conor pauses for a moment, and then, "You said something about a Telling. What is that?"

Grandpa breaks in with, "That's tomorrow, and it will explain a lot more, but for now we need to eat and get back to Nashville and meet with Janet at her office."

"Yes, I must be getting back to the village," Graybeard adds. Then, turning to Conor, in a soft voice, "Lad, I know you must be really confused, but the next two days will clear everything up. Take it one step at a time, and I will see you tomorrow."

With that, Graybeard walks to the corner of the table and climbs over the edge, descending out of sight. Conor leans over and watches as the tiny man climbs down the table leg. All the years Conor has been coming to his grandparents' home, he had never noticed that the pattern carved into the wooden table legs made a perfect ladder for someone Graybeard's size.

When Graybeard reaches the floor, he tips his hat to Conor and walks behind the stove, where he disappears from sight. Conor turns and leans over still further and that's when he sees, for the first time, a small little door that, when closed, is almost invisible.

"Wow," is all he can say as he sits back up.

Grandpa smiles, adding, "You will start noticing a lot of things around here we modified to help them get around."

Conor sits in silence for a moment. Then finally he asks, "Grandpa, you said I need to change schools again. Why?"

Grandpa answers, "Well, you need to come back here, because you should be closer, now that you will be the Tinys' guardian. That is, I hope you will be." The older O'Brien stops talking as it hits him, *What will we do if our grandson refuses to take over? I never even thought he might not be **able** to or even **want** to."*

Looking at his grandson, he says, "Conor, I'm afraid we just assumed you would do this, but we don't want you to think you **have** to. It's true; in the past when it came time for another O'Brien to take over, each has gladly taken up the task. But that doesn't mean **you** must."

"Well, I believe I want to, Grandpa. It... it just, it's just... I'll miss my new friends, that's all."

13

"I know, and we are sorry to put you through this again, but it will be better if you live here with us."

"I guess I understand, but I just got settled at school. Hey, wait. How will I get to school? The school bus doesn't come clear out here. I rode -- I mean, used to ride -- the bus when we lived in our house in..." The memories of home and his mother and father suddenly fill his heart.

Grandpa, seeing Conor stop and tears starting to fill his eyes, tries to lighten things up,

"You're right; the bus doesn't come way out here. I guess we'll just have to buy you a car."

"A car! Wow, great! But wait, you and Grandma can't afford to be buying me a car, can you?"

"I'm pretty sure we can; we do have a little money." Both grandparents snicker. "The truth is, we have all the money we need, Grandson."

"I get it. Your leprechaun friends gave you a pot of gold!" Conor jokes.

"You could say they did, but in a roundabout way." You see, they arranged for your great-great-great-grandfather to get controlling interest in several very large companies -- like that Micro what's-its-name company you thought your dad worked for; we own that, along with about a half dozen other big companies. I don't know all the ins and outs myself, but that's why we need to meet Janet at her office and get you to sign some papers."

"Janet **who** and sign **what** papers?"

"Janet Cook. She's our lawyer, confidant, and the CEO of our company, and when you sign the papers, you will get complete control of Hawk Industries."

"Hawk Industries? That's one of the largest corporations in the US!" Conor almost yells. "How can...?"

"Well, you really won't have complete control until your 21st birthday, but you will have all the benefits and funds you will need to help keep the Tinys safe."

"Me and Hawk Industries?" Conor repeats.

"Yep," Grandpa grins. "You really must try and keep up, Grandson," he adds with a chuckle. Conor once again sits with his mouth wide open in total confusion.

14

Chapter 3
The Attorney

After saying goodbye to Grandma and her wishing them Godspeed, the two settle into the backseat of the town car for the return trip to Nashville. Grandpa tries to answer Conor's many questions about the Tinys, Janet, and Hawk Industries, but he always ends with, "After today and the Telling tomorrow, this will all make more sense."

"Is the lawyer aware of the Tinys?"

"Well, I trust Janet as much as I trust you. I told her about them, but she's never seen them," Grandpa then adds. "I figure she thinks I'm a little off in the head." He chuckles.

Conor sits quietly for a few moments, "Grandpa, I love and trust you and everything, but if what you say is going to happen at this lawyer's office today. I just wonder how in the world I can possibly handle anything as large as Hawk Industries. I'm still in high school; what do I know about running a company, let alone a huge corporation?"

His grandpa smiles, "Conor, how old are you?"

"I'm 17."

"And what have you learned about how to handle things in life?" Grandpa continues.

Conor mulls the question for a minute and then answers, "I've always tried to learn as much as I can, to put my trust in the Lord, and try to make the best decisions I can."

"That is how you are going to handle Hawk Industries. Besides, you still have a few years to learn the ropes before you need to take over, that is if you want to. As for me, when it became my turn, I decided to hire good people like Janet to do the day-to-day running of the company. You may choose to run things yourself, and if you do, I know Janet will be a good teacher."

It is just before noon when Ed turns into the parking structure of the large office building in downtown Nashville. A short walk to the private elevator and the ride up to the ninth floor brings them to the entrance of the office of Hawk Industries' CEO, J. L. Cook. As they enter, the receptionist smiles, pushes a

15

button on the intercom, and says, "Ms. Cook, they are here."

Seconds later, the door to her office opens to reveal one of the most beautiful women Conor has ever seen. She looks to him like she is maybe in her 30s and somehow, very familiar. She smiles and walks up to Grandpa and gives him a big hug, "Grandpa, it's so great to see you. As your personal attorney, I have all the forms prepared and ready for signing, as you requested."

She steps back, looks at young Conor and continues, "And you must be Conor the Fifth. I've heard so much about you, I feel like I've known you forever," as she shakes his hand.

"Please come in," she steps aside and then follows them into her office.

Waiting on the couch is Brittany.

"BRITTANY! What are YOU doing here?" Conor shouts.

"What are YOU doing here?" She asks as she jumps up.

"How... What's going on?" Conor questions.

"Mom had me fly in from LA last night and asked me to come with her to the office today. That's all I know!"

"She's your MOTHER?"

They both stop and turn to look at Janet and Grandpa, who are both grinning at them.

Janet is the first to speak. "We thought it was time for you two to find out a few things."

"What things?" Brittany asks.

Janet gestures to the couch and chairs. "Let's all sit down, and we will explain." When they are seated, she continues, "Conor, after you lost your parents, you became your grandparents' sole surviving heir. The O'Briens are the largest stockholders in Hawk Industries, which makes you heir to a very large fortune. It was your grandfather's wish that you change schools to better protect you."

"Protect me? From what?"

Grandpa answers, "I haven't told you before, but we don't believe your parents' plane crash was an accident!"

"WHAT?"

"We found evidence the fuel system had been sabotaged," Janet answers.

"But, who would do that? Dad and Mom never hurt anyone!

16

WHY?" Conor asks with tears in his eyes.

Grandpa comes over and puts his arm around his grandson. "We don't know who or why. We only know it was not an accident. That's why we sent you to the private school in Los Angeles where Brittany was attending. We did ask her to keep an eye on you, and we were both very pleased when you became friends"

Conor thinks about all this for a minute and then turns to Brittany and smiles. "So, you've been spying on me, huh?" he says with a big grin as he pokes her in the ribs.

She tries to wiggle away from him. "Yes! But you never did anything worth reporting back to Mom about. You lead such a dull life." She laughs.

He looks at her. "And this coming from the president of the Geek Club." Everyone laughs.

Conor reads and signs all the paperwork and security forms that give him access to Hawk's many company buildings and offices. Janet explains, "With your ID card, you are allowed to enter any building the company owns. Just remember, you must be accompanied at all times by an adult. Do you understand?"

"Sure. I have the run of the place as long as I'm on a leash."

"You shouldn't take it that way, Conor. We have many government projects at Hawk, and there are rules we all must follow," Janet points out.

"Sorry, I shouldn't have made a joke of it," Conor says.

"I apologize also. I'm afraid I take this job very seriously, maybe TOO seriously at times."

Janet hands him a list of all the companies owned by Hawk Industries:

- Micro Technologies.
- Hawk Aeronautics.
- Mason Toys.
- Reavis and Sons Commercial Construction.
- Morgan Metals.
- Hawk Oil and Gas.

Handing him a cell phone, she says, "This has my office, home, and cell numbers; you can reach me anytime, day or night. Conor, I love your grandfather and would do anything for him, and now my job is to help you. Oh, he's a bit strange," looking

17

over at Grandpa napping on the couch, "with his talking about little people and all, but I know he's a good man, and from what I've learned of you, it runs in the family."

"It sure does, Darling. Are y'all done yet?" asks Grandpa from the couch.

"You need to co-sign a few papers and then we are finished. By the way, Grandpa, I do have an idea on how we can keep the kids in school together -- if that's what they want?"

Both of the teenagers say, "Yes!"

"Okay; how about if we set up our very own private school right here at our headquarters. I've looked into hiring a great private teacher and what could be more secure? Brit and I have a large home and Conor can stay with us during the week and go home on the weekends. What do you two think?"

Brittany speaks up, "Wait a minute; you mean now? Let me get this straight. I have to change schools, too, and quit living in LA and move back in with my mom. Cool! I'd love to!"

"Hey! When Grandpa buys me a car, we can ride to school in style," Conor announces.

"A car! Do I get a car, too?" Brittany asks as she looks at her mom.

"We'll see," Janet answers. "So, how do you feel about that, Grandpa?"

"We might be able to work something out," he replies with a grin.

Conor, who has been unusually quiet, turns to Brittany, "How about you and I go talk for a minute?"

Brittany can see he has something he is concerned about, "Sure! Mom, we need to take a break."

Janet looks at Grandpa, who nods his head in approval.

The teens get up and leave Janet's office. They start walking, when Conor stops. Brittany looks at him questioningly.

The two are standing in the middle of the wide-open reception area -- with the secretaries' desks out in front of offices on both sides -- and the secretaries are all looking at them.

" I really want a Coke!" Conor says.

"Me, too, but we need an escort, remember!" Brittany whispers.

Brit looks around and then goes over to the nearest secretary,

18

"Excuse me. Would you mind escorting Mr. O'Brien and me to the cafeteria?"

The young woman smiles, "Mr. O'Brien? Of course, I will." She stands up, pauses, and continues, "May I ask what you are looking for, Mr. O'Brien?"

"Brittany and I want a cold drink and a quiet place to talk."

The young secretary comes closer and whispers, "Weren't there any drinks in your office?"

"My OFFICE?"

"May I show you?" she smiles as she opens the door right behind her desk.

When the three enter the executive office set up just for him, the young lady announces, "Mr. O'Brien, this is your office and I'm Mandy Lewis, your secretary."

Conor stands in amazement, while Brittany shakes Mandy's hand, "Hi, I'm Brittany."

"Yes, I know, Miss Cook -- pleased to meet you." She then goes over to one of the bookshelves and swings it out to reveal a drink center full of Cokes and snacks. Then she continues, "Want to see your other rooms?"

"OTHER rooms?" Conor and Brittany say at the same time.

"Yes, Sir. There are four rooms connected together to form your office complex. This is your main office," she says as she indicates the area they are in. "Over here," she adds as she takes them through a door to the right of his desk, "is your work area, complete with computer station and a design desk."

"A design desk?" Conor questions.

"Oh, this is a special type of computer drawing desk that your grandfather thought you might like."

"What's special about it?"

'Watch this," she says, as she picks up the pencil laying there and draws a big smiley face on the desk; she then reaches over to a flat keyboard he hadn't noticed before, and pushes "Print." A printer comes to life and a copy of the drawing prints out.

"Wow! I can for real use this!"

"Well, I'll leave you two to enjoy your drinks. I'll be right outside if you need me. And welcome, Mr. O'Brien," she says as she turns and starts for the main door.

"Miss Lewis," Conor calls to her.

19

"Yes, sir?"

"You mentioned four rooms; where are the other two?"

"Oh! Sorry, Sir! They're right here behind this wall." She presses on what looks like just another wall panel, which opens to reveal a bedroom. "And that door leads to the bathroom."

"Thanks, Miss Lewis, but how about we stop with the 'Sir' and 'Mr.' or 'Miss.' I'm just Conor. Okay, Mandy?"

"Why, of course Mr.---I mean Conor."

After the secretary leaves the office, Brittany says, "What are you going to do with all this?"

"I don't know, but it's way cool, huh!"

"Yes, it is," she answers as they each get a soft drink and go over and sit down in a seating area with a big couch and soft chairs in one corner. "So, what's on your mind? I know something is bothering you, so give."

"Ok. It's the **private school** thing. I just don't know."

"What about it? Don't you want to be back here in Tennessee?"

"It's not that. It's just – well, to tell the truth -- I feel a little weird getting all this special attention. You know, a private teacher just for you and me. What do you think?"

After considering the question for a minute, Brittany says, "I have an idea!"

"What?"

"How about we ask Mom to find some underprivileged kids to attend classes with us? You know -- share what **we** get, with them."

"Hey, that's a great idea; let's go ask her!"

They return to Janet's office and explain what they had come up with. Liking the idea very much, she agrees to find some kids who would benefit from a private school. "I'm very proud of these two!" she whispers to Grandpa.

Conor is beginning to feel maybe all this is going to work out. *"After all Brittany and I get to be back home in Tennessee. I get a CAR and a OFFICE. This is so COOL!"*

Grandpa gets up from the couch and walks to the desk, picks up a pen, and is done in less than a minute. "We're done now, right? It's time for us to be heading back."

"Conor, I mean it. Call me for any help you need," Janet

20

adds.

She opens the door, and as Conor steps out, he stops and looks at Grandpa. "I would really like for Janet and Brittany to be with us tomorrow at the Telling."

"The Telling?" questions Janet.

Grandpa smiles at his grandson, "You're the boss!"

"Okay, then." Conor turns to Janet and Brittany and gives his very first order: "Janet and Brittany, be at Grandpa's house in the morning. And dress for the country," Conor says over his shoulder as they enter the elevator.

"What's the Telling?" Janet asks again, but they were gone. "I guess we'll find out tomorrow!"

Chapter 4
The Storm

The village of the Tinys is in Eastern Tennessee, not far from Jamestown, nestled in the beautiful woods high up on the Cumberland Plateau. This flattop mountain range runs from the northeast corner southward to the southern border of Tennessee. On the plateau are a few farms and small communities like Jamestown. The people living in this area are some of the nicest anyone would ever meet. The forests are full of tall oaks and towering pines, and they can be very dense. The area is sparsely-populated, making it a perfect place to hide the Tinys.

In the Tinys' village, two brothers are arguing. The discussion ends when the younger brother stomps out of the house.

A short time later, through the bedroom window, Eric sees Bryan leaving the village earlier than usual. Noticing Bryan is carrying a pack and his bow, Eric quickly dresses and is out of the house, trying to catch up. He heads in the direction he had seen his brother go and soon spots him. "Bryan, wait up!" Eric shouts as he runs to catch up.

"What do you want?" Bryan asks, as he turns to face his older brother. "Why don't you leave me alone?"

"Ah, come on," Eric says as he reaches Bryan's side. "What's wrong? Where are you going?"

"I just want to get away," Bryan answers hurtfully. "So go back!"

"Not until I get some answers. Are you still upset about last night's meeting?"

"Yeah. So?" Bryan huffs as he turns and heads deeper into the woods.

"Look, Bryan, you knew you weren't old enough when you asked. How did you expect them to react? You know the rules say you must be 16 to become a scout. It's only seven months until your 16th birthday. That's not too long."

"It's not only seven months, and you know it! The counsel only picks new scouts once a year. That means I need to wait a whole year, Eric. A whole year! They could let me start now. I can do everything any scout can. I can hunt, fish, set traps, and scout, and I'm better with the bow than most. I can even hide and move in the forest better than you!"

"Hey, don't remind me. I don't want anyone to find out my little brother is better than me in the woods," Eric says with a grin and a chuckle.

"So, you finally admit I'm better than you," Bryan retorts, not returning Eric's laughter.

Again, Bryan turns away and continues on.

"Bryan, wait! Why are you going? You don't have to leave." Eric pleads again.

Over his shoulder, Bryan remarks, "I will live in the forest. You know I can!"

"Boy! What a stubborn kid," Eric mumbles to himself and then yells to his brother, "Okay, but why don't you at least wait until after the storm."

Bryan stops short and turns to face his brother. "Storm?" He questions, looking skyward.

"Yes, storm," repeats Eric. "You can read the skies as well as I can. You just forgot to look."

"I don't care if a storm is coming. I'll hole up in a tree."

"A tree! Now that's a good idea," Eric says sarcastically. "The perfect place to be, in the middle of a thunderstorm, you know, with lightning and wind."

"Ha! Got you again," Bryan grins, and points at his brother. "I know lots of trees that have already been hit, so there! Lighting does not strike the same place twice." With that, he heads off into the forest.

Shaking his head, Eric starts back to their house. Knowing he must go after his brother, he begins his mental checklist of the gear he'll need. "It's going to be a long day," he says under his breath.

The rain starts as he nears his house.

"Eric!"

He turns to see who is calling and finds Dina standing under the eaves of the house next door. He waves, and she motions for him to come over.

"Now what?" he mumbles to himself, knowing all along

23

what she wants. Dina has been following Bryan around like a lost puppy since they were 5 years old. Everyone knows they are a couple.

When he is close enough to hear her, Dina asks, "Where is he going?" pointing in the direction Bryan went.

"Into the woods to pout!" Eric replies sarcastically.

"There's a storm coming. Why is he going into the forest in a storm? Why didn't you stop him?"

By now he can see the tears forming in her eyes. "He'll be okay," he says as he tries to console her. "I tried to stop him, but you know how he gets when he's upset. Don't worry -- I'm going after him."

"Please hurry!" she says, looking toward the woods.

"I will," replies Eric as he turns and runs into his house. By the time he gets his gear together, the rain is coming down hard. The morning sky is growing darker by the minute. Standing on his porch while he adjusts his pack, he looks up at the threatening clouds; the way they roll and turn is not a good sign. The storm has him very concerned. Heavy rain can mean flooding and possible high winds. He must find Bryan and bring him back -- and quickly!

He moves to the side of the porch and picks up his star staff. As he lifts it, its weight reminds him of its purpose. Gary, the village's fix-it man, designed the star staff, coming up with this new staff design after watching a porcupine defend itself from a much larger animal. The staff is made up of three separate shafts that are pointed on each end. They're connected at the center to swivel, so that when a Tiny is in danger, the staff can be opened into a six-point, three-axis star. It works as a great defense against large animals. When open, the star staff is big enough so all a Tiny needs to do is hold onto the center and duck under it. The points sticking out in three different directions provide a sharp protective shield.

Shouldering the staff, Eric heads for the woods.

The area between the woods and the village is clear of grass and brush, but he stays on the path anyway. The path is packed down from constant traffic and won't muddy as fast as the rest of the area.

"Now, which way did he go?" Eric says to out loud.

24

"Maybe he's headed for the Owl Tree" comes Dina's voice from behind a nearby tree.

"What? Where are you...?" Eric asks but is quickly cut off.

"That's his favorite place for thinking," she finishes as she steps out from her hiding place. She is dressed to travel and carrying her pack, as well.

Seeing her face, Eric abruptly says, "No! No way! You're not coming!"

* * * * *

By the time they get near the old Owl Tree, the rain and wind are getting worse, and Eric is starting to worry. "Dina," Eric shouts over the noise of the storm, "even if he isn't here, we better stay and wait out the storm."

"But..." she starts to say.

"No buts! I let you come along because you said you would listen to me, and I say we stop here!"

"Okay!" she concedes in a tired voice. She is used to traveling in the forest, but not in the middle of a storm, let alone one as bad as this. The rain and the wind have taken its toll, and she is soaked through. Even though she is concerned about Bryan, she knows he is totally at home in the forest, and he will be safe. She hopes.

Eric stops at the base of the tree and waits for Dina to catch up. Looking around, he can see the tree at one time had been hit by lightning, caught fire, and the insides burnt out. The years of weather had worn away most of the burnt wood, and birds and other creatures, from time to time, have made the Owl Tree their home. Signs of old nests are visible all around.

When Eric looks up at the top, he notices this tree is taller than most of the others in the area. The branches at the top spread out like a 10-fingered hand reaching up into the sky. Its leaves long ago left its branches, and against the dark, stormy clouds, the bare and bent branches look like a giant, sinister hand, reaching up to grab the sky.

"Come on, Dina; let's get inside." He sees an opening at the base in between two of the larger roots. They climb over the roots and enter the Owl Tree.

25

Once inside, they notice a big hole in the center going high up to a big opening that is allowing the rain to pour directly on them. Eric is working his way around the debris, trying to find a sheltered spot, when a field mouse scurries out, brushing past Dina. Screaming, she jumps back and loses her footing.

Eric, who is busy clearing a path, turns in time to see the mouse disappear outside and Dina fall into a puddle.

Bryan, sitting all snug and dry, high above in an abandoned squirrel's nest, hears the scream. Jumping up, he grabs his bow and runs to the edge of the nest. He looks down and sees the mouse leave the base of the tree.

"That scream sounds like Dina," he says to himself. Then he hears what sounds like Eric, laughing.

"Hey, who's down there?" he yells. Eric's head pops out, and he looks up to see his brother. "So there you are. It's wet down here. How do we get up there?"

"You climb up the bark. Start just to the left of the hole for the best way." Bryan ducks back out of the rain. Then it hits him. *"We. Who's the 'we' with Eric?"* he asks himself.

Looking down again, he sees Dina climbing up in front of Eric. "Dina!" he yells. "What are you doing here?" Then without waiting for Dina to answer, he yells to Eric, "Why did you let her come?"

Dina and Eric reach the nest and climb in. Immediately Dina goes over to the other side farthest away from Bryan. She sits down, pulls her knees up, wraps her arms around them, put her head down and curls up into a ball, and tries to warm herself. Eric, knowing what is about to happen, wanders over to the side and pretends to be looking for something in his gear. Meanwhile Bryan stands dumbfounded, looking from one side to the other. Nothing is said for almost 5 minutes.

Feeling the tension, Eric goes over to the opening, looks skyward and realizes it's turning a dark gray-green.

"Bryan!"

Bryan glances up from checking his own gear, with Eric motioning for him to come closer. Bryan can tell by the tone of his voice and the look on his face that something is terribly wrong. Going over to Eric, he checks outside. At first he looks down, but seeing nothing unusual, his eyes return to his brother's

26

face. This time, following Eric's eyes, he discovers what has Eric so disturbed.

Eric asks, "Is there a cave nearby?"

Shaking his head, Bryan replies, "No, only trees for at least a mile."

"We must get out of this tree and find some better place to wait out the storm," Eric announces.

From the tone of their voices, Dina instinctively realizes something is not right. "What's wrong?" she asks Eric.

"You tell her," he instructs Bryan.

"Tornado weather!" is all he manages to get out before Eric shouts.

"Funnel cloud!" as he points out the cloud to Bryan.

"Is it on the ground?" Dina asks, rising to go to them.

"No, only about halfway down, but it's moving right toward us!"

As the funnel cloud moves closer, the wind picks up, and all the trees around them begin swaying and bending. Branches break loose and they, along with leaves and other debris, begin flying through the air. Just then, a large furry head appears at the opening to the nest. Eric and Bryan jump back, immediately going into defensive postures, weapons at the ready.

"Blue Boy!" Bryan shouts as he recognizes his friend, the large blue-gray squirrel. Blue, seeing Bryan, continues inside out of the wind and rain. Eric, is still holding his spear at the ready.

"It's okay, Eric! He's my friend, Blue," Bryan reassures him. Bryan and Blue exchange nods. Blue then checks Eric cautiously and moves past him, going deeper into the nest. Turning his attention back to the storm, Eric moves to look outside.

"HERE IT COMES!" Eric yells. "MOVE BACK INSIDE, AND FIND SOMETHING TO HOLD ONTO!"

Bryan glances around frantically and spots a place where the inside of the hollowed-out tree forms a stump.

"Come here!" he shouts over the roar of the tornado. Pulling Dina over to the stump, he digs in his pack and grabs a rope. "Eric, come on!" he yells over his shoulder. Eric is still standing near the opening, watching the funnel move closer. "Eric, we can tie ourselves to this!" Bryan shouts as he starts to wrap the rope around himself and Dina. Seeing what Bryan is doing, Eric

27

moves to join them, just as the Owl Tree twists suddenly. Looking up from tying the ends of the rope together, Bryan sees his brother knocked off his feet and slammed into a nearby wall. "Eric!" screams Bryan helplessly.

With a great tearing noise, the top of the old Owl Tree -- including the part they are hiding in -- is torn from the rest of the tree. Spinning and rising, they are lifted higher and higher into the air, and their world becomes a tumbling, twirling nightmare.

Chapter 5
Missing

Graybeard stands on the hill west of the village. This is one of his favorite spots. He likes to start each day by coming up the hill to check and make sure everything is in its place. From that vantage point, he can see the entire village. Graybeard loves the morning right before the sun comes up; the air is still and quiet. He watches the lights coming on in the different homes, as people are getting ready for another day. Their little village is very peaceful. "How long will it stay this way?" The Tinys' leader wonders aloud.

As he watches, he notices the door of Gary's house open, spilling light onto the street. Gary comes out and starts walking toward him as he does most every morning. The village blacksmith and fix-it man, Gary is also an inventor. You can always find him in his shop at the back of his house, working on something. His love of things mechanical is only exceeded by his devotion to his lovely wife and his son.

Graybeard nods a "Good morning" to Gary as he comes closer. Then he turns his attention back to the village, looking for his friend, the teacher. Mr. Vaughn should be leaving the schoolhouse about now, although he is sometimes late joining them on the hill. Graybeard looks closely at the schoolhouse to see if any lights are on. The teachers' quarters are in the rear of the building that serves both as the school and the church.

"Ah," he says aloud, "he's up," as a light comes on.

Gary reaches the crest of the hill, "Good morning Dad. Quite a storm we had last night!"

"Yes, it was, I even thought for a while there that we might have a tornado!" replies Graybeard.

Gary suddenly hears something crashing through the branches overhead. Looking up, he sees a pinecone falling toward them. Grabbing Graybeard up off his feet, Gary dives quickly to one side. The pinecone makes a crashing sound as it hits the ground exactly where they had been standing.

"Phew!" exclaims Graybeard, "Thank you son for saving me! Are those pine cones getting bigger, or is it just me?"

"You're getting smaller," laughs Gary while helping his

father up. Turning to check where the pinecone landed, he says, "No need for thanking me. I was looking out for me, too," With a slight grin on his face and a friendly pat to his father's back, he adds, "That would have started our day off badly."

"Or ended it," replies Graybeard as he straightens out his clothes. "And today being the Telling Day."

"Ah, yes!" Gary says, remembering his Telling Day, a day of importance for the children. "So today they learn about our origins."

"The ones old enough to know need to know now," Graybeard answers. "Our history will help them understand why we are here in the forest and why we must remain here. I often worry about the young ones wandering too far or even wanting to leave. I don't even want to imagine what would happen if the outside world found us."

"Will Grandpa O'Brien be joining us?" asks Gary.

"Yes, and if all goes well with his grandson, we will be introducing him at the Telling as well,"

Gary frowns as he questions his father, "What will we do if he turns down Grandpa's request?"

"We will trust in the Lord as always. God has cared for us thus far, and I don't believe He will stop doing so now," answers Graybeard.

"I do trust in God, but it's hard not to worry some," remarks Gary as he notices the door of the schoolhouse open. "Ah! Here comes Vaughn now. Let's ask if he has any ideas about what to do if things do not work as we plan."

Before Vaughn can even reach the bottom of the hill, Dina's mother, Ann, runs up to the teacher.

"DINA IS MISSING!" she exclaims.

"Missing?" repeats Vaughn, "You mean she is not home? Maybe she is over at Bryan's. You know how she dotes on that boy," he comments. Vaughn is the teacher, historian, and a scientist. He is constantly looking for new things to learn and is a member of the village council.

"No! I checked with Bryan's mother. He and Eric are gone, as well, and they did not sleep in their beds last night! She told me their packs aren't there, either. I went home and checked; Dina's pack is gone, too! What can those kids be up to? Have

30

they run away?"

Graybeard and Gary notice something is wrong and come down from the hill to find out. "What is it? What is wrong?" asks Graybeard.

"Dina, Bryan, and Eric are gone, and Ann thinks they ran away," explains Vaughn.

By now Ann is crying. "Where could they be?"

Graybeard puts his arm around her shoulder, "Now, now; I don't think they would do such a foolish thing as run away. They probably went hiking in the woods, got caught in last night's storm, and are holed up in some cave or tree. They will be back soon. Let's split up and ask around if anyone in the village knows where they went."

Gary stops by the home of his sister, Kasandra, to see what she might know. He knocks, but there is no answer. "She must be out early making a house call," he says to himself. "I'll go back home and check with Lois." As he starts down the street, he sees Kasandra heading for his house. "Hey, Kas!" Gary calls, but the village healer is deep in thought and doesn't hear him. She is preoccupied with getting her long, blonde hair tied back in a ponytail. He notices her coat pockets are filled with the morning's herbs and cures she was out gathering.

Having just turned 30 and raising her young daughter on her own, she is the youngest widow in the village.

"KASANDRA!" Gary shouts, and she turns to find her brother approaching. "Oh, hi, Brother. What are you up to this morning?"

"It's some of the teenagers -- Ann's girl, Dina, and the brothers Eric and Bryan seem to be nowhere around," he answers. "Have you seen them?" he asks as they enter his house.

Gary's wife, Lois, looks up from her cooking and, seeing Kasandra, says, "Hi, Kas!" Then noticing the worried look on her husband's face, she stops what she is doing and turns to ask, "What in the world is wrong?"

"We are missing three of our young people," Gary answers. "And I asked Sis if she saw anything."

"That's where I saw them!" Kasandra says, snapping her fingers and turning to face Gary. "Last evening, I was coming back to the village from gathering herbs. I saw Eric and Bryan

31

near the woods. I could tell, even from a distance, they were arguing. After all these years of watching those two fight, I'm afraid I didn't pay them much attention. And with the storm already starting, I was hurrying to finish my rounds. Just as I entered the house, I looked back and noticed Bryan heading toward the woods, and Eric heading for home. I wasn't too surprised about Bryan going into the woods -- surely he knew the storm was coming and would return before it hit. Later, on my way to bring some herbs to Lois for Trey's arm, I saw Eric with his gear and staff entering the woods. Thinking it a bit odd, I told Lois."

"Yes, I remember you did say there was a storm coming, and you saw Bryan going into the woods, but we both really didn't think much of it at the time," Lois comments. Then she turns and sets the pan she was stirring off the stove and starts for the door, "Come on" -- she waves back at Gary and Kasandra --"let's go find out what this is all about."

Down the main street of the village, they meet up with Dina's mother. She is crying, "I looked for her everywhere. I checked her room, and noticed her pack and walking stick are not there! Why would she leave? Where could she have gone?"

"Now, now," Lois says reassuringly as she wipes the tears from Ann's cheeks with a part of her apron, "I'm sure she didn't leave the village. She must have stayed at someone's house last night because of the storm."

"But I've looked **everywhere** and asked **everyone**. No one's seen her!"

Just then Trey, the son of Gary and Lois, comes walking up. "Seen who?"

"Dina's missing, and her mom can't find her. Have you seen her?" Lois questions Trey.

"Yeah! I saw her going into the woods near Bryan and Eric's house."

"When?" Dina's mother asks.

"Last night, just before the storm came," he answers.

"Was she with anyone?"

"Nope."

"Did she have her pack?"

"Uh...yeah, maybe...she was carrying something, might have

32

been her pack."

"Did you notice if she returned to the village?"

"No, I went over to Kara's house."

"Wait a minute!" Lois exclaims. "Kasandra, you said you saw Bryan going into the forest just before the storm? We had better go check with Eric and Bryan's parents."

"Bryan!" Dina's mother says, almost to herself. "Dina did say something yesterday about Bryan. Let's see... she said something about him being upset with the council."

"The council?" questions Lois.

"Yes. Dina seemed very upset about it," Ann adds.

"Trey!" Lois calls to him just as he heads for their house. "Do you know anything about the meeting yesterday?"

"Nope," he replies, "and I'm late for work," he says over his shoulder as he heads off.

"Gary," Lois says sadly, "I'm worried now! We need to find out what's going on and where these three teenagers are."

Nodding in agreement, Gary says, "Okay, let's go check with Eric and Bryan's parents."

Graybeard and Vaughn had been checking with some of the villagers and now met up with the others as they arrive at the boys' house.

"No one has seen either of them since last night right before the storm hit," Graybeard announces as he joins the group.

"I think it's time we ask the scouts to go try to find them," Gary adds.

"Yes! I'll send them right out," Graybeard agrees. Then turning to Dina's mother, he says, "Once we find them or get any information, I will come and tell you."

"Thank you all for helping," she says as Lois and Kasandra take her to her house to wait.

33

Chapter 6
Journey Home

The funnel of the small tornado never does touch the ground. However, as it passes over the old Owl Tree, the top of the tree and the three Tinys get caught in its swirling winds. The force of the winds twists and breaks the top third of the tree off, with the tree snapping right where lightning had done the most damage years ago. The outstretched branches at the top act like an open umbrella, catching the wind and strong up-drafts, carrying the treetop and its Tiny passengers away from their village.

As the tree snaps, it spins violently. The spinning makes the rope around Bryan and Dina feel like it is going to cut them in two. Dina screams and faints. Bryan fights to hold her up. The tree keeps spinning and twirling as Bryan prays, "Lord, help us!"

Just then the spinning starts to slow, the top third of the tree and the three Tinys begin to suddenly descend. With a loud splash, the tree lands in a lake -- hitting the water, trunk first. With the branches overhead, the tree is driven partly under water. As the tree submerges, water rushes into the nest where the Tinys are holding on for dear life!

When the water reaches Eric, he comes to, only to find he is clinging onto a very wet squirrel that has been gripping a branch with its claws and holding on as tightly as he can. Eric shakes his head, trying to clear his dazed and confused mind. "What's... Where... Got to find Bry..." The water rushing in makes it hard to see.

Just then the tree lays out flat on the lake, and floats on the surface. As the tree comes up, it rolls to where the opening of the nest is facing straight up.

When Blue Boy sees the sky, he climbs out from inside the floating tree with Eric still hanging on to him.

Bryan is struggling to untie himself and Dina, who is just starting to come to. He yells, "HOLD YOUR BREATH!" Suddenly the tree begins sinking into the water, with the hole in the tree filling fast. As the rope drops away, the two swim for the surface, gasping for air as they break through. They find the nest and start looking around inside. Bryan turns to Dina. "Do you see Eric? I don't see him anywhere!" He dives down to search for his

34

brother.

"Hey!" comes a voice from above. Dina looks up and sees Eric peering into the nest.

"Eric!" She exclaims. "You're all right!"

"Yeah, just a little groggy. Where's Bryan?"

Bryan suddenly comes to the surface, and Dina points up.

When he spots his brother, he grins from ear to ear. "Hiya, Bro!" Eric, who is lying on his stomach -- looking through the hole in the tree and down into the nest -- smiles and passes out. Bryan and Dina scramble out onto the floating tree. When they reach Eric, they roll him onto his back. Opening his eyes, he asks, "What happened?"

"You passed out," explains Dina. "You must have hit your head when you were thrown around. " As she searches for injuries on his head, she finds a large lump on the right side, just behind his ear. Turning to Bryan, she says, "There's a knot here and most likely a concussion to go with it. We will have to watch him for a while to make sure he stays awake."

"I'm okay!" Eric insists as he starts to sit up, wobbling as he does.

"Yeah, sure you are," Bryan says sarcastically as he pushes him back down. "I need to check out our situation, so just lay back and relax awhile."

"Okay," Eric grumps, and gulps as a wave of nausea hits him.

* * * * *

The light of dawn finally peeks over the trees to find the three Tinys and a big fluffy squirrel cuddled together on top of the floating prison.

It's been a long night, with Bryan and Dina taking turns trying to keep Eric from sleeping.

Bryan looks around to find they are floating in a small lake about 300 feet from the shore. That's not far for a Big, but to a Tiny it's more like 1,800 feet. Noticing Blue up on the highest branch, Bryan moves to join him.

"Where are you going?" Dina asks.

"Just up to get a better look around."

35

Eric sees what Bryan is going to do, "Be careful; don't make the tree roll over."

"Okay!" replies Bryan as he starts up a branch, moving slow and easy. But, the tree starts to roll after only a few steps.

"HOLD IT!" Eric shouts.

Bryan quickly moves back down. With each step back, the tree rights itself. Blue scurries down from his perch and stops on the trunk, where he turns to his friend and chatters loudly at Bryan. Moving carefully, the worried squirrel goes to the other end of their floating prison.

"What was that all about?" questions Eric.

"He was scolding me," explains Bryan, "for rocking the boat." He smiles and shrugs his shoulders.

"Well, you had it coming," Dina says.

"Okay! Okay! I'll take it easy!"

Bryan tries again, moving up the branch slower and stopping every few inches; at each point, he tests for any signs of roll. Finally, he makes it up to the highest point. Looking around, he notices they are slowly moving toward the shore.

Climbing back down, he gives them the bad news. "We are being blown to the shore," he tells the others. " Also, I took a good look around, and I don't recognize anything."

Eric ponders the situation for a minute, and then asks, "Do you remember which way we were carried?"

Bryan, going back in his mind to the time just before the funnel hit, "...I remember the clouds were moving northeast."

"Northeast?"

"Yes."

"That's not good," Eric announces with a sigh. "We might be very close to a town, and that means Bigs. We must be careful, very careful!" Holding his head and thinking out loud, Eric starts mumbling, "My head hurts like blazes. I probably have a concussion. We are far from home, lost, and too close to a Bigs' town. How am I going to get these kids home safely?"

Suddenly, bubbles come out of the end of the log, right where the tree broke off. Blue scampers past them, heading up into the branches. They each look at Blue, puzzled, and then where the bubbles are forming. Just as the trunk starts to sink, Bryan yells, "Run for the branches!" He and Dina grab Eric to

36

help him up.

"I'm okay!" he insists as he shakes loose of their hold, only to weave, stumble, and almost fall into the lake. Again, they grab him and lead him up to the branches. By the time they get up on a branch, the tree trunk is so far under water that only a few feet of the branches remain out of the water.

Everyone looks over at Blue, who is chattering like crazy with his fur standing straight up.

"Now what's wrong?" Eric asks, as he adjusts the star staff, which is secured to his back. Bryan checks in the direction Blue is looking.

"I don't see anything." Climbing up to where his furry friend is, Bryan again takes a look at the shore they are drifting toward. "Dog, dog!" he shouts!

To the Tinys, who are only 12 inches tall when fully grown, a big dog like a German shepherd is something to avoid, and avoid at all costs.

Bryan carefully climbs back down to be with the others.

Eric is on his feet, steadying himself by holding onto a nearby branch. Dina moves closer to Bryan, and Blue is still chattering.

"Did he see us?" asks Eric.

"I don't know," Bryan replies. "I'll go back up and find out."

"Go very slowly this time, and maybe he won't spot us. If he hasn't already," Eric adds.

"Okay!" Bryan says over his shoulder as he moves to climb the branch again.

"Bryan! Be careful" Dina cautions, not wanting him to go any higher.

Bryan climbs slowly up the side of the branch facing away from the shore in hopes he won't be seen. But with all the noise Blue is making, he doesn't have much hope. *"Maybe,"* he thinks to himself, *"maybe the dog will just see Blue and no one else."* Reaching the place on a branch where he is at the same height as Blue, he slowly peeks around and sees the dog looking their way. The dog barks at the squirrel, turns, and runs into the underbrush.

"He ran off!" he tells the others. "I don't believe he saw us -- only Blue."

By this time they have drifted close to shore. The tree stops

37

moving when the submerged trunk hits the bottom.

Dina looks around and -- seeing it's too far to shore to swim -- asks, "How are we going to get to the bank?"

"I don't know. Swim?" Bryan comments.

Dina points at the water, "Do I need to remind you two that Tinys don't like to swim where we don't know the size of the fish, turtles, or whatever might be in there. We could become fish food if we're not careful."

Eric, studying their situation, notices that some of the outstretched branches reach the bank, but they are too far off the ground for the three to drop from.

"Okay! I think I know how we can get to shore," Eric announces as he begins climbing out on a limb. "Follow me."

"Wait a minute, Eric!" Bryan says. "We can't drop from up there."

"I know, but if we all go out to the end, our combined weight should cause the branch to lean over far enough for us to jump down."

"Oh! I understand. Sure, that should work," Bryan, says as he helps Dina out onto the branch where Eric is almost to the end.

However, when all three of them get as far out on the limb as they can get, the branch is still standing not bending.

"Now what?" Dina says.

"Well, I thought that would work," replies Eric, still holding his aching head. "Let me consider this some more."

They all sit on the end of the branch, trying to figure out how to get down, when Blue solves the problem. He simply scampers out to the end of their branch, and his added weight does the trick.

"Whoa. Hang on!" cries Eric.

When the branch starts to tip and move closer to the ground, Eric warns, "We all have to jump at the same time! Jump when I say 'Go!' Ready...GO!"

All three Tinys drop to the safety of the ground, but Blue stays on the branch as it swings back up. As it passes close to the branches of the tree on shore, Blue makes a picture-perfect jump, climbs up into the tree and disappears in the leaves.

Bryan and Dina stand up and start brushing themselves off. Bryan looks around to see where Blue went. Not finding him, his attention returns to his companions. Dina notices Eric still sitting on the ground, holding his head and weaving back and forth. She calls Bryan, "Bryan, Eric is hurting a lot. We've got to get him back home to the healer."

Bryan kneels down by his brother. "What's wrong, Eric?"

"It's my head. The jump made it hurt even worse! I must rest...I'm SO...sleepy."

"No!" shouts Dina. "He can't go to sleep with a head injury!"

"I know," Bryan says. "You've got to stay awake, Brother! You know you can't sleep now."

"Yeah, I know," Eric answers weakly, "but I'm so tired."

"Get him on his feet!" Dina instructs. The two help Eric up, having to hold on to him because he is so dizzy.

Eric tries to clear his head with a small shake, and then says, "Bryan, keep heading southwest...move away from here fast."

Bryan takes a bearing on the sun and turns facing the correct way.

"Grrrr!" Standing in their way, growling and showing his large teeth, is the dog.

Bryan quickly moves to shield Dina. Eric unfolds his star staff and positions himself between Bryan, Dina, and the dog.

"Get under the star, Dina," Eric whispers quietly, fighting to stay standing while holding onto his star staff.

39

Having never seen a full-size dog up close before, Dina is frozen in her tracks.

"Dina!" Bryan yells, as he turns and grabs her arm, forcing her under the star staff.

Hearing Bryan yell, the dog stops growling and cocks his head to listen. Eric notices the dog is wearing something around his neck.

"Bryan -- he is wearing a name tag; he's tame!" Eric points at the collar. "Call out his name." He then slumps to the ground.

Bryan moves so he can see the tag. Just then, Blue jumps from the tree overhead and lands between the dog and the Tinys. The dog growls again. Blue arches his back and flips his tail, challenging the dog. Bryan needs to move from behind Blue's big, bushy tail so he can read the dog's name.

"Come on, Blue!" he says more to himself than the squirrel. "Hold still so I can see his name better!"

After moving back and forth a few times, he gets a clear look. "Jack?" he says out loud. "What a name for a dog!"

"Call out his name," Eric suggests weakly. "His name!"

Bryan runs to a spot closer to the dog than he really wants to be and yells, "Jack, no! Jack, no!"

The dog stops growling and looks at Bryan. Bryan wants to run but instead moves closer and the dog lowers his head. Bryan remembers how Blue likes to be scratched. "Good boy, Jack!"

By now the dog is sniffing him. Bryan reaches up and scratches him gently near his ear.

Slurp! Bryan gets licked. The force of the tongue nearly knocks him down, and he is wet from knee to shoulder. "Hee, hee!" -- Bryan laughs --"He's friendly, alright. Good boy, Jack!"

Blue, seeing the danger has passed, scampers into the woods.

Dina comes closer to Bryan and the dog.

"I want to pet him! But I don't want to get licked like you did."

Eric comes up behind them, walking slow and using his staff as extra support.

"You know, you might have wound up as his lunch!"

"I don't think so. He responded to my voice commands," Bryan answers.

"Yeah!" Dina says, turning to look at Eric. That is her

mistake. Slurp! She gets sideswiped with a wet tongue. "Oh, yuck!" she lets out. "I thought you said he was friendly!" she punches Bryan in the shoulder like it was his fault. "Yuck, yuck, yuck!"

Bryan and Eric both laugh.

"We need to get going," Eric ends the fun by saying. "We must get away from where the Bigs are."

"Okay," Bryan answers, as he scratches the dog's ear once more and starts off into the woods. Dina and Eric follow.

Cocking his head from side to side, the dog watches them leave. High in the trees, Blue is watching, too, and then he takes off in the same direction -- except he takes the high road, going from tree to tree.

They are heading southwest, the direction they assume their little community is. As they move through the woods and as the hours pass, Eric is growing stronger and no longer feeling dizzy. His head is clearing, and now he is concerned about finding out just where they are and how much further they need to go. He stops and asks, "Bryan, do you have any idea where we are?"

Bryan, who has been paying more attention to Dina than to their surroundings, stops and looks around, but all he sees is forest.

"No, I don't. I'll climb this tall tree and take a look around!"

"Okay!" Eric says, and he sits down on some grass to rest.

Bryan quickly climbs about 100 feet up in the tallest tree nearby. As he reaches the top branches, he first looks in the direction they are going and then all around.

"What can you see?" Eric shouts, but Bryan is too high and the wind up at the top of the tree keeps him from hearing Eric.

Dina sits down next to Eric, "It's hot, and I'm getting thirsty!"

"Yes, me too," Eric replies. "We need to find water soon."

Bryan sees they only have around 100 yards of forest left before they will come to a cornfield.

"There's a farmer's cornfield ahead; maybe we can find some corn that's ripe," he yells down the 100 feet to the two on the ground, but they still can't hear him. Just then he hears a loud noise coming from the direction they came. He shouts as loud as he can, "Something is coming this way!"

Seeing his brother can't hear him, Bryan jumps off the

41

branch he is on and falls 20 feet to catch a small branch. Then he drops again and lands another 20 feet down. He screams at the top of his lungs, "Something is coming this way!"

Eric sees that Bryan is almost halfway back down the tree.

Bryan points to the direction the thing is coming from, "I can't see, but it's moving very fast and making a lot of dust," he tries to tell Eric. Then he spots it! What he sees is trouble, and it has four wheels! He yells, "Get off the trail -- it's a four-wheeled vehicle and it's coming right for you!"

Seeing how the machine is able to drive right through big bushes and over small trees and rocks, Bryan warns, "Get behind a big tree, fast!"

Eric jumps up and grabs Dina's hand and pulls her behind the nearest tree, just as the four-wheeled demon comes crashing through the bushes and right over the area where they had been resting only a moment before! The driver has so much dirt and mud on his goggles that he doesn't even see them running! Barely missing the tree they are hiding behind, the rider cranks on the throttle and spins the tires, sending dirt, rocks, and grass flying right at the two Tinys. A large rock barely misses Dina's head as she ducks.

And then it's gone, and all that can be seen is a trail of dust as the roar of the engine fades away.

"Are you okay?" Bryan yells, as he starts further down.

"Wait! We're okay," Eric answers. "Stay up there, and get a bearing that will get us out of here!"

"Oh! Right!" Bryan says as he climbs back up, takes out his compass, and looks around for landmarks he can recognize. Down on the ground, Eric helps Dina up. They start wiping off the dirt that completely covers them. Bryan spots a landmark he recognizes. He looks down to see if Eric is looking up, but he isn't, so Bryan finds a pinecone and drops it near them.

Eric looks up to see Bryan signaling him to come up. Eric climbs about halfway up the tree when Bryan yells, "I can see the Jamestown Airport light!"

Eric stops and asks, "What direction?"

"About three miles to the west." Bryan points in the direction as he answers.

Eric pauses for a minute and then asks, "Can you see the

runway?" If the runway was visible, he was thinking, he could take a bearing (find what direction to go) off of it, since the runway runs north and south.

"No! It's too far away and hidden by the trees and hills."

Bryan begins to climb down when he hears an airplane. He stops and watches the aircraft as it passes overhead.

"Hey, wait! I see a plane!" he yells, keeping an eye on it. "It might be landing!" When he sees the landing gear come down, he gets excited -- "It is landing!" he exclaims. He quickly returns to the top of the tree and watches. When the plane lands, he checks his compass. Finally he exclaims, "I've got it!" and climbs down.

Once he is back on the ground, he pulls out his compass again, finds witch way is north, and then squats down. Brushing aside some leaves, he draws a map of sorts on the ground.

"Okay! Here we are," he says as he points to the X he drew, "and here is the airport. We need to head this way, and by the end of the day, we should be here, HOME!"

It is hot and slow going through the farm fields. None of them like being surrounded on all sides by corn stalks 6-feet high. They can't see more than a few yards, except straight down a row. They do climb up a corn stalk to pick and eat some ripe sweet corn along the way. After walking through the corn for nearly two hours, Bryan holds up his fist for them to stop. He puts his hands behind his ears so he can hear better and slowly turns back and forth to try to locate the direction of whatever it is he hears.

"What do you hear?" Dina asks.

"I'm not sure, but I think I hear a machine," Bryan answers.

"Which direction?" questions Eric?

Bryan points out across the field to his left and slightly behind them. "It sounds like it's over there."

Dina grabs onto his arm. "Is… is it coming this way?"

Bryan is still trying to get a fix on just where the sound is coming from. Now they are all trying to listen! Bryan takes Dina's hand from his arm and tells her, "You stay here with Eric. I'll go find out what this is and where it's headed!"

Eric holds up his hand to stop Bryan. "No, wait! We shouldn't separate! You might get in trouble, and we won't know it!"

Bryan runs off in the direction of the noise and shouts over

43

his shoulder, "Who **me**? I never get into trouble!" Then he is gone and out of sight as they stand there, waiting.

Eric sighs and then mumbles, "I really hate it when he does that!" and smiles at Dina.

Bryan runs about 60 feet when he enters a clearing made by the machine as it cuts and picks the corn. All he can see is row after row of cut corn stalks. He looks down the edge of the row still standing, and what he sees frightens him to death! A giant combine is coming right at him! Its tires are huge and crushing the ground beneath them. On the front is an enormous blade that is shearing the corn stalks off just above the ground.

He quickly turns around and runs back the way he came, to warn the others. He fears his companions are standing right in the middle of the machine's path. He tries to shout, but the machine is too close, and now the noise is very loud and getting louder.

He runs as fast as he can, knowing he is crossing the very path of this behemoth! He tries to keep an eye on the ground for his tracks to make sure he is going back the way he came. His quick estimate of how wide a path the machine cuts is about 30 feet. He knows the thing is now dangerously close, and he is not sure he can make it past the area it's now cutting. All the noise, dust, and wind are only adding to his fear and dread. The ground is shaking and the noise is deafening; the dust is now so thick he can hardly see or breathe.

That's when it happens -- his foot strikes a rock, and he falls. As he hits the ground, what little air he had rushes from his lungs. His mind screams, *"GET UP!"* His heart is pounding! Panic slams into his mind. Just when he thinks he won't make it! A pair of hands reaches out and grabs him. Pulling him out of the way of the machine as it passes with a roar.

"GOT YOU!" Eric shouts.

As the dust clears, Bryan catches his breath and says, "Thanks, Brother, I thought I was a goner for sure! We must get out of this field and fast! That thing will be coming back this way any minute now!"

"Okay! Lead the way," Eric adds, making sure Dina is right with them as they move out of the corn and into another problem... open ground!

Eric is quick to see each of the rows of cut stalks is about 30

44

feet apart and there is only open ground between each row.

"If we go this way, the driver of the machine will see us!"

"Yes, I know, but we cannot go back in there!" Bryan points to the standing corn.

Just then Dina shouts, "Look!" She points at another machine across the rows of cut corn stalks on the far side of the field. "This one is picking up the stalks and throwing them into a truck!"

Bryan and Eric both look at where she is pointing. Bryan again looks down the row they were standing near and sees the first machine coming back their way, cutting its next row of corn.

"We had better hide and fast!"

Eric, busy watching the other machine, turns to see what Bryan is talking about.

"We are going to get caught between these two machines if we don't get out of this field now!"

Dina, who is looking at the row of cut stalks, advises, "We should go over this row of stalks and hide from the cutting machine. Then run along the row after it passes."

Eric and Bryan both yell, "GO!" and they climb over the stalks just in time to hide when the combine passes nearby.

They spend the rest of the day running, jumping over cut stalks, watching out for the big machines, and hiding. By the time they finally get out of the cornfield and back into more forest, they are hot, dirty, and tired.

Determined to get home, they continue. During the next few hours, Eric grows stronger as he recovers from his concussion. The last mile or so of simply walking through the woods, compared to the tornado the night before and the encounter with the machines in the cornfield, has been a breeze.

The trio finally arrives back home after their long and hazardous journey -- just in time for tomorrow's Telling Day! All the families greet them and ask them what happened, and they explain about the storm and the trip back. Graybeard, upon hearing how Bryan took charge when Eric was injured, asks Eric if he might speak to him in private.

They quietly slip away from the crowd and go over to Graybeard's house. Once inside, Graybeard asks Eric to tell him about the storm and their trip home and not to leave anything out. Eric tells him all he remembers. Finally, after about an hour, Graybeard questions him, "Do you think Bryan is ready to be a scout? Or is he still too young?"

Eric knows whatever he says would weigh heavy on the council's decision.

"Yes, I do think he's ready. After seeing him in a situation like we were in, he PROVED IT!"

Graybeard considers for a minute and then says, "Very well then; that's what I will recommend to the council."

Chapter 7
Telling Day

The sun is washing the last of the dawn's gray away when Janet pulls into the driveway of the O'Brien home. She has been there many times before on business; a few times she has stayed the weekend just to visit. She likes it here, away from the rush of the city, and her favorite time of day is the early morning, when the forest is just waking up.

Conor bounds out the front door and down the steps. "Good morning," he says as Janet and Brittany get out of the car. He smiles at the sight of them, dressed in blue jeans, T-shirts, and tennis shoes. Brittany's mom does not look at all like the lawyer he had seen the day before.

"It's really great you're here," he continues. "Come on in. We're in the kitchen. Would you like some fresh coffee, tea or hot coco?"

"Sounds good," Janet replies with a smile as they enter the house..

In the kitchen, Janet introduces Brittany to Grandma, and there are welcoming hugs and greetings. They sit around the table with steam rising from the coffee cups and the two teens are sipping on hot coco. After a moment of awkward silence, Janet asks, "Okay, we're here, so what's all this about the Telling?"

No one says anything for a moment. Conor clears his throat, "Well, you know how Grandpa has mentioned the Tinys to you a few times."

"Yeah -- remember, I told you," Grandpa adds, smiling.

Janet sits back in her chair, looking at Conor like he had big floppy ears and was wearing a top hat. Slowly she says, "Yes; what about it?"

"Well, that's what Brittany, you, and I are going to find out about today!" Conor announces with a big grin on his own face -- like those words explain everything.

With a sigh, Grandma interjects, "Sweetheart," as she shakes her head and covers Janet's hand with hers, "I know they both sound a bit crazy right now, but if you will just bear with us for a few more hours, this will all make sense."

47

Janet looks into her eyes and just says, "Yes, Ma'am." As she thinks, *"What's wrong with these people? Lord, you know I love them. Please don't let them be completely nuts!"*

Conor changes the subject, talking about being up most of the night, mulling over the decision about changing schools and all that has happened.

Grandma asks Janet how she is doing, making small talk as they wait and Grandma works at filling a picnic basket. It isn't long before Grandpa stands up and announces, "Sun's up. It's after 6; time to go!"

"Where?" Conor and Janet both ask at the same time.

"We will need to take a little walk. You didn't figure the Telling was going to be here, did you?" replies Grandpa. With that, they all go out the back door, cross the backyard, and follow a path leading into the woods. As they follow Grandpa, they move in and around trees and foliage. After traveling for a little more than a quarter of a mile in silence, Grandpa stops and says, "This is where we wait!"

There is a fallen tree beside the trail, so Grandma sets down her basket and takes a seat. Grandma directs Janet, Brittany, and Conor to take a seat next to her. Grandpa stands in front of them and explains, "Now, you are going to be the only three people, with the exception of Grandma and me, that the majority of the Tinys have ever seen. What I mean is, the surprise, excitement, and, well, whatever feelings you are going to go through, will be the same for them."

At this point, Brittany looks really nervous, so Conor reaches over and takes her hand in his. She squeezes his and holds on tight without looking at him.

"There are things we must be careful about," Grandpa continues, "like where we step and stand. We don't want to be hurting anyone!" Grandpa goes on: "Don't talk too loud or yell. Oh! And don't interrupt while the Telling is being told!"

Then Grandpa falls quiet as he rubs his chin, considering if there is anything more to say.

Suddenly, a small voice is heard from a nearby bush, "Old friend, since you have them scared already, can I play? Arrrrrrrr!" Graybeard yells as he bursts out of the bushes and runs down the trail at them, waving his arms. Janet and Brittany

48

scream, Conor jumps, and Grandma laughs.

Grandpa just smiles as he announces, "Oh, yeah. I forgot to tell you -- they do love having fun and a good joke!"

When everyone calms down, Grandpa adds, "Conor, would you like to do the introductions?"

"Sure." He turns to their guests and motions to the little man. "Janet, Brittany, may I present Mr. Daniel O'Doul, known to all as Graybeard. He is the elder and leader of the Tinys and the only one I've met so far," he adds.

Graybeard walks up to Janet and extends his hand. "I'm sorry. I just couldn't resist having a little fun at your expense. After hearing so much about you two and Conor, I feel like you are family."

Then he turns to Grandpa, "You said they were pretty." Then, glancing back at Janet and her daughter, he says, "My Ladies, you are BEAUTIFUL!" as he removes his hat with a flourish and bows to them.

Janet blushes, and then, staring down at the little man, asks, "How is this possible?"

Grandma puts her arm around her shoulder and softly says, "Stay with us, dear; you will understand shortly."

Graybeard turns to Conor, saying, "Lad, you made a wonderful decision to include them in our small band of confidants. I have felt Janet needed to be aware of us long before now."

He then turns back to Grandpa. "I have things to attend to before the festival of the Telling starts. So if you would like, you can take them by the village and show them around. It's all but deserted now because everyone is heading for the clearing." Then he adds, "You know where you are to be seated for the ceremony." With that, he tips his hat to the ladies – young and old -- and with a wave is off up the trail.

Grandpa instructs, "Follow me," and they all continue down the path in the direction Graybeard went. After about 50 yards, they come to another path that leads to the right, away from the main trail. They follow the new path.

"This trail encircles the village," Grandpa explains. "For their protection, the village is surrounded by sticker bushes and wild berries with no apparent openings or paths leading in."

Grandpa stops at a rocky area covered by bushes. He steps on one rock and then another, which releases a rope and pulley system raising the sticker bushes just enough to allow them to enter. Once inside the barrier of bushes, they find another path.

"If you will just come this way, you can see most of the village from here," Grandpa says over his shoulder. The vegetation thins out and they stop at a grove of beautiful trees, where they see what looks like a picture out of a child's storybook. Hundreds of small, houses nestle among the trees. Some are built up in the lower branches of the trees, with rope walkways leading from one to the other, but most of the houses are on the ground. There are small little gardens all around. Some houses are painted bright colors and each has a distinctive door design. The houses and the grounds around are kept neat and clear of any rocks, twigs, leaves, or pine needles. The five visitors stare in wonder at the sight before them.

There are stairways built into the sides of tree trunks leading to the homes off the ground and ropes hanging down with knots for climbing. Conor gazes in awe at elevators with more ropes going to hand-cranked winches for hauling items up to the homes. Janet counts six water wells spaced throughout an irrigation system leading to all the gardens.

50

"It takes my breath away every time I see the village," Grandma says.

"Good heavens; this is amazing!" exclaims Janet.

"Amazing is definitely the word!" Brittany replies, as they continue on around the path with "Wow," "Look at that," and "Unbelievable" being the extent of the conversation.

When they reach the main trail again, Grandpa stops to tell them, "When we get back to the house, I will show you how to inform them you are coming out here, so there are no surprises. Always remember to never walk through the village. Stay on the paths; we don't want anyone getting hurt."

With that being said, he waves them on: "Let's go." They follow him on down the walkway for another 40 yards or so until he again stops and motions for them to leave the walkway. They walk behind some tall brush until they come upon two wooden benches, placed about 4 feet apart. Then Grandpa whispers, "You three sit here, facing the brush. Be as quiet as you can. Things

51

will all start in a few minutes."

He and Grandma sit on the other bench and wait.

Conor, Janet, and Brittany sit down and soon begin to hear voices coming from the other side of the brush. Some are talking, others are laughing, and a low mummer comes from others. Slowly there are more and more voices, and they grow louder with each second. The three of them are so excited they can hardly sit still. Through the brush they can see glimpses of bright colors and movement, but nothing more.

Graybeard stands on a knoll to one side of the big clearing, watching the villagers enter and take their places. Some sit on little wooden benches placed in a semicircle around the speaker's platform, and some prefer to sit on the naturally-formed seats of tree roots, rocks, or grass encompassing the clearing. He smiles as he looks around the area.

"Gary and the rest of the volunteers did an exceptional job this year," he begins. He takes note of the two teachers with the children 12 years and under sitting in one section. The teachers will take them on a field trip to the stream after he makes the introductions, and before the Telling starts. He takes in a big breath, lets it out, and heads for the speaker's platform.

Noticing the children 13 and older seated in the front row, he says to himself, *"Only nine children!"* Just before starting up the steps, he turns to look for Kasandra, the village healer. He spots her over by the main entrance, just coming in. Looking around, she notices him motioning her over. She waves back and starts working her way through the crowd. She stops along the way to adjust a bandage or two and to inquire if her remedies are working.

He is patiently waiting when she finally gets to him. "Good morning, Father," she says as she hugs him. "Good morning, Daughter. How are all your patients doing? Well, I hope."

"Very well!" She smiles at him, knowing he is teasing her about how long it took her to reach him.

They both notice things are about to start, and they take their seats on the platform.

As they sit down, Graybeard sees most of the people have ceased their greetings to one another and are starting to settle

52

down.

Kasandra nudges her father, "Come over to my house tonight after the Telling. I made fresh-baked oatmeal cookies." Knowing how much he loves her cookies, she tries to get him to come over as often as possible, especially since her mother passed on. She doesn't like him living alone and worries he's not eating right or taking good care of himself. But he insists he is getting along just fine.

"Cookies! Ah," he replies with a big grin. "I will bring some fresh milk."

By now the people have all entered and found seats. Graybeard stands and moves to the center of the platform. As he walks over to the podium, he recalls his first Telling -- oh, so long ago. Looking down at the bright faces of the young ones seated close to the platform, he sees the same expressions of excitement and wonder that he had known those many years before.

He smiles and raises his hand to quiet the people.

"Welcome to the festival of the Telling. Before we start, we need to introduce our guests. We have five Big people with us today! I would like to start with the two you all know very well, our beloved friends, **Grandpa Conor and Grandma Faye.**"

Graybeard turns to the right with a sweep of his arm -- and like magic, the brush in front of them slides to the side. The crowd breaks into applause as Grandpa and Grandma stand and wave to all. Graybeard looks to the right of the stage and gives a thumbs-up to Gary and three other men, who had pulled the ropes that parted the bushes. When the applause dies down, he continues.

"As we all know, the Lord called home their son, Conor the Fourth and his wife Sara, last year. They will be missed, until we see them again in Heaven.

"Tonight, we add three more dear friends to our trusted circle. You have heard me and the elders speak of them many times. I am proud all of you finally get to meet Janet Cook, her daughter Brittany, and Conor O'Brien the Fifth!"

Graybeard turns to the left with a sweep of his arm, and the bushes shake but don't move. Off to the side, he sees four men straining on the ropes, but nothing is happening. There are a few

53

chuckles and hoots from the crowd and then a loud SNAP! As the rope breaks and the four men land on their rears.

The bushes start to fall over; Conor catches them and starts sidestepping them to the left with his head over the top, grinning. The whole place breaks into a roar of laughter, with some Tinys even falling off their seats, holding their sides.

Conor goes back to Brittany's side, and the three of them are caught up in the contagious laughter. The grandparents and Graybeard, along with the crowd, burst into a 5-minute belly roll! When everyone finally quiets down, the ice has been broken, and a warm feeling of friendship settles over all.

After wiping the tears of laughter from his face, Graybeard raises both arms and in a loud voice proclaims, "Hear ye! Hear ye! Hear ye! I proclaim this to be the time of the Telling to the fifth generation in the America."

An overwhelming "Hooray!" comes from the crowd, along with more applause. The two teachers with the youngest children line them up, and they soon leave on their field trip. Among the group is Angela, the teacher's daughter, and Ahnika, Kasandra's daughter.

The teenage Tinys seated in the front row are all now totally focused on Graybeard, who says, "You are the next generation," as he spreads his arms to indicate all the teenagers. Looking up and scanning the crowd for the faces of their parents, he continues, "It is time you learn from **where** we came and **who** we are!"

The oldest of the children, Trey, thinks to himself, *"**Who** we are?" I know **who** we are. We are **kids**, **people**. What does he mean, **who** we are?"*

Trey looks up to hear Graybeard saying, "...are not normal size for most humans, you see; we are smaller, much smaller."

Now Conrad's hand shoots up, as if he was still in the classroom.

Graybeard is having a hard time holding back a smile as he addresses Conrad: "Yes, Conrad; what is it?"

"What do you mean, we are smaller?"

"Well, Conrad, most of the people living on this Earth are 5 to 6 feet tall. Your dad, although he is tall for a Tiny, is only a little more than 1 foot tall."

54

The children consider this for a few seconds and then there are a few "Oohs" and "Aahs," along with some puzzled looks.

"Let me explain," continues Graybeard.

"We are, or rather, **you** are the fifth generation since we were brought to this country from England in 1919. Now I know you've studied some history in school."

Most of the children nod their heads "Yes."

"You know we live in the state of Tennessee, which is in the country of the United States of America. You also know about towns and cities. But what you do not know is that we are living here away from towns and cities for our protection! We must remain separated and away from the Bigs!"

This time Chais shoots his hand up. He is one of the boys known as the "Three Musketeers," because they were all three born within a 10-day period of each other. Also, the three of them are always seen running around together.

"Yes, Mister Chais?"

"You said 'Stay away from the Bigs!'"

"Yes!"

"A big WHAT?" This brings laughter from the crowd.

"No, not a big, I mean...not...ahem... What I meant to say was to stay away from the big people. That's what I meant. We Tinys call them Bigs."

Another hand goes up, this time belonging to Brandyn.

"Yes, Brandyn?"

"Why must we stay away from the Bigs? Are they bad people? Would they hurt us?"

"No!" Graybeard answers. "Most people are not bad, but some -- just a few, mind you -- are too curious, and that's not good for us."

This time it's Dowen, another one of the Three Musketeers, who raises his hand and asks, "Why is being curious bad?"

"Well, it's hard to explain... All right, think of it this way. When you see a baby animal, you want to hold it, play with it, and keep it, right? Some of the Bigs see us kind of like that – not that they consider us animals, but they would want to pick us up and play with us, and most likely want to keep us."

"Because we are small, like some of their toys?" questions Dowen, who has been taking this all in.

55

"That's right, like a toy," says Graybeard, enjoying all the interaction with the kids.

"Are there any Bigs living near us?" asks Nathan, the younger brother of Conrad and the third Musketeer.

"No, Nathan. They live very far from here, except for Grandma Faye and Grandpa Conor. We are safe here, in the forest."

Kariya, who is the youngest child at the Telling, raises her hand.

"Yes, Kariya. What is your question?"

She stands up. When she does, the top of her head is barely even with the heads of the other children still seated. "Have you ever been hurt by a Big?"

Graybeard smiles as he pulls on his beard, "No, I have not. My best friend is a Big." He points to Grandpa, Conor O'Brien III. "Yes, yes -- I know I said Bigs were bad for us, and it's true with a few exceptions -- and the O'Briens are a very special exception.

"Now, you all know Grandpa and Grandma O' Brien, and you know they love you and would never hurt you. Well, Conor, their grandson, and Miss Brittany and Miss Janet love you too, and they only want to help keep you safe. I know it's hard for you to understand that some people, big or small, can do bad things, but that's a lesson you **must** learn. The world, outside of our little village, is full of people and things that could hurt you. But let me emphasize: Most people of all sizes are good. The thing you need to remember is it's better for us if the world outside does not know of or ever find out we even exist."

Graybeard continues: "You see, it was the great-great-great-grandfather of Mr. O'Brien who brought my great-great-great-grandparents here to live in America."

Half a dozen hands go up all at once.

"Wait, wait," Graybeard says. "Now that you know about the Bigs, tomorrow at school your teacher will tell you all about our history and how we came to be here."

This time Vanessa, the oldest girl, raises her hand. "Yes, Vanessa?"

"Why can't you tell us now?"

"Well, I..."

56

"Please!" is the cry from all the children.

"Well I...suppose... If you really want to know!"

He is having a hard time holding back a grin. He loves to tease the young ones. "Okay!" he says, and he bursts out laughing and signals the teacher to come up.

The teacher, Mr. Vaughn, comes up on the platform next to Graybeard; he smiles, and winks. Then, turning to face the children, he finds them all sitting quietly, watching his every move and gesture. As he pulls up a stool nearby, he sits, readying himself for the stories he loves to tell the most. He, too, remembers how excited he was at his first Telling.

He begins... "The best way to explain our history is through the Telling. These stories are told to each and every generation."

Graybeard walks up to Mr. Vaughn and hands him a large, leather-bound book.

"Before I start, let me explain this book." He holds it up so all can see.

"This is very old, as you can tell, and it contains the records of our lineage, first written by John Ashley. This account you are about to hear has been handed down to each generation. This is the only written record of our forefathers and of us Tinys. Each generation adds its part. Mr. Vaughn opens the old book and carefully turns to the first page.

"Our story begins with..."

Chapter 8
1657AD Rescue

The year is 1657. At Corth Castle in England, young Count Edward Hawk is worriedly pacing the floor. He had just summoned his two best men, Luke and John. He has known these men all of his life -- they served his father before him and are like older brothers. Entering the count's sitting room, a servant announces, "Sire, they are arriving and will be here in a moment."

"Very good; send them straight in!" replies the count excitedly.

John and Luke had been at the practice field training and testing their fighting skills as they wait for the count to send them on a special mission. Now he has called for them, and both are ready to go anywhere for this man they love as a brother.

The mood in the old castle is one of grief and despair, with so many bad things happening recently.

Edward's father, Count William, had fallen ill and died only a few months before. Just a year earlier, Edward's mother had passed quietly in her sleep. The sudden loss of his wife had taken its toll on Edward's father and his health failed rapidly. Now Count Edward, at the young age of 18, is alone and in charge of a large estate in the north of England, with several businesses in England and elsewhere that his father had founded. Losing both of his parents in such a short amount of time had hit Edward hard, but the duties of running what is now Hawks & Company help keep him busy.

Now **this**! A mad man named Hobart and his band of cutthroats has captured some of the little ones, and no one knows where he has taken them. Hobart is a ruthless pirate who fled France a few years before to escape hanging.

Edward's father, Count William, had discovered the Tinys about the same time as Hobart's men had stumbled upon them. Count William, with a few of his men and the help of the Tinys, had defeated Hobart and captured most of his men. Unfortunately, Hobart and a few others had managed to get away.

Now Hobart has returned to England with more men and is getting his revenge by capturing a group of Tiny men.

58

Fearing for his little friends, Count Edward had sent men out to scour the country looking for the Tinys. Finally, after almost a month of searching, he has news!

John and Luke climb the stairs to where the count is waiting. They come to the open door of the sitting room and hesitate, as it is not proper to enter without being acknowledged.

"Come in, my friends!" the count tells them, "I have news to share." He motions for John to close the door as he puts one finger to his lips. When the door closes, he comes over and greets them with a slap on the shoulder. "Come, sit. We must not let anyone overhear our plans."

"Good news, Sire?" Luke inquires.

"Aye! I have! Our spies have found out where he is holding them, and we must be quick before he moves them again. He has brought them back to the ruins of the old Dunmore Castle that he's been using as a base. It's only two days' ride from here, and once we are there, we will mount our attack and take them back!" announces the count.

John is the first to speak up. "Sire, if we mount a full-scale attack, surely they will know we are coming and hide the little ones again."

As the count's champion and lifetime friend, he is very loyal to the Hawk family. At 5-foot 7-inches tall, he is average size, but he is stronger than he looks and extremely versed with the weapons of the day.

Count Edward stands, slowly paces back and forth, and ponders the situation. "Of course you are right, John," he says, "but what can we do that will not alert them?"

"We should take only a small band. This way we can hit them," John starts to say.

"No, wait!" Luke interrupts. "The best way to get inside is for only two to go. John and I must go. We can sneak in by dressing like Hobart's guards. Bluff our way in, and fight our way out, if we must. They will not expect only the two of us." Luke, John's best friend and fellow orphan, is also the count's champion.

Count Edward and John both nod their heads. "That could work," agrees the count. "But what of me? Surely I must go!"

"No, Sire! You would be in great danger, and should we be

59

discovered, it would be hard for us to protect you," John explains. "You are better-needed here, for if we should fail, then who will try again, if not you?"

"Aye! You are right again, my friends. It will not be easy, staying here while you two go off to fight my battles. But let it be done as you say."

"But what of this Hobart? Why did he take the little ones in the first place?" asks John.

"As you know, Hobart and my father clashed a long time ago when the Tinys still lived in the dark forest. When he was driven off, Hobart swore he would come back."

"A few years ago he returned from France with what I'm sure was ill-gotten wealth and bought that old run-down castle. He hadn't bothered any of the Tinys or us until he captured some of the Tiny men while they were on a quest."

"The Tinys had wanted to go back to the dark forest where they once lived to retrieve something of value they had left there long ago in a cave. The little ones had decided it would be best to travel without an escort, trusting that it would be easier for them to travel unseen. But Hobart had placed a spy in Corth Village. That's how he knew of them and when they would be alone," answers the count.

"But why has he taken them?" questions Luke.

"Hobart is a man mad with power and wealth. I have been told he believes the little ones hold the knowledge of how to conjure up gold," the count explains. "What a fool! He is convinced they know how to turn lead into gold. He must be beating and torturing them, trying to get the secret out of them, a secret they never possessed."

"Why don't they just tell him of the treasure that is here and save themselves from all that pain?" John asks.

"That, my friend, you will need to ask them yourself. They have always been loyal to my father, and me as well. I pledged to protect them and have failed. You must bring them back!"

"Aye, that we will, Sire, and as for Hobart, if I find him, I would have him at the end of my sword!"

The count sends them off with "Go now, and Godspeed to you both!"

Two days later, John and Luke drive their wagon into the

60

small village next to the old castle where Hobart is holding the little ones. No one pays them much attention. They manage to find two of Hobart's men patrolling outside of the village and quickly relieve them of their uniforms, which fit well enough. They are unnoticed, as the villagers are accustomed to seeing Hobart's men traveling back and forth. After waiting until nightfall, John and Luke enter the village; as they get closer to the back gate of the old castle, they can see there are only two guards on duty. As they slowly approach the gate, one of the guards comes to the center of the road, blocking their way. "Halt!" he commands.

"Whoa," John tells the team of horses as he brings them to a stop.

"What be your business here?" the guard demands.

"Hobart's business, you fool," Luke answers. "Who else would have us out in the middle of this damp night? I could be home sleeping next to my wife with my dog to keep my feet warm."

"Aye, tis a big fat dog he has!" jokes John. They all laugh.

"Go on then, and get your work done so you can go home to your wife and fat dog!" The guard laughs as he waves them through.

Once past the gate, they swing around, placing the wagon so they have a straight run at the gate when they escape. Climbing down from the wagon, Luke whispers, "Hopefully, fooling the cell-guards will be as easy."

John looks over at him to see a big grin on his face.

They manage to get into the cellblock without encountering anyone. When they see two very big men guarding a single cell, they decide this must be the cell holding the little ones. John walks up to the one he assumes is in charge. "Hobart instructed us to transport these creatures" -- he says, pointing to the cell holding the little ones --"to a new location right away!" and starts for the cell.

The head guard holds up his hand. "Let me see your orders!"

"But of course," John says as he reaches into his cloak, draws his knife, and points it at the guard's throat. "Will this do?" he asks jokingly.

Luke, too, has his knife out and pressed against the other

61

guard's belly. With his free hand, he reaches over and takes the guards' swords and tosses them aside. John removes the cell keys from the first guard's belt and forces the two into an empty cell, where they tie and gag them. After locking them in, they open the cell where the little ones are, telling them they have come from Count Hawks.

John and Luke get them all outside; helping about 24 Tinys get into the wagon. Suddenly, the next shift of guards comes around the corner. The rainy night is dark, so the guards can't see the Tinys being lifted into the wagon, but they do notice the two big men.

"What's your business here?" one of the guards demands.

"Hobart's business. Who wants to know?" John answers.

"I do, the captain of the guard," the captain announces.

John, trying to buy time so Luke can finish getting the little ones into the wagon, walks over to confront the two Hobart guards. "Oh, good evening, Captain. I didn't recognize you in the dark." Before the captain can see John is not one of his men, John attacks, punching the captain on the chin and sending him falling backward to land on the ground, out cold. John then pounces on the remaining guard and wrestles him to the ground before the guard can draw his sword.

Meanwhile, Luke picks up the last of the little ones and places him inside the wagon.

John manages to hold the second guard at bay until Luke can join him. John prays, *"I hope no one hears us fighting."* Before the guard is able to call for help, Luke knocks him unconscious with the butt of his sword.

The guards at the gate are inside a hut, trying to keep warm, and don't hear the ruckus. John and Luke quickly climb onto the wagon and start for the gate. The same guard that had stopped them when they entered comes out to stop them again. He holds up his lantern to see who it is. "And where be ye off to now?"

"You can bet it's not home to his wife on this cold night. That's for sure," John responds.

The guard remembers them. "Ah, yes -- the one with the wife and fat dog!" Moving aside, he lets them pass.

The guards are still laughing at the fat dog joke as the wagon disappears into the night.

62

After leaving Hobart's castle, they don't head straight back to Corth Castle, but instead go the other way in an effort to throw off any pursuers. Soon they make their way back to the small village they had passed through earlier. They leave the old wagon and retrieve the coach they had hidden nearby.

After traveling the dusty, tree-lined roads for two days, the team of four fine horses is tiring, and it is taking all of his strength for Luke to maintain control of the coach and its precious cargo.

"It has been a long, hard journey," John thinks to himself as he sits inside the coach looking out at the woods. He hopes their success will please the count.

"Can you see the castle?" John asks from inside the coach.

"Not yet," Luke answers, adding, "but it will be glorious to be home again." "But what of Hobart himself, the one who did this foul deed?" Luke questions, with a scowl and fury in his eyes. "If only we could have gotten at him. But we hadn't enough time, more's the pity."

As the coach turns and starts up the last of the winding roads that will take them through the hills to the castle they call home, John again turns his attention to the view alongside. This trip has been sad and dangerous and he longs to forget it. Concerned that Hobart's men would soon be closing in on them, he prays they can reach Corth Castle before Hobart does.

The view outside of the coach reminds John that it is fast becoming fall. The forest is ablaze with color. He has always liked this time of the year, with the cool nights and clear, bright days. When he was a lad, he would walk for hours in the woods, just looking at the bountiful colors and listening to the leaves crunch under his footsteps. He loved the forest and missed that part of his youth. Back then, there was always a new mystery just around the next tree or beyond the gully ahead. There were plenty of places to hide and play and time to daydream of knights who fought from tall horses in shining armor. He loved to dream of gleaming swords, colorful banners, and decorated shields of old.

John's daydreaming is cut short when the coach hits a rut in the road, jarring him back to the present, just as Luke yells, "WHOA!"

John turns to see what it is that has caused Luke to give such an order.

Luke starts yelling, "It's burning, it's burning! The castle is burning! What kind of trouble is this now?"

John, seeing a glimpse of smoke and flames, tells Luke, "Quickly now, turn off the road, and head into the woods over there," as he points to the right where the trees are dense enough to hide the coach.

Luke asks, "Did you see?"

He finds the answer in his friend's expression.

"Aye that I did! Lord, have mercy on us all, for what we have brought upon our count."

Luke's head sinks to his chest in despair, "How did they know to come here? We did not reveal ourselves to them. What kind of magic is this that they can find us so quickly?"

"It's not magic, my friend, but the devil's work, I be thinking," John says as he moves to the front of the coach just in time to see the reins drop, and the horses slow to a stop.

"Come now, Luke!" John says as he jumps down to retrieve the reins. "We must not let them find the little ones. I will drive, and you watch our backs to see if we are followed."

Climbing up onto the driver seat, John snaps the reins. "HAW!" he shouts at the team of horses. Looking back, he sees his friend standing up at the back of the coach, facing the rear.

"Hmm. Seems like I remember a gully not far from here," John announces.

"Aye! I remember; it's through there," Luke points to his left. "It should be large enough to hide the coach."

"Haw, now!" John shouts, as he again snaps the reins on the backs of the horses. "Haw, now!"

With a jump, they all pull at once, sending the coach and its passengers deeper into the woods.

As the coach lunges forward, several tiny "Oohs," "Ouches," and even a few yells can be heard coming from the back of the coach.

"Sorry!" John says. "We should have warned you. Is everyone alright?"

"Aye!" comes a reply from within a hidden compartment. "We are all alright. You just caught us by surprise."

64

As they move through the woods, Luke keeps looking to their rear to ensure they are not followed. Once again, he calls to those inside the coach. "It will only be a little ways more, and then it will be safe to stop and let you out."

"Aye, thank you, Sir. We can use a wee walk in the woods, if you catch my meaning!" replies the tiny voice from within.

After they travel about 400 yards into the woods, John finally turns the coach into a gully. Pulling back on the reins, he says, "Whoa! Whoa now!" as he pushes on the brake lever with his foot to bring the coach to a halt. As the coach stops and the dust settle, John and Luke look around to make sure they are safe. John climbs up on top of the coach to get a better view.

"Do you see any sign of Hobart's men?" asks Luke.

"No, not a sign. We're safe enough here. Let's get them out. It must be quite hard on them, being crammed in there for so long, besides being chased across the country by the likes of Hobart and his evil bunch."

Luke enters the coach and lifts the rear floorboards to reveal a secret compartment, which had been added for the sole purpose of hiding and transporting their tiny passengers.

Inside are 24 tiny men. As they stand up, most are rubbing their eyes in the transition from the dark compartment to the bright light of day.

John comes around from the front of the coach to the rear, lets down the tailgate, and helps their passengers one-by-one down to the ground.

After everyone is out of the coach, the oldest man looks up at John. "We owe you our lives and much gratitude, Sirs. What can we say or do to repay you two for saving us?"

"You need not thank us, Sir, but give your thanks to God. For it was only with His help and by His hand that our Sire -- whose castle now burns, no doubt by the hand of Hobart -- did we learn of you and your plight."

The old one lowers his head, closes his eyes and says nothing out loud. All the other tiny men, who have been listening all along, stop what they were doing and lower their heads as well. After a few moments, the old one ends with, "Amen" and raises his head, and the others do the same.

The old one, seeing the look of surprise on John's face, asks,

65

"Did you suppose, Sir, because we are small and different from most, that we would not know and worship the Lord our God? I did as you suggested and gave thanks to the Lord for our deliverance and also for you, Kind Sirs, our deliverers."

Somewhat taken aback and embarrassed, John then replies, "Forgive me; I did not mean to imply such. I do admit, though, that up to now, I had not thought of you and yours as men and women, but more like children. My humble apologies."

The old man smiles at John. "You, Sirs, of all the big people, owe no apology."

"Thank you! May I inquire as to how this was done to you? How did all of you come to be so small?"

"We are as we have always been, small in stature and small in number. This has been so, for as many generations as any can remember," the old one answers. "Are we safe here?" he asks. "Shouldn't we be moving on before they find us?"

Luke returns, having gone back the way they came to cover their trail.

"I hid our trail as best I could, but the coach wheels dug deep ruts that I can't cover up, and I fear they will lead them to us."

Looking down at these precious little ones, John asks, "Is it true you are all that is left of the ones who were caught?"

"Yes!" answers the old one. "We are all that remains. We started with 36 men, but now only 24 are left after suffering under the hand of Hobart."

Luke reminds his friend, "John, it is growing near dusk. We should be safe here until morn, don't you agree?"

"Aye. These people need to rest and eat a meal. Will you care for them while I go and see what has become of our homes and the count?"

"I will, but you must take care not to be seen by Hobart or his men," Luke warns.

"Fear not. I will return before the night has passed," he says as he unhitches the lead horse and climbs on. "If I do not return, you alone must see them to safety, my friend."

Luke shakes his friend's hand, adding, "God willing, we will both take care of them. Now go, and God be with you!"

John spends an hour going the long way around to come up from behind the castle. It is not quite dark yet, and when he gets

66

closer, he sees it is not the castle that is burning, but farmers burning off the fields after finishing the harvest. John is relieved that he and Luke were wrong about the fire, but he is still very cautious as he approaches the back gate of the place he calls home. Knowing most of the guards, he calls out before getting too close, "Hail the castle!"

The guard answers back, "Who say ye?"

"John Ashley."

The door on the gate flies open, and the guard comes out.

"John? Is it truly you? We thought the worst had befallen you!"

"I am fine, my friend, and how is the count?" John says as he rides up to meet the guard he now recognizes.

The guard comes up to the horse and takes hold of the bridle, "He is well and worried about you and Luke. He left orders for you to see him straight away. What news do you bring?"

John dismounts and starts across the courtyard, turning with a wave: "First, I must see my count, then you will know. Have someone tend to my horse."

"Aye, Sir!" the guard replies and hands the reins to a servant standing nearby. "Here, see to his horse."

Once inside, John finds Count Edward sitting alone in his library. He rushes in with a happy shout. "Sire!"

"John!" the count shouts with joy. "Thank the Lord you are safe!" Forgetting protocol, he gets up and runs over to greet the friend he has known all his life. They clasp each other's arms. "I thought you and Luke might be lost to me!"

"And we feared for you and the castle when we saw the smoke and flames!" answers John.

"The castle? Smoke? What smoke?" Edward questions, leading his friend over to sit next to his chair. Then, the light of knowledge comes on his face. "Oh! You saw the farmers burning the fields."

"Aye, and we thought Hobart had burnt this place," John answers.

Edward looks at John with concern. "This man would do such a thing? Surely he would not dare to come against my men and me. Not after what my father did to him at the dark forest."

"That and more, my count!" John exclaims. "Hobart is a

67

terrible man. He treats his subjects with contempt and cruelty. He mistreated the little ones so that scarcely 24 men are left!"

"Only 24, you say? Why? When he captured them, they counted more than 35! What did he do to them?"

John shakes his head. "We have yet to learn the truth of his deeds."

Edward paces back and forth, pondering what he has been told.

John, who was captain of the guard for Edward's father and who has known Edward all his life, thinks as he waits, *"He has grown into a fine man that William would be proud of!"*

Edward slumps in his chair, his head in his hands, and tears in his eyes. "I have failed them."

"No! My friend. You saved them twice. Once when your father and you brought them here to live and learn and become the God-fearing people they are today, and now from the likes of this Hobart. But this madman is very powerful, and he will not stop until he finds them again," John reminds Edward.

"Yes, I know you are right. In order to protect them, I have gathered all of the Tinys from their village nearby and had them brought here inside the castle. But if Hobart is as powerful as you say, these walls may not shield them. We must guard them at all costs. My father and I swore to protect them and keep them safe. Now we must do what I fear the most!"

"What is it you fear, my Count?"

"I must ask a great deal of you, my friend."

"Ask what you may, and I will give as I can," John replies.

"You must take the little ones far from here."

"What? Take them away? But they are your friends. How can you watch over them if they are far from you?"

"We must do this. They will not be safe if Hobart knows where they are," Edward continues. "Go get Luke and the little ones and bring them here for now. We will make plans as to where you must go to keep them safe and away from Hobart."

John does as he is commanded and soon returns with the Tiny men and Luke.

While the Tiny men and their families are being reunited, Edward tells Luke of his plan to have the Tinys taken far away from Corth Castle.

68

"Aye! I can see you are right, but how are we to do this, and where can we take them that would be safe?"

"Are you both willing to give up your home here and take on this task?" the count questions.

"Aye! You know John and I have no family here. It was your father, God rest his soul, who took us in as orphan children and raised us as his own, and so we leave little behind, save you, Sire. We will leave this castle we call our home with heavy hearts, for I suspect we can never return."

Edward stands and says, "It falls to you and John to take them and care for them. I have thought and prayed on this, and I believe you must go far from here, even as far as Ireland!"

"Ireland? That is wild country. How would we live?"

"I can help. I possess great treasures and as much as you need, you shall have!" exclaims the count.

"But, my Count, we will only need a small ship that Luke and I can sail, and the supplies to see us through."

Count Edward looks long at his friends and smiles. He goes over and pulls on the cord hanging nearby, summoning his servant. He turns to his friends, "You, Sirs, are truly my champions and my friends. You shall have all you need." A servant appears in the doorway; Count Edward turns and instructs him, "See to it that John and Luke receive all they ask for, and send in the Captain of the Treasury."

"Very good Sire!" The servant replies and instantly leaves to do his count's bidding.

"The Captain of the Treasury?" John questions. "My Count, we need only some food and a few supplies for the journey. We cannot take any of your fortune."

"Ah!" exclaims the count. "That's where you are mistaken, my faithful friend. You see, it is not my fortune -- the treasure belongs to them!"

"Belongs to the little ones? But how, I have seen this treasure, and it fills most of the catacombs beneath this very room? How did they come by such a thing?"

The count smiles and motions for his friend to sit down as he continues, "As you recall, it was my father who first came upon them in the dark forest these many years ago. They were trying to live in the forest, because they feared the big people; they thought

69

we were giants, so they stayed mostly in caves. My father stayed with them for some time, befriended them and asked if they would come to live in his castle. He swore on his honor to protect and provide for them. At first they were reluctant, but after he took a few to see the castle, they agreed to come and live here."

"After they had grown to know him and the family as friends and providers, they told him of a treasure they had found in a sea cave. They took him to it and told him to take it back to the castle and to use it to help both his family and them. This treasure consisted of 35 chests of gold coins, 200 chests of silver coins and bars, eight chests of diamonds, and other jewels. Most all of it remains here today, and you! Sir, will have whatever the little ones need of it."

"But we cannot travel with such a treasure. It is far too dangerous to do so," John notes.

"I will ship some to you, after you are settled. Now go, and may God bless you and Luke and each who choose to protect these little ones. I will miss them as I would miss my own children."

After bidding farewell to John, Luke, and the Tinys, the ship full of supplies and around 400 little ones leave on the long journey to Ireland.

Mr. Vaughn closes the book of the Telling and looks down at the children to see them all sitting quietly, wondering what comes next.

Trey is the first to speak, "What happened to them? Did they go to Ireland?"

And the others were all saying, "Tell us more; tell us more, please!"

"Well, we don't have any written records of what happened next. We can only speculate. But we assume they did indeed go to Ireland and most of them stayed there for a long time. We do, however, have a record that tells us some of them must have returned to England; and then, and later on in 1917, they got in real trouble! Do you want to hear that account?"

"Yes! Yes!" all the children yell.

So the teacher opens up the Telling book once more and begins to read...

70

Chapter 9
The Raid of 1917

The Big peoples village of Blyth is on the rugged northeast coast of England. A group of Tinys also lives alongside the big people. Blyth is a small, out-of-the way place not well known or traveled. It's an ideal place where the little ones can live and work in harmony with the villagers. They have been in Blyth since the mid-1700s; some chose to live in the village, but most live in the caves nearby. These little ones are the descendants of those rescued from Hobart the Terrible back in 1657 and taken to Ireland.

One of the village fishermen, a big person and his 9-year-old son are out fishing, like they have been so many times before. They sail out much further than usual, because fishing is very poor close to shore, and they need a good catch, for it has been weeks since they have caught anything.

A huge storm comes up very suddenly and carries them far out to sea. The year is 1917, and England is at war with Germany. The storm blows them dangerously close to waters patrolled by the German Navy, and as luck would have it, a German gunboat spots them and stops them for questioning. The Germans naturally assume the fisherman is there to spy on them. They beat him and try to get him to confess he is a spy, but he doesn't. The German captain becomes very angry and tells the man they will beat the boy and throw him overboard if the man does not confess. The fisherman becomes very afraid and wanting to save his son, tells the captain the only secret he knows. He tells them his village hides a great treasure of gold. The Germans do not believe him at first, so they pick up his son and start to throw him overboard, but the man cries out and tells them to look under his son's shirt. Sitting the boy down on the deck, they pull his shirt off over his head and find a strip of leather tied around the boy's waist with a small pouch attached. One of the sailors pulls the pouch loose and opens it to find a single gold doubloon.

"Gold!" he exclaims, holding it up for all to see. "Das is gold!"

71

Seeing this as a chance to become wealthy, the German captain decides he will raid the village and grab the plunder for himself; however, he tells his crew they are going there for the fatherland and the war. It is very dangerous to go near the coast of England, and the captain knows this. But the chance to find a great treasure is too much to resist.

"Take these two below, and put them in the cell!" he commands his men.

"Lieutenant Kruger, bring us about and set a course for the coast of England," the captain orders.

"Ya vol, my captain!" Kruger answers as he nods to the helmsman and then watches to make sure they are on the correct course. Seeing they are now headed for the English coast, he tells the captain, "On course, Captain."

"Das is good," replies the captain. "Maintain a sharp lookout for Englander ships. We do not want to get our strudels shot off, now do we"? He laughs at his own joke and then starts to leave the bridge. "I will be in my cabin. Notify me when land is sighted."

After the captain leaves the bridge, one of the junior officers, a young man of 19, approaches Lieutenant Kruger. "Sir, our standing orders are - -not to go near the Englander coast- -;"

"Ya vol Hendrix, I know what our orders say, but he is the captain."

Later, as they approach the coast, Lieutenant Kruger orders the captain to be notified and the prisoners brought up to the bridge. As they step through the hatch with the prisoners in front of the guard, the guard gives the fisherman a shove, sending him sprawling onto the deck.

"That will be enough of that!" shouts Kruger.

Snapping to attention and clicking his heels together, the guard responds, "Ya vol!"

Lieutenant Kruger notices that the hands are tied on both the man and the boy. He points to the ropes and orders the guard, "Remove those."

The guard starts to question the lieutenant, "But the captain…"

"Never mind that!" snaps Lieutenant Kruger. "I said remove them!"

72

The guard takes his knife from his belt and cuts their bindings. When he is done, the lieutenant orders him off the bridge. "That will be all. You are dismissed!" The guard turns red in the face, but without saying anything, snaps to attention, salutes, and leaves the bridge.

The lieutenant takes the boy by the arm and leads him over to the forward-facing windows where he can see the coast. "Is that where you live?" asks Lieutenant Kruger in a soft voice. As the boy sees his village, his expression is all Kruger needs to know.

"Yes, Sir," answers the boy.

"Sub Lieutenant Hendrix!" Lieutenant Kruger commands.

Hendrix comes to attention. "Yes, Sir," answers the sub lieutenant, who is at his station on the other side of the bridge. "Come here," Lieutenant Kruger orders. "I have an assignment for you."

Hendrix crosses to stand by the lieutenant; Kruger bends down and whispers something in his ear. The sub lieutenant looks at Lieutenant Kruger with a questioning expression, then smiles, "Yes, Sir! Right away, Sir!" He then takes the two prisoners by the arms and leads them off the bridge.

A knock on the door awakens the German captain. After rubbing the sleep from his eyes, he demands, "Yes, what is it?"

"Sir, Lieutenant Kruger wishes to report we have arrived at the Englander village, as per your orders."

"Very well. I'm on my way."

"Yes, Sir!"

The captain dresses quickly, joining Lieutenant Kruger on the bridge, and he asks, "Any sightings of enemy vessels?"

"Nein, Sir," replies Lieutenant Kruger as he steps down from the captain's chair and stands aside.

"Did you see any troops in the village?"

"Nein, Sir, only a few civilians."

"Civilians? How can you be sure they are not soldiers merely dressed as villagers?"

"Captain? Sir, this is not a military installation, and we are deep in Englander waters. We should leave."

"Leave? Not until we find the treas… I mean destroy the

73

enemy! Bring the guns to bear!" orders the captain.

"Nein! Captain -- you can't do this!"

But the captain ignores the lieutenant's pleas and orders, "Fire!"

The grass, mud, and stick huts are no match for the heavy guns of the German ship. The villagers never had a chance.

* * * * *

Elizabeth O'Rourke has been in the village only a few days. Traveling from Ireland only a week before, she is on a mission to try to locate the lost group of little people thought to be in this part of England. She is the only big person who knows about the little ones in Ireland, or more clearly, the only one who has had contact with them and knows where they are. Her father had been taking care of them until his passing, and she has been looking after them for the past five years. Before his passing, he told her he had lost contact with the group in England and wanted to try and locate them. She promised her father she would try to find them.

When she arrives at the village of Blyth, she tells villagers she is looking for an uncle who is her last remaining relative.

Earlier that day, while she visits with one of the villagers who invite her to her home. Elizabeth is looking around the house while her host is busy making tea. Suddenly, she sees a rug crumpled up where someone had bumped it. Bending down to straighten the rug, she notices a trapdoor under it. She quickly straightens the rug and acts like she hasn't noticed anything.

"A trapdoor?" she says to herself. *"Can this be the clue she has been looking for?"*

Just then the German shelling begins. The lady of the house runs out to see what is happening and is immediately hit. Elizabeth is looking out the open front door when she sees the woman fall. Just then the windows blow in, and she falls to the floor, crabs her purse and crawls over to where she had seen the trapdoor. Opening it, she drops into a dark tunnel. Being more afraid than she has ever been before, she does the only thing she can -- she crawls as fast as possible in the only direction the tunnel leads, hoping she is moving away from the attack and

74

toward the hills.

She crawls about 100 feet in total darkness, scraping her knees as she goes, when she thankfully sees a dim light ahead. Overhead she can hear and feel the exploding shells, as the house she was in only moments before, collapses. She falls on her face and covers her head with her arms, fearing the tunnel will collapse. But it doesn't. She lays still for a while, sobbing, and then she hears a voice, a tiny voice coming from up ahead in the tunnel.

There it is again, closer this time. "Are you all right?" the wee voice asks as the tiniest of hands touches her arm. She raises her head to see one of the little people standing there.

"Thank God, I found you!" is all she can say before she faints!

* * * * *

After the shelling stops, the captain orders Lieutenant Kruger to form a shore party and search the village. Kruger and his men try to search through the wreckage of the destroyed and burning huts, but the damage is too much, and the fires still too hot. Lieutenant Kruger orders his men to spread out and find whatever they can.

He is alone when he comes around the last remains of what had been the village meetinghouse. He notices, through the smoke, what looks like two children standing next to an injured man. When he passes through the smoke and comes nearer, he sees that what he thought were children look more like miniature men, not children at all! Suddenly the two little men see him, and they try to run. He yells at them to halt. The smoke blows around him again, and he loses sight of them. By the time the smoke dissipates, they are gone.

Just then he hears his ship's horn sounding the recall. Turning back toward the shore, he spots the reason for the recall. A British ship is approaching at full speed. The ship is a cruiser, a much larger ship than the Germans', and the cruiser's guns can shoot more than a mile further than the German guns.

As he runs back to the shore boat where his men are clambering aboard, he shouts for them to shove off. Climbing

75

back on board his ship, Lieutenant Kruger is met by the captain.

"Well, did you find any treasure?"

"No, but I saw something amazing!" Kruger tries to explain.

"I don't care about what you saw unless it's the gold!" shouts the captain.

"Did you look everywhere?"

Unable to contain his anger at the captain for being so stupid as to destroy the village before they even had a chance to look for any treasure, Lieutenant Kruger answers, "No! You destroyed everything! We couldn't even get near most of the huts because of the damage and fires!"

"Nothing? You found nothing?" exclaims the captain, choosing to ignore his first officer's anger. "Nothing! I risk my career, and you found nothing! Get out of my sight!"

Lieutenant Kruger leaves the bridge and goes to his cabin.

Meanwhile, the Germans pull up anchor and start running from the British cruiser.

Now, below deck and in his cabin, Lieutenant Kruger is still furious with the captain. *"I tried to tell this stupid man what I saw!"* he said to himself. *"Now I will fix him. I'll record everything that has happened in my journal, and when we get back to port, I will report what he did!"* Kruger sits down at his writing table, opens up his journal, and starts writing.

Back on the bridge, the captain shouts, "Where are the fisherman and the boy? Bring them to me!" As the first shells from the British cruiser explode just off their bow.

"Return fire!" orders the captain.

"No!" interrupts Sub Lieutenant Hendrix. "Sir, they just want us to heave to. If you fire, they will destroy us!"

"We can outrun them!" the captain says, and he again orders, "Full speed, man the guns, and prepare to open fire!"

"Fire!"

Just then the sailor who had been told to get the fisherman and boy returns. "Captain, the prisoners are gone."

"Gone!" shouts the captain. "How could they get away? Where did they go?"

But before the sailor can answer, the British ship returns fire and a broadside of all her guns finds its target with deadly results. The British guns prove to be more accurate, striking the smaller

76

German ship and killing everyone on board.

* * * * *

Meanwhile back in the tunnel, Elizabeth wakes to find the little man trying to revive her.

Patrick is begging, "Please, it is only a few more feet; you must crawl, and then you will be in the cave where you can stand up."

Getting to her knees, she continues to crawl into the cave and finds it lit by only three candles. She slowly stands and looks around, seeing another little man. This one is older, standing off to one side. Patrick is talking to the older one, quietly, so she can't hear. "She said, 'I have found you,' and she was not surprised to see me."

Quinn, the old one, looks up at her. "You are not of this village," he says.

Elizabeth sits down on the cave floor so she can see them better and replies, "No, I am from Ireland, and I was sent here by the Tinys who live there."

"I have no knowledge of anyone living in Ireland," Quinn says, trying to find out who she really is and her reason for being in the village. He heard she is looking for a lost uncle. She smiles and reaches in her pocket and retrieves a small, leather pouch. She sets it down on the floor and opens it.

"I do not lie, nor do I fault you for your suspicions. See for yourself the proof of what I say," pointing to the open pouch.

Patrick starts to move over to the pouch, but Quinn stops him. "Wait, I must see this proof myself!"

He walks over and looks inside to find a ring. "A ring belonging to a big person is no proof of what you say!"

Elizabeth slowly reaches inside and removes the ring, turning it around so Quinn can see the crest inlayed in the red stone.

He smiles from ear to ear.

"Sounds like perhaps the British troops are arriving!" announces Elizabeth.

"Yes!" answers Patrick. "We must not be found here!"

"Is there a back way out of here?" asks Elizabeth.

77

"There is, but I'm afraid the opening is too small for the likes of you, my friend," Quinn answers.

"Then you two go quickly. I will be fine! I will not give you away to them or anyone else!"

* * * * *

After the German ship was attacked and stopped...

...An English Navy search party is now looking for survivors in Blyth.

Someone yells, "You there in the cave, come out, or I'll toss in a bloomin grenade, I will!"

"Oh! Please don't -- I'm English!" Elizabeth calls out.

She then turns to the two Tiny ones and said, "Go now! I will come back as soon as I can."

"God keep you, Miss!" the old man says, and they disappear from sight.

She turns back to the tunnel entrance and yells, "I'm coming out; don't shoot!"

Standing nearby, British Lieutenant Hobart yells at the sergeant, "Throw it!"

"I can't do that, Sir."

I ordered you to throw a grenade!"

"Sir, I can't -- there's a lady in there!" answers the sergeant. Now Hobart is waving his pistol all around and getting red in the face as he commands, "That's an order, Sergeant!"

"Yes, Sir, but as I explained, that's a civilian in there, Sir!"

Right in the middle of all this, Lieutenant O'Brien and the rest of the Marines walk up.

"What is going on here?"

Hobart turns around, "This man refuses to obey a direct order. Arrest him!"

Lieutenant O'Brien looks over at the Marine sergeant.

"What's this all about, Sergeant?"

"Sir, the lieutenant here ordered me to throw a grenade into that tunnel, and it appears that there is a civilian woman in there!"

O'Brien turns back to Hobart, "Is that true? Is there a woman in that tunnel?"

Hobart is outraged at being questioned and replies, "I gave a

78

direct order, and he" -- he says, pointing to the sergeant -- "refused to obey it!"

While this is going on, Elizabeth has managed to crawl back out of the tunnel and is standing beside one of the Marines, "May I say something?" she calmly asks.

Lieutenant O'Brien turns to see, although a bit ruffled and dirty, one of the most beautiful, redheaded women he has ever laid eyes on! "Yes, Ma'am!" is all he can say.

She continues, "My name is Elizabeth O'Rourke. I am here visiting, and they...I was..."

While she is talking, she looks around at the destroyed village and the home where she had been, only moments before. Seeing the massive devastation, she stops speaking, breaks down, and cries out, "Heavenly Father, what have they done?" as tears roll down her face.

As the anger builds up inside her, she turns and points at Lieutenant Hobart. "This man wanted a grenade thrown in the tunnel without finding out who or what was in there!" she says, pointing to the tunnel she had just exited. Then she stands face to face with Hobart. "You! You would have killed me if the sergeant here had not questioned your order to throw a grenade in on me!"

Lieutenant O'Brien turns to Hobart. "Harry, why in the world would you do that?"

"I don't have to answer that!"

Lieutenant O'Brien, recognizing that something is very wrong with his onetime friend, orders, "Lieutenant Hobart, you are relieved of duty and will stand down. I'm placing you on report." Turning to the Marine sergeant, he says, "Sergeant, you will witness my orders."

"Yes, Sir!"

After seeing all his men gathering around, Lieutenant O'Brien says, "Alright, men -- the village is secure, and only this one survivor has been found. Sergeant, form a burial detail and tend to these poor souls!"

"Yes, Sir! Right away, Sir," the sergeant replies, and he turns to the Marines. "Fall in!"

The men all snap to, and then the sergeant assigns them to details. "Corporal, take six men and get these people buried

79

proper-like."

"Yes, Sergeant!" they answer, and leave to tend to their assigned duties.

"Murphy and James, stand guard on the beach. George, you and Smith watch this side of the village and the road."

"Yes, Sergeant!"

After the men move out, only Elizabeth, the sergeant, and the two lieutenants are left, and Lieutenant Hobart starts in again.

"I gave an order, and he refused to obey," he repeats, still waving the pistol around. The sergeant, who is standing closest to Hobart, waits for the right moment and then simply reaches up and disarms him.

"I'll take care of this, Sir, if you don't mind," the sergeant announces as he tucks the pistol in his belt. Turning to address Lieutenant O'Brien, he inquires, "Would there be anything else, Sir?"

O'Brien, trying desperately to hold back a laugh, shakes his head and tells the sergeant, "No, thank you, Sergeant; carry on."

"Sir!" answers the sergeant as he salutes, turns, and walks off swiftly.

Lieutenant O'Brien remarks, "Harry -- and you too, Miss O'Rourke -- we better go down to the beach and wait for our ship."

Harry Hobart is still standing there with his mouth open and holding his hand like he is still holding the gun.

Taking hold of Hobart's arm and leading him, Lieutenant O'Brien starts off. He turns back to see Elizabeth still standing by the destroyed house, "You, too, Miss! You best come along with us until we can figure out what to do with you. As you can see, there is nothing you can do to help here."

Elizabeth runs to catch up. Walking alongside of him, she says, "I guess you are right, Lieutenant. I can return later for my things, if I can even find them." All the while, she's thinking to herself, *"What in the world am I to do now? I can't just leave the little ones here all alone to deal with this awful mess..."* She halts abruptly as if she has forgotten something. Lieutenant O'Brien stops and turns around to see what is wrong.

"What is it, Miss?"

"I need to go back and find my bag. It has all my money and

80

things. Can you help me try to find it?"

"Yes, Ma'am!" He looks around for the sergeant, and seeing him on the beach, he calls him over. "Sergeant!"

The sergeant snaps around, "Sir?" Seeing the lieutenant waving for him to come, he takes off on the run. When he reaches the lieutenant, he snaps to attention and salutes.

Lieutenant O'Brien returns the salute, "Sergeant, I need you to take over here while I return to the village to help Miss O'Rourke find some of her things."

"Yes, Sir!"

"And have the corporal stay with the lieutenant." He points to Lieutenant Hobart, who stands nearby, staring out to sea. "Signal me when the ship comes back."

"Very good, Sir."

As they walk back to the devastated home where she had been visiting, the lieutenant asks, "What brings you to England, Miss O'Rourke?"

She is deep in thought, worrying what to do about the little ones. "Oh! I came here looking for some long-lost friends," she explains, not wanting to lie to him. "And you may call me Elizabeth, Lieutenant." She smiles.

Smiling back at her. "Well then, you must stop calling me Lieutenant. Conor O'Brien at your service. Now, what is it we are looking for?" he asks as they arrive at the remains of the home.

She starts looking around in the rubble and picks up a few items of clothing and personal things like a comb and brush. She finds her coat, but on close examination, sees a large hole in it.

Trying to lighten up the mood and seeing the coat, Lieutenant O'Brien jokes, "Boy! It's a good thing you were not wearing that!"

She laughs and tosses the coat back on the rubble pile. Then she realizes there is a way she can talk to the little ones without the lieutenant knowing. "Lieutenant, uh...I mean, Conor. I can't find my purse. Would you be a dear and make sure the remains of this house don't fall down and block me in while I go back in the tunnel and search for my purse?"

"I'll go, and you stay here!" he offers.

"Thank you, Lieutenant, but I know where I sat, and I assume you are a bit too big to get through the opening to the

81

cave."

"Well, okay; but here, take my torch, and be quick about it!" he orders with a big grin.

"Why, thank you, Conor," she returns to addressing him by his name. "I won't be but a moment," she says as she jumps down and crawls into the tunnel. Inside, she doesn't find the little ones as she had hoped, and she sits down to ponder what to do next.

"Are you alright in there?" calls Conor.

"Yes! I'm still looking for it," she answers.

"And what is it you are looking for, Miss?" a small voice asks. She quickly turns to see Patrick, the young man who had found her in the tunnel, smiling up at her.

"Oh! Thank God! I was so worried I would not see you before I had to leave."

"Leave?" questions the little man.

"Yes, the Navy officer is insisting I should be taken with them, and I can't refuse to go, or they might wonder why I would want to stay with no one left alive here. You do understand, don't you?"

"Why, yes, of course! And you must not worry about us. We have all we need right here in these caves."

From outside Conor asks, "What's taking so long, Elizabeth? We need to get back to the beach."

" I found my purse," she calls out. "Just one more quick look around and I'll be out." Then she says to Patrick, "I will be back with supplies and the means to get you out of here and to Ireland just as soon as I possibly can."

"Godspeed, Elizabeth O'Rourke! We will await your return." He then turns and is gone.

Chapter 10
Love and Betrayal

When the British warship returns and sends a long boat to retrieve the shore party, Lieutenant O'Brien orders all the men to board the boat, and as they all climb aboard, he turns to Elizabeth. "You should come along with us, Miss O'Rourke,"

"I can't go. I must stay and..." -- she looks back at the still-burning village -- "and help!" she says weakly, not really believing any of the villagers are in need of help anymore.

Standing next to the shore boat, Lieutenant O'Brien reaches out his hand to her. "Come along now. There's nothing to do here."

Turning, she takes his hand, and they board the boat.

When they get out to the cruiser and board, O'Brien asks Hobart to take Elizabeth to the mess hall while he reports to the captain. Hobart, who has been quiet for some time, starts another of his rants, "Oh! I see. Send me off on an errand so you can fill the captain's ear full of nonsense about me. Well, you're not getting away with this! I'm going up to report that Marine who refused my order, straight away!"

Lieutenant O'Brien looks around to see if anyone saw or heard Hobart's comment. Determining the passageway clear except for the three of them, he grabs Hobart by the front of his coat, lifts him up, and slams him against the bulkhead. BAM! "Look here, you sorry, spoiled-brat of a man! If you try that, I will beat you to a pulp! Now take our guest to the mess as I said."

As the lieutenant releases his hold on his coat, Hobart's head and shoulders slump down as he slowly turns and starts down the passageway. Elizabeth gives Lieutenant O'Brien a questioning look. "Go with him; it will be all right," he assures her.

She reluctantly starts after Hobart; however, after a few feet, she turns and looks back with the same questioning look. Lieutenant O'Brien, who is still standing there watching them, sees her look and shoos her with a wave. "Go on, go on!" he coaxes with a smile.

Once on the bridge, Lieutenant O'Brien reports to the captain all they found in the village. He also explains how he has placed Lieutenant Hobart on report and why.

"Where is Lieutenant Hobart now?" asks the captain.

"I had him escort Miss O'Rourke to the mess," answers Lieutenant O'Brien,

"Miss O'Rourke?" questions the captain, and then he remembers Lieutenant O'Brien reporting bringing her on board. "Very good, Lieutenant. Well done! Now to other matters, did you find anything in the village that might give us a clue as to what in the blazes the Germans were interested in?"

"No, Sir!"

"What about this...what's her name? Does she know anything?"

"Elizabeth O'Rourke, Sir. I don't believe so. She said she was just visiting from Ireland, Sir."

"Ireland, is it? Hmmm!" the captain says. He starts rubbing his chin and seems to be thinking about something.

"Sir?"

"Yes?"

"Did we find anything aboard the damaged German ship?" the lieutenant asks.

"I understand they found the ship's logs and a journal."

"Was there anything in the German logs that might explain their attack?"

"What? Oh, nothing, nothing at all! That will be all for now, Lieutenant," orders the captain.

"Very good, Sir!"

"Oh! And see to it you question this O'Rourke woman a bit more on the subject, and send up Lieutenant Hobart."

"Aye, Sir!" The lieutenant dashes off the bridge and hurries to the mess hall.

While all this is going on, Lieutenant Hobart and Elizabeth arrive in the mess. When they sit down, a young orderly comes over and asks what they would like to have from the kitchen. Hobart, still in a funk, just waves him off, but Elizabeth stops him with a request. "I wonder if I might have a cup of tea, if it's not a bother."

The orderly smiles, "Right away, Miss, and it's no bother at all." He tips his hat, and goes for the tea.

Ignoring that interchange, Hobart is still stewing. *"I'll fix*

84

him; my senior -- my foot," he says under his breath.

The orderly returns to the table with a pot of tea and some biscuits. Elizabeth thanks him with a smile, and, not wanting to set off another rant, simply asks Hobart, "Would you care for some tea, Lieutenant?"

"Tea! Can't you see what O'Brien is doing? He is trying to ruin me. The dirty little..."

"Dirty little what?" questions Lieutenant O'Brien as he walks up to the table.

"What?" is all Hobart can get out.

Lieutenant O'Brien looks at Elizabeth, smiles, and points at the chair next to her, "May I join you?"

"Please do," she replies and returns his smile.

Hobart starts to say something but before he can, O'Brien turns to him and says, "Oh! The captain wants to see you now!"

After Hobart leaves, Lieutenant O'Brien sees the orderly across the room and holds up Hobart's tea cup. The orderly nods in acknowledgement and brings him a fresh cup. Elizabeth picks up the pot and pours him a cup of tea.

"Biscuit?" she asks, offering him the plate.

"Thanks, but no," he says as he looks in the direction Hobart went. "What was he going on about this time?"

"He kept saying he would get even with you, and he seems like the kind who would try. I don't believe he is in his right mind. Is he always like that? I mean, I thought you called him a friend back there in the village, didn't you?"

Lieutenant O'Brien shakes his head. "I thought at one time we were friends, but after training and being assigned together, things changed."

"How do you mean?"

"Well, you see, I received my commission one month before he did."

"One month? I'm afraid I don't understand."

"You see, in the Navy, time of commission makes a big difference in who is put in command of jobs we are assigned. An officer, who is commissioned even a day ahead of another, outranks him. Because I received my commission before Hobart, he is obliged to follow my orders, not the other way around, as he would like it. This all has to do with ego -- his, I mean. That and

85

the fact that once on board, he found out I'm from America, and he hates Yanks!"

Elizabeth sits quietly with a funny look on her face. "You mean to say all the stuff that went on in the village was just to spite you?"

"Yes 'Um! I mean, "Yes, Ma'am. I'm afraid so." He shrugs. "You will have to excuse my American slang. Sometimes it just slips out."

She laughs, "I like the way you Yanks talk!"

"Why, thank ya, Ma'am!" he says with his best southern drawl. They both laugh.

An orderly comes up, "Your cabin is ready, Miss."

"Which one?" questions Lieutenant O'Brien?

"The executive officers quarters, Sir," the orderly answers. "Will that be all, Sir?"

"Yes, thank you," says the lieutenant. Then to Elizabeth, "I will be glad to show you to your quarters. But first, if you are not too tired, I need to ask you a few questions."

"Questions? What about?"

"The village, and the attack mostly. Do you mind?"

"No, not at all!" she replies.

"Okay, then. Let's start with why you were there. I remember you saying you were visiting. Is that correct?"

"Yes, I had been there only two days." Staying with her story of looking for her uncle, she continues, "I was trying to find my uncle who I thought might be living there."

"Did you find him?"

"I'm afraid not. It seems he had moved on, and I'm not sure where he went."

Then, Lieutenant O'Brien asks, "How did you manage to get into that tunnel?"

She tells him about the house and the woman preparing tea and seeing the trapdoor. Then she remembers the attack and starts crying. "The whole thing was so brutal and senseless!" she exclaims as she sobs.

"Here, now!" Lieutenant O'Brien says, as he takes his handkerchief out and hands it to her. "I am sorry that we must go over this right now. It is important for you to try to recall as much as possible while it's still fresh in your memory."

86

Still sobbing, she says, "I know; it's just so sad!" as she dabs her eyes.

"Do you have any idea what the Germans were doing there or what they were looking for?"

"I'm afraid not."

Then he asks, "Do you understand German?"

"Yes, I do. I studied German in school."

"Did you overhear anything that might be helpful for us to understand what their mission was?"

She stops sobbing and looks at him for a moment, trying to figure out what sort of man he is. She knows she needs help getting back to the Tinys, and she wonders -- *"Can the lieutenant help me? Would he help me? How can I ask him to help? After all, we have just met."* She knows she has liked him since she first saw him, but *"Is he to be trusted with such a secret?"* she asks herself. *"What would be his reaction if I tell him?"* She decides to give him a little information to see how he reacts.

"I heard the one called Lieutenant Kruger telling his men to keep looking for something."

"Did he say what they were searching for?"

"I couldn't quite make out what he said because of all the crashing and burning of the house."

"Do you have any idea what it might have been?"

Just then a seaman comes up to the lieutenant, salutes, and hands him a piece of paper. The lieutenant returns the salute and takes the note.

"Excuse me, please," he says to Elizabeth as he turns away and scans the message, which says: "Have you deduced any useful information in your talks with the lady?" The captain had signed the note.

Lieutenant O'Brien takes out his pencil and writes, "None so far," and hands it back to the seaman. "Return this to the captain," he orders.

"Very good, Sir!" the seaman replies as he wheels around and heads down the passageway.

The lieutenant wonders what to do next; then, noticing how tired Elizabeth looks, he decides to take her to her quarters so she can rest a bit. He smiles and remarks, "We've been at this long enough. Let's get you to your room so you can freshen up and rest

87

before the evening meal."

He stands and holds out his hand. She takes it, and he gently pulls her to her feet and leads her down the passageway.

As they walk, he is remembering their conversation and has a feeling she knows something she is not revealing. He had already dismissed the idea back in the village, when he saw her reaction to the destruction and deaths, that she might be a spy. He is confused and conflicted between trying to find out what the enemy was up to and his wanting to get to know her better. He was attracted to her right from the first, and the attraction is growing with each minute he spends with her, but something in her manner or her eyes tells him she is in trouble and needs help.

As they reach the door to her room, he notices they are still holding hands. He likes holding her hand -- very much so. Opening the door for her, as she starts to enter, he asks, "If it's all right with you, I will be by to take you to the evening meal."

She steps just inside the room, turns around, and smiles. "Thank you. I would like that."

The evening meal is quiet, with little conversation. Lieutenant Hobart is not around. Evidently he had been assigned some grungy job as punishment for his actions in the fishing village. He is not missed! Elizabeth and Conor sit looking at each other with silly grins on their faces. A lot is said, but few words are spoken.

Then the lieutenant snaps out of it and remembers something.

"I almost forgot -- I have one of the German officer's journals. You did say you could speak German?"

"Yes, I can," she replies.

"Can you read it, as well?"

"Yes, I can read and write German. Why?"

"Well, if you don't mind, we can, or rather, you can read what's in the journal. Maybe we can find out just what they were after. If you're up to it?"

"Why, yes, I can do that. When do you want me to start?"

"Right now, if that's all right? I just need to run down to my quarters and get the journal."

"Fine. I'll wait right here," she answers.

——————— Copyright 2015 Gary E. Reavis, Sr. ———————

When he enters his room, Hobart is there, looking very upset. "So, you had to go and put me on report, did you!"

Lieutenant O'Brien, trying to make light of the thing, says, "Look, you are the one who went a little cuckoo, today in front of the men. I had no choice in the matter, and you know that."

Then he goes over to his desk, picks up the journal, and walks out.

Hobart is steaming and mutters softly to himself, *"I'll get even with him, so help me!"*

A few minutes later, Hobart starts for the dining room, ready for supper.

Lieutenant O'Brien returns to the table where Elizabeth is waiting, and as he sits down, he hands her the journal. "Here it is."

She opens the journal, and starts to read it aloud. At first it contained what would be normal day-to-day entries. Then right at the end, on the last page, she finds:

March 12th, 1917
We had come out of a very strong storm and were patrolling just off the Dutch coast when we came upon a small fishing boat. An Englander and his 9-year-old son were onboard. The captain, assuming they were using the guise of fishing to spy on our ship movement, ordered the fishing boat brought alongside. The two Englanders were brought onboard for questioning. Sub Lieutenant Hendrix, who speaks English, was the interpreter. The Englander claimed to be just a fisherman, and said they had been blown off course by the storm. But the captain would not accept his answer and had him bound and beaten. However, the man would not confess to spying, and after searching their boat, I found no evidence or spying equipment.

The captain became so angry, he had one of our men pick up the young boy and threaten to throw him overboard. The Englander pleaded for his son's life. When they tied the boy's hands and feet, the man broke down, crying and saying he was not a spy but he would tell the captain a secret if it would save his son. He whispered for only the captain to hear; telling him there of a large treasure hidden in his village. Again, the captain doubted him, so he had the men pick up the boy and hold him

89

over the side of the ship. The Englander fell to his knees and begged the captain to look in the small pouch tied around the boy's waist. When the captain opened it, he found a gold coin inside. It appeared to be a very old coin, and that got the captain's attention. The captain hid the coin from us.

Then the captain disobeyed our standing orders not to go near the Englander coast, and he ordered us to go to the village of the fisherman. When we arrived at the village, the captain ordered us to fire and had it destroyed, even though I told him we could see no signs of a military outpost there, and all we saw were civilians.

The captain called me aside and told me about the coin and the treasure story. Then he sent me ashore with a patrol to search, not for the enemy or to see if there were any survivors, but to look for this so-called treasure! However, the damage was too great, and because of all the fires, we could not do a good search. But while looking around, I saw something amazing! I saw two men that appeared to be only as tall as my boot! I tried to tell the captain; he, of course, had heard all the old stories of leprechauns, fairies, and the like and did not believe me. He was only interested in the treasure...

Elizabeth gasps!

90

Chapter 11
The Journal

Lieutenant Hobart is just about to enter the ship's mess hall when he overhears Elizabeth reading from the captured journal. He stops just out of sight and listens. When he hears Elizabeth gasp, he chances a quick peek around the door and sees her drop the book and starts to cry!

Conor, not knowing what is wrong, is trying to console her. "What is it, Elizabeth? What's wrong?" he asks.

She turns and buries her head in his shoulder and cries. "I've betrayed them!"

"Betrayed who? The Germans?" Conor questions.

Elizabeth leans back in shock and pounds on his chest. "No, no, no!" Then she sinks back against him, and as he put his arm around her, she softly whispers, "The little ones!"

Conor still doesn't understand what she is so upset about. "Don't tell me **you** believe in those fairy tales about little people and leprechauns and the like?"

Elizabeth raises her head and looks around to make sure no one else is nearby, but she does not see Hobart hiding in the passageway. Looking Conor in the eyes, she announces, "I must help them. I have faith that you can be trusted, Conor. Lord, help me if I'm wrong!"

Conor is even more confused. "What are you talking about?"

She goes on, "I need your help, and I don't know where to start!"

"Is this about the attack?"

"No! Well, yes, in a way… the attack has caused the problem. It's the German journal!" she says as she picks up the book. "This thing must be destroyed!"

"What? What's in this book that makes it so important that it must be destroyed? I didn't hear you read anything that would be a military secret."

Elizabeth hesitates, and then continues, "It has nothing to do with military secrets. It's the story the fisherman told the captain. You see, I know it's true!"

"What? Are you telling me there really is a treasure in the village and that's what the Germans were after?"

91

"Yes!"

Hobart hears someone coming down the passageway, so he heads back to his room. Once inside, he starts his plotting. He thinks, *"That's it! I'll get even with him but good! I'll go back there, grab the treasure, and I'll be richer than even my father. Even more, with the treasure, I'll destroy Conor's life!"* Hobart laughs aloud.

Back in the dining room, Elizabeth is saying, "We can't talk here; let's go to my room."

"Okay!" Conor answers with a puzzled look on his face. They get up from the table and head for the executive officer's quarters. Once they arrive, Conor stops with his hand on the doorknob, "Perhaps I shouldn't enter your room?"

Elizabeth touches his arm and pleads, "Please, I can't chance anyone overhearing what I'm about to tell you! Trust me. I can explain everything!"

Inside, Elizabeth sits on the bed, and she indicates for Conor to sit on the desk chair.

"I must tell you -- I am having a hard time accepting this story of treasure. It's a bit much to swallow!"

"I know, Conor, but you must believe me when I tell you this is what I heard the Germans talking about!"

"Okay! I know that's what you said you heard, and I have confidence in you. However, I find it hard to consider that a German officer would risk so much based on a fisherman's tall tale."

Elizabeth knows somehow she must convince this man, whom she has grown to like very much, that she is telling the truth. But how can she tell the secret and yet protect the little ones?

She takes a long look at Conor, and in him she sees goodness and caring. She wants to trust him, and she realizes she needs to – and so she asks him outright, "Can I trust you to help me, Conor O'Brien?"

"Trust me? Of course you can! But that's not the question. The question is can I trust you? I still don't know what you were really doing in the village and why you alone survived. Elizabeth, there is going to be an investigation by the Naval Command, and I need to have answers for them!"

She jumps up. "Investigation? Why? What are you talking about?"

Conor goes over to her and takes her hand. "Don't you realize you are under suspicion?"

"What? Suspicion of what?" she asks, and she starts pacing around the room.

"Please believe me. I don't think for a moment you had anything to do with what the Germans did. But the captain wants me to find out why you were in the village and how you came to survive when everyone else was killed."

Elizabeth sits back down on the bed and begins sobbing. "But I told you -- I was looking for someone, and I found the tunnel just before the attack!" she replies between sobs.

Conor sits down next to her and put his arm around her. He knows she is telling the truth about what she told him. He also feels she is keeping something from him, a deep secret. He decides to just go ahead and ask her. "Elizabeth, I believe you are holding on to a secret you want to share. But you are afraid, and you don't know if you can trust me. Elizabeth, with God as my witness, you can trust me. I like you very much and I want to help!"

When he says that, she throws her arms around his neck and cries even more. When she finally stops crying, she looks up at him and confides, "I was in the village, trying to locate a group of tiny people I believed live there."

Half joking, he says, "More fairy tales?" but this time he is smiling.

She frowns at him and continues, "I was sent to England by the group of little people called Tinys that I care for in Ireland."

"Wait! There are more of them in Ireland?"

"Yes! My father was their benefactor for many years, as was his father and his before him. Because my father had no sons, it fell to me when he passed. When the war broke out, my little ones grew concerned about the others living in England. They asked me to go and try to get them to come back to Ireland. I told the villagers I was looking for an uncle, so as to not disclose my real task. However, it appears the villagers knew of the little ones

93

and were helping to hide and care for them. As I told you, I had just located the trapdoor to the tunnel when the attack came. I managed to get inside and crawl back about 20 feet, and that's when I found the little ones. They are still there, waiting for me to return and help them leave. Now do you believe me?"

"Yes, I believe you about the little ones, as you call them, a group of small people, but the part about a treasure" -- Conor looks at the floor and with a sigh continues -- "I just don't know."

"Why is that?" she asks.

"Well, I find it hard to believe anyone big or small who had a fortune would choose to live in such a remote and backward place as that village."

She looks at him with a twinkle in her eye, "You would if you were afraid the big people would harm you or steal your treasure. You would find an out-of-the-way place and do things like start a myth about leprechauns and fairies." Then she slowly and deliberately says, "Especially if you are only 12 inches tall!"

Conor sits there with his eyes wide open. Then he softly asks, "They are this tall?" as he holds his hand a foot above the floor.

"Yes!"

After the ship docks at Harwich the next morning and following morning muster and a quick check of the duty roster, Conor goes to Elizabeth's cabin to see if she would like to get something to eat. He knocks on the door. When she opens it, he sees she is dressed and ready for a new day.

"Good morning, Elizabeth. Would you join me for breakfast?" Conor says, with a big smile on his face.

"I would be delighted!" she replies, with a smile as big as his.

Just then, their joy of seeing each other is interrupted by an announcement over the loudspeaker.

"Lieutenant O'Brien, report to the bridge!"

"I guess breakfast will have to wait. I'll be back as soon as I can. Of course, you may go on ahead if you like," he tells her.

"No -- I will wait here for you," she replies.

He heads up to the bridge, wondering what this is all about. He has been given leave of all of his other duties to try to get to

94

the bottom of the German attack. Now he is trying to figure out what he will tell the captain if he asks what he has discovered.

As Lieutenant O'Brien enters the bridge, he notices the captain talking to the same Marine sergeant from the landing party. When he gets closer, he hears the captain say, "...and the sailor was on deck watch when he saw Lieutenant Hobart leave?"

"Yes, Sir, at 5:30 this morning," answers the Marine.

"Very good, Sergeant -- you have your orders. That will be all!" Then turning to the lieutenant, he inquires, "O'Brien, did Lieutenant Hobart sleep in his bunk last night?"

"Why, I expect so, Sir. I retired a bit late, but I thought I saw him sleeping when I came in. Why? What's the problem?"

"The problem is I've been informed that some things are missing from the ship. Money and even a pistol, so it appears we have a robbery on our hands," the captain explains.

"A robbery on one of Her Majesty's ships?" asks O'Brien,

"Yes, indeed, and that fool Lieutenant Hobart has gone missing without leave!" the captain explains more.

"AWOL? Why that stupid...oh! Excuse me, Sir!"

"That's quite all right, Lieutenant; I feel the same way. What a downright stupid thing to do. He shouldn't need money -- his father is well-to-do, you know."

"Yes, Sir, I know. But why did he do it?" questions the lieutenant.

"That's what I wanted to ask you, Lieutenant. Do you have any idea what this might be all about?"

"Why, no, Sir -- not off-hand, other than him being upset about me putting him on report."

"Hmm. Well, you ask around, and see what you can find out," commands the captain.

"Very good, Sir!"

O'Brien salutes and starts to leave when the captain asks, "Oh, by the way -- did you uncover anything from talking to Miss O'Rourke? Anything I might want to put in my report to the admiralty?"

"No, Sir. I don't think so, Sir," he answers, not wanting to give away Elizabeth's secret. But he knows he must tell the captain something. "A journal from one of the German officers described an incident where an English fisherman who was

95

captured by them told a tale of lost treasure. That's what they were searching for – at least, that's how it appears."

"A what? Treasure? Well, you can be sure I won't be telling tales of treasure in my report! That will be all, Lieutenant."

"Aye, aye, Sir!"

The lieutenant leaves the bridge, almost running to tell Elizabeth the news.

She is still waiting patiently in her room when he arrives and knocks on the door. As she opens the door, he rushes in and closes it behind him. Conor takes her hands in his and tells all that went on and how he told the captain about the treasure story and that the captain would not be including it in his reports. They hug and kiss, and then start for the dining room.

Coming closer to the room he shares with Hobart. Conor stops and says to Elizabeth, "I better go in and check to see if that rat took any of my money when he took off!"

Going straight to his locker, he looks inside. He picks up the little box he kept some odds and ends and a few dollars in, and, sure enough, the money is missing.

"Well, he cleaned me out!" Conor tells Elizabeth, who is waiting in the passageway at the open door. He puts the box back, closes the locker door and starts to leave when he notices something else is missing from his desk.

"The journal," he whispers. "It's gone!"

After finishing breakfast, Conor tells Elizabeth he has some leave time coming and he will go to the captain and request it now they are in port.

The captain looks up from reading the request form and says, "Off on a spot of leave, is it? Jolly good! And what of Miss... what's her name?"

"Miss O'Rourke, Sir!"

"Yes, yes, of course, O'Rourke! From Ireland, as I recall!"

"Yes, Sir! I'll be escorting her back to the village to see about getting some of her things."

"Very good. Carry on!"

"Aye, Sir!" And he goes quickly to meet Elizabeth!

As they leave the ship, Conor sees a fellow officer getting into a truck on the dock and shouts, "Hey, Hartford -- how's about giving us a lift to a decent restaurant?"

"Sure thing, Yank; hop in!" his friend replies. A few minutes later they are climbing out of the truck and thanking Hartford for the ride.

Conor tells Elizabeth, "I will try to hire a car here. We probably won't be able to find one, once we get up the coast."

"All right. Then I'll go to the deli on the corner and pick up some sandwiches and things for the trip. I'll meet you back here," Elizabeth says.

After two hours of trying everywhere, Conor fails to find anyone who has a car he can rent. He finds Elizabeth sitting in a booth at the restaurant.

"Did you get a car?" she asks.

"I'm afraid not. There are so few cars around, and most of them are being used for the war effort."

"What will we do?"

He plops down beside her, "I've been thinking and I have a plan," he answers.

"Good. What is it?" she says with a sigh of relief.

"Okay! First, we take the train to Newcastle, and then we hire a truck or a team and wagon, load up some supplies, and head for Blyth."

"What about Hobart? Could he know about the treasure?" she asks. "Maybe that's why he stole the journal and went missing."

"I agree," Conor says. "He must have read it or overheard us talking last night. He's just crazy enough to try to go there, so we must hurry!" Then he hesitates.

"What's wrong? What is it, Conor?"

"I'm a bit embarrassed. You see, I don't have very much money on me, and we don't get paid until a week from now."

"Oh! Don't worry -- we have plenty of money, see!" she says as she reaches into her pocket and pulls out a large roll of bills.

"Where in the world did you get that?" he asks.

"Well!" Elizabeth says as she puts the bills back in her pocket, "While I was out shopping, I noticed across the street a little coin shop that is owned by the nicest little old man. I showed him some coins I had, and he got really excited and offered to buy them at a very reasonable price, so I sold some to

97

him."

"Coins? What coins?" he questions.

"They were like these," she says as she opens up her bag to reveal about 30 solid gold doubloons! She laughs at the look on his face and then gets up and holds out her hand, "Let's go catch the train, and on the trip I promise to tell you everything!"

"Everything?" Conor questions as they walk out of the restaurant and head for the train station.

98

Chapter 12
Hidden Treasure

Lieutenant Hobart was able to catch an earlier train, and he arrives in Newcastle hours ahead of Conor and Elizabeth. He, too, is unable to find a car or truck to drive to the village, so after considering it for some time, he decides to call his father in London.

"Hobart residence!" the butler answers the phone in his usual dull tone.

"Jameson, this is Harry. I must speak to my father straight away!"

"He is having his breakfast, young sir, and you know he cannot be disturbed at breakfast."

"But this is an emergency. I must insist!"

"Very good, but you know he will be most angry with you," Jameson adds, as he goes to tell his master that his son is on the telephone. When he enters the room where the senior Hobart is, he announces himself with, "Ah, hum, beg your pardon, Sir, but young Harry is on the telephone, and he insists that he speak to you right away! I did tell him you wish not to be disturbed, but..."

Hobart looks up over the morning paper, "What, Harry on the phone? You know I'm not to be bothered! Oh, very well; put him on."

When the butler hands him the phone, the senior Hobart says, "Well, what is it now, Harry? I'm having breakfast, you know!"

"I'm sorry to disturb you, Father, but I need you to send our car and driver up to Newcastle right away."

"Newcastle? Whatever for?" his father asks.

"I'm stuck here, and I must get over to Blyth, and there are no cars to hire out here."

"What the deuces are you doing in Newcastle? I thought you were on your ship, out to sea and all that!"

"Yes, Sir, I was, but I left the ship..."

"You what? Harry, you can't just leave the ship! Are you on leave?"

"Well, no, Sir; I just left."

"You went absent without permission? Don't you know there

is a war on? They can have you shot for that! You get back to that ship straight away! I will not stand for a Hobart being shot for desertion -- do you hear me?"

"But, Father, I must find the treasure!"

"Treasure? What nonsense are you talking about now? Now, you listen to me, young man..."

"But it's the treasure that Grandfather used to tell us about in his stories!" Harry insists.

"Poppycock and fairy tales, that's what my father put into your head. Poppycock, I say!"

"But I found a journal!" Harry tries to explain.

"Now you listen to me, Harry. I'm sending my chauffeur to fetch you and take you back to your ship. Is that understood?" his father demands.

Suddenly, Harry Hobart gets an idea! He will let his father think he would go back with the chauffeur, and when he gets to Newcastle...

"Alright, Father. I'll come back. Please send the car for me."

"Good. I'll have it sent up right away! By the by, where will he find you?" asks Hobart senior.

"I'll just wait here at the train station," Harry answers, with a wicked grin on his face and his hand on the pistol, tucked into his belt and hidden under his coat.

Elizabeth and Conor are able to get tickets on the next train to Newcastle. On the train trip, they get to know more about each other, and as each mile passes; they fall more and more in love.

She tells him about how she takes care of the little ones in Ireland, and how long ago the little ones used some of their treasure to help their caretakers. Many companies were started, and they have now developed into a large corporation called Hawk Industries. "With each new caretaker, the business is passed on to them, and they become the head of Hawk Industries."

"Hawk is a funny name for a company. Where did that name come from?" Conor asks.

"The name was chosen to honor the two men who first helped the little ones. They were men of wealth -- an English count named William Hawk and his son Edward. William and his

100

son were responsible for finding the Tinys. After his father's death, Edward went on to care for and educate the Tinys. With the Tinys' help, he founded Hawk and Company. That was around the year 1660."

"Now, tell me more about you and your family," she says.

Conor leans back in the seat and, taking her hand, "It all started long, long ago, when I was very young!" He laughs, and she smacks him on the arm. Then he turns serious. "My family is from the South. My father builds boats -- fishing boats mostly, but we do make a few sea-going yachts. My grandfather and grandmother came to America in 1850. When they first married, they settled in South Carolina. Grandpa was also a boat builder."

"Where did your grandparents come from?" Elizabeth asks.

"They came from Ireland. If I remember correctly, they were from a small fishing village near Dublin."

The two spend all the remaining travel time telling each other about their families and themselves. By the time they finally reach Newcastle, they are happy and have almost forgotten all about Hobart -- that is, until they step off the train.

Upon entering the station, Conor spots Hobart, sitting across the room, facing away from them; Hobart evidently has not seen them enter the station. Conor starts to go over to tell him to go back to the ship and to turn himself in before he gets into even more trouble. However, before he can do that, things start happening.

The chauffeur arrives in front of the station with the Rolls Royce. Then just as Hobart is about to confront the chauffeur with the gun, forcing the chauffeur to give him the car, another vehicle pulls up, and inside are two Marines!

As Hobart goes through the station door to meet the chauffeur, he sees the Marine sergeant from the ship. He quickly pulls the pistol from his belt and fires, but he misses the sergeant and hits the corporal in the left arm.

Seeing Hobart pull out the gun, the sergeant returns fire and hits him in the leg, knocking him down and sending Hobart's pistol flying.

Conor, who is trying to get to Hobart and stop him, runs over and picks up the pistol.

101

Hobart is lying on the sidewalk, yelling and whining in pain and holding his wounded leg.

The sergeant, seeing Hobart is no longer armed, turns to aid the corporal.

Meanwhile, Elizabeth is trying to calm Hobart down and get his wound bandaged. When the sergeant finishes dressing the corporal's arm, he comes over to where Hobart is lying and salutes Conor. "Sir, I have orders to return this man to the ship!"

Conor hands him the gun, saying, "Very good, Sergeant; carry on!"

"You and the young lady will be okay?"

"Yes, Sergeant, we will be fine," replies Conor.

Then he notices that the Marines had arrived in a truck, and he gets an idea!

"Sergeant, where did you get that lorry?"

"From the motor pool, Sir."

Conor takes the sergeant by the arm and walks him over to the Rolls.

"How would you and the corporal like to ride back to the ship in that?" he asks, pointing to the Rolls.

"Sir?"

"I don't believe either of you can drive that lorry. The corporal is wounded, and you have this dangerous prisoner who must be watched at all times. I'll commandeer that Rolls and the driver to take you back to the ship, and I will return the lorry myself."

By then the sergeant has caught on to what the lieutenant is suggesting and smiles, "Yes, Sir; that would be most helpful."

The sergeant, the corporal, and Hobart get into the Rolls, and drive off. Conor and Elizabeth take the truck and head for the fishing village.

* * * * *

Once at the village, it takes some time to convince the Tinys that Conor wants to help. After getting a few of them to meet him and talk with him, they all finally come around. As Elizabeth watches how he talks to them, how he listens to what they have to say and is concerned for their safety, she is becoming convinced

102

that this may be the man for her.

As the Tinys approve of their new member, they get to work gathering up all their belongings and anything else they can load on the truck, including many wooden crates.

Conor is so busy helping to load everything that at first he doesn't take notice that each of the crates has strong canvas bags attached to hooks screwed into the sides of all four corners. The crates are hanging by the straps with the bags up in the air like they are filled with gas like a balloon, but they are not puffed out like a balloon. After 20 or so heavy crates, he finally asks, "Elizabeth, what in the world do they have in all these crates of farm equipment, and what's in the bags attached to them?"

Elizabeth motions for the next crate in line to be put aside. The four Tinys that are carrying it lift the crate up over their heads and just shove it in the direction of the two big people. The crate floats through the air a few feet and then slowly settles to the ground. Conor goes over and puts his hand on one of the bags and pushes down. It takes a lot more pressure than he thought it would, but he does get the bag to go down; as it does, however, it feels to him like the bag is full of rocks.

"Be careful and open one of the bags and reach up inside..." Elizabeth instructs, but one of the Tinys yells, "NO! WAIT!" As he comes over, he reaches into his pocket and pulls out a little red rock and puts it in Conor's hand, saying, **"Careful; don't open your hand or it will fly up and away."**

Conor stands with the little rock in his hand, not sure what to do after that stern warning.

Elizabeth comes over and gently takes the red rock out of his hand. She holds her hand upside down and opens it. The rock stays in her hand and doesn't fall, like it is glued to her palm. Closing her hand, she looks around and then climbs up into the canvas-covered back of the army truck. She motions for Conor to follow her, and when he gets next to her, she holds out her hand and lets go of the red rock. The red rock flies straight up to the canvas top and stops. Conor looks up at the rock and back at her. "You mean to tell me those bags are all filled with red rocks?"

"Yes, and that is how they can move those heavy boxes," she replies.

"Where did they come from, and how do they rise up like

that?"

"They were found long ago in a cave, but I'm afraid we no longer know where that cave is. Its whereabouts have long been forgotten. As for how they do what they do, no one knows. That remains a mystery."

"But look! This is what's inside the crates." She picks up a pry bar and opens one of the crates. Inside, all he can see is straw -- until she moves the straw aside to reveal several canvas sacks. "Open one!" she says with a grin.

Conor reaches his hand in to open a bag and finds gold coins, hundreds of gold coins like the ones he had seen in Elizabeth's bag back in Harwich. He whistles. "So, this is the treasure the Germans and Hobart were after!"

Elizabeth smiles and explains, "This is only a small part of the fortune that was given to the little ones by Count Hawks, with the two groups each having a small portion they use to help those who help them -- like the villagers that were here," she says sadly.

"Like I told you on the trip up here, they invested a great deal of the fortune in building the companies that make up Hawk Enterprises. Oh! And we have a few banks!" she smiles again at her last remark.

He sits down on one of the crates. "You mean to tell me they own banks?"

"But, of course! Where else would they keep most of their gold and silver?" she giggles.

A Tiny jumps into the crate, closes the sack, covers it back up, and climbs out as others close the lid and re-nail it shut. All Conor can say is "Wow, you guys work really fast!"

The Tiny man looks up at Conor and winks.

Conor steps down from the truck, stands back, and for the first time takes a good look at how these Tiny people all worked together to load the truck. They had put together a wooden path from the cave to the back of the truck. He can see that some of the wood is charred.

"They used wood from the village to make the path and the ramp up to the truck," he thinks to himself. As he investigates farther, he sees there are no wheels under the crates and boxes that are being brought out of the cave. The things they are

104

moving are simply floating in air, being lifted by the bags of red rocks. Conor stands in amazement, smiling.

Elizabeth, who has been directing most of this, comes over to him. "What are you grinning about?"

He puts his arm around her shoulders. "Oh, I was just watching them at work and how they manage to move all of those large crates. It's just so amazing to see!" Having secured all the little ones in the truck, along with their treasure and belongings, Conor and Elizabeth set out for Maryport on the west coast of England -- where they would meet a ship for Ireland. Elizabeth has planned their whole journey. While in Newcastle, she had made all the arrangements with a company the Tinys' own to have a cargo ship waiting for them in Maryport.

Once they are on the road, a lot of the Tinys come forward into the cab of the truck to talk with Conor. They all seem very interested in the fact that he is from America. They ask him many questions about where he lives and his family. He enjoys answering their questions and talking to them.

As they talk and ask questions, he sees these people have an amazing lust for life and knowledge. To his surprise, they are all well educated.

After things quiet down for a while, he turns to Elizabeth in the passenger's seat. "They really love to learn, don't they?"

"Yes! I've found them to have some of the brightest minds of anyone I've ever met. I consult with them, and they help me with company decisions all the time."

Quinn, the eldest Tiny who Elizabeth had met in the cave, comes up to the cab to sit and watch Conor drive. After a while he asks, "Is it hard to learn to use your hands and feet to move those pedals, the steering wheel, and the levers all at the same time?"

Conor, who has been shifting through the gears as they climb some hills, answers, "No, not really, but it does take a bit of practice to be good at it."

"Why do you need to be good at it?" questions Quinn.

Conor smiles and answers, "You need to be able to coordinate the moving of the gears in order to make the truck move smoothly and safely."

"Ah! I see," Quinn acknowledges. Then he sits silently and

just watches for a few miles.

As the trip progresses down the road, the Tinys ask Elizabeth to come into the back and talk with them.

Quinn asks, "Elizabeth, you have been taking care of our brothers and sisters in Ireland for more than five years now. Isn't that correct?"

"Yes, that's right. Ever since my father passed, I've cared for them. Why do you ask?"

Quinn looks around at the others, and they all encourage him to continue, "Well, we've been talking. We really like you and Conor." He pauses for a second. "We wondered if you would be our caretaker, as well?"

Many from the group respond enthusiastically with a "Yes!" or a "Yeah!"

Elizabeth happily says, "But of course. When we get to Ireland, I will take care of you, also."

Suddenly the responses change to "No!" and "Not there!" She is puzzled, "I don't understand," she says. "What's wrong?" At the same time, the Tinys all shout, "America -- we want to go to America!"

She is taken aback and announces, "I can't take you to America!" Then Quinn remarks with a smile, "Yes, you can, if you go with Conor!"

They all yell, "Go with Conor, go with Conor!" and start laughing.

When they reach Maryport, Elizabeth directs Conor to the warehouse owned by Hawk Enterprises. Once they are safely inside and the door closed, the Tinys all start talking to her excitedly. Conor gets out of the truck and walks around to the back to see what all the commotion is about.

"What's all the fuss?" he asks, opening the back so that they can all get out.

Elizabeth climbs down and looks back at all the anxious faces, shrugs her shoulders, and says, "They all decided that they don't want to go to Ireland to live."

"They don't? Don't tell me they want to go back?"

"No! They don't want to live in England, either!" Elizabeth answers.

Conor looks at all the faces that are smiling up at him. They

106

look as if they are about to burst with anticipation.

"Okay -- so where do they want to live?"

All of them let out a big, "In America with you and Elizabeth!" Then they all laugh in unison.

Ultimately, the Tinys decided they would stay in Ireland until the end of the war, as it would be far too dangerous to try to go to America once the Americans had joined the fight against Germany. What they didn't realize is that it would be two more years before the war would end.

Conor helps get the Tinys settled in Ireland before he has to return to his ship. Over the next two years, he manages, -- as often as he could get leave -- to come see Elizabeth and visit with the Tinys. After about a year of visits, Conor asks Elizabeth to marry him. She, of course, said "Yes," but they agree to wait until the war is over and he gets his discharge.

Conor has heard that Harry Hobart was charged with leaving his post without permission. The charges for shooting the corporal somehow had gotten dropped after the corporal mysteriously came into a large sum of money. The last Conor heard was that Hobart's father had bought Harry's way out of the Navy and all the trouble he was in. Conor doubted that would last long.

WWI finally ended in 1919. Shortly thereafter, Conor was discharged from the British Navy and Elizabeth and Conor were married a month later. By the time they were ready to come to America, some of the Tinys had decided to stay in Ireland. One of Elizabeth's male cousins agreed to care for the Irish Tinys, and Conor and Elizabeth brought about half of the Tinys to America.

They lived in South Carolina for a few years, but finally moved and settled in Tennessee.

* * * * *

Mr. Vaughn announces, "The end," and closes the book of Telling.

One of the children raises a hand.

"Yes, what is it?"

"Is Conor and Elizabeth our Conor the V's great-grandfather

107

and grandmother?

"No, they were his great-great-grandparents."

With no more questions from the teenagers, Mr. Vaughn takes the book and returns to his seat.

Graybeard gets up, goes to the podium, and raises his hands to quiet everyone. When he sees that the kids have settled down, he says, "Let us close the Telling with a prayer." Lowering his head, he begins, "Heavenly Father, as we gather together to celebrate another telling of our history, we give thanks to You for the O'Briens and now Janet and Brittany who have joined them in helping to keep us safe here in Tennessee. We ask that You bless those that bless us and forgive those that would do us harm. Everything else we leave in Your hands. Amen!"

Looking up, he shouts, "Now, let's eat and have some fun!"

Chapter 13
The Hobarts

Present Day England

The headquarters for Hobart Industries, Ltd., is based in London, England. The massive complex covers a quarter of a mile. The main office building, where President and CEO Randle L. Hobart has his office, is a 10-story giant. His office alone occupies a large portion of the top floor. Inside are some of the most expensive pieces of furniture and artifacts to be found in the world. Randle is young, in his early 20s; his brown hair and his manicured nails are perfectly groomed. He wears a suit costing more than most people make in a month. There always seems to be an air of superiority about him.

His secretary announces over the intercom, "Sir, you have a call on line two."

"Who is it?" he asks gruffly.

"It's Mr. Simms of Simms Shipping," she answers.

"Simms! Good. Put him through," he replies, rubbing his hands together like he is going to get something he has always wanted. "Hello, is that you, Simms?" he asks smoothly.

"Yes, it's me. Now you listen here, Hobart. You can't get away with this sort of thing!"

"Why, Simms, what are you talking about?" Hobart inquires with a smirk on his face.

"You know good and well what I'm talking about!" Simms yells. "You can't do this to me! I made a deal with your father. You can't just stop supplying us overnight. This is outrageous!"

"I can, and I will if you don't take my offer," Hobart announces hatefully.

"Why, you little sneak. Just because my son caught you cheating in college..." Simms starts.

"Look, Simms... you have a choice -- your yacht or your company! Make up your mind, and I want an answer, NOW!"

"Oh, all right; you can buy the yacht, and at your price, but you will live to regret this, Hobart. Mark my words!" Simms warns, giving in to Hobart's blackmail and slamming down the phone.

Outside the office, his secretary can hear Hobart laughing like a madman. Reaching down, Heather Baryl turns off the recorder hidden in her desk.

Later that day, sitting behind his enormous desk, Randle Hobart is talking on the phone.

"I don't care what you have to do, or who you need to do it to. I want controlling interest in that company today!" He slams the phone down and yells, "How I hate incompetents! Why can't I find employees with brains?"

Getting up from behind his desk, he starts pacing around the room thinking: *"Why did you go and die without telling me about them?"*

Randle sits once more behind his desk and remembers all that has happened in the last three years. When his father had died of a heart attack, Randle was called home from college to assume control of the family business. In the last six months, he has starting to flex his corporate muscle, and he likes it. The power and control he has over others is intoxicating. Hobart Industries is one of the largest holding companies in the world, with hands in commercial airlines, shipping, oil, and mining, to name a few industries. If it is a multi-million dollar company, you can bet Hobart Industries holds stock in it.

Randle recalls the last time he spoke with his father. He was home from college and staying at his family's estate in England. The conversation with his father runs through his mind.

* * * * *

"Well, got caught cheating again, did you?" his father asks. The fact that Randle had been asked to leave three of the top universities in the country did not set well with his father.

"It was my roommate; he turned me in, the dirty..."

"So, what are you going to do now?" his father interrupts.

"I am going to fix him for good!"

"No, no! I meant about finishing school. I can care less about what you do to whomever. Or how you do it. But you WILL finish college. Is that clear? How can I turn over the company to

110

Copyright 2015 Gary E. Reavis, Sr.

you if you can't even finish college?"

"School is boring! Why do I need to finish? You control the company and can do whatever you want. If you say I'm in, the board will have to allow it."

"Sure I could, but it's not the board I'm worried about. There's someone higher up that worries me!" his father explains.

"Higher up than you? How can that be? You own the company!"

"Son, I manage the company. I guess it's time I told you. I was waiting until you finished college, and you were ready to take over, but now is as good a time as any."

The next words his father said burned in his memory. "It's your aunt: my older sister holds total, unyielding control of Hobart Industries, and I'm nothing more than her puppet!"

"And now," Randle says to himself, "Now, I'M the puppet!"

His private phone ringing brings him out of his thoughts with a start. "What?" he yells as he answers the phone.

The calm voice of his secretary is on the other end of the line. "Your aunt is on line one, sir."

"What! No! I can't talk to her right now. Uh, tell her I'm out of the office."

"Yes, sir!" Miss Baryl replies and then clicks back to talk to his aunt. "I'm sorry, Miss Hobart, but Mr. Hobart seems to be out of the office; may I take a message?"

"Out is he? Well you give him this message: I will be in London on the 13th, and I expect to see some results!" The aunt hangs up.

The intercom on her desk buzzes and she answers. "Yes, Mr. Hobart?"

"What did she say?" he asks, sounding like a schoolboy who knows he is in trouble.

Miss Baryl gives him the message. Without even acknowledging her, he clicks off. She mutters to herself, "And I thought your father was hard to work for. But you, young Mr. Power-Hungry, take the prize!"

Later the same day, while going through some of his father's old files in one of the drawers, he comes across an old key. He calls his secretary.

"Miss Baryl, I need you."

As she enters the office, he holds up the key. "Have you seen this before?"

"Yes, Sir," she answers, after taking a closer look at it.

"Do you know what it's for?"

"I believe it's for your father's secret safe."

"Secret safe? What secret safe?"

"The one hidden under your desk, Sir."

"I didn't know... Why didn't you inform me of this?" he questions, starting to get angry.

"You never asked, Sir," she replies with a slight smirk in her voice. "Will that be all, Sir?"

By now he has turned his attention to the desk. "Yes! Yes! Go!" He waves his arm at the door. "Call maintenance, and send someone up to move this desk," he orders, still looking at the huge, wooden desk his father used every day. "No, wait! I will do this myself!" he announces, changing his mind, not wanting anyone knowing the location of the safe.

She turns again to leave, wanting to get back to her own desk. He stops her with yet another question, "Who else knows of the safe?"

She turns back to face him and replies, "Now that your father is gone, only you and I, Sir"

"Good! That will be all," he says with another dismissing wave.

As he studies the finely carved wooden desk, he wonders if he can, indeed, move it. "Why, this thing must weigh 500 pounds!" he exclaims as he walks around the desk, looking at the floor trying to find the safe. "Hmmm, no seams or cracks I can see. Where can it be?"

Getting down on his hands and knees, he crawls around under the huge desk, tapping here and there to see if he can determine where there might be a hollow place. After about five minutes of crawling and tapping, he gets up and moves around to his chair. Sitting down in disgust, he reaches over and hit the intercom button, "Miss Baryl."

"Yes, Sir?" comes her quick but exasperated reply.

"Miss Baryl, would you come in here, please."

112

"Right away, Sir"

Upon entering his office, she crosses the enormous room to stand in front of his desk.

"Are you sure the safe in the floor is under the desk?" he questions.

"No, Sir."

"What? But you said it was under the desk in the floor."

"Sir, I simply said the safe is under the desk. I did not say it was in the floor."

"Oh! Okay!" he exclaims, more interested in finding the safe and its contents than reprimanding her for not explaining the whereabouts in the first place.

"Very well, then; that will be all." And again she is dismissed.

By the time she closes the door, his attention is fully back to the desk. He kneels down and looks underneath but sees nothing to indicate a safe. Sitting back down in his chair, he glares at the monster of a desk as he turns the key over and over in his hand.

"Where can it be?"

He likes a good puzzle, but he is growing tired of this one. "This key fits a lock to a safe," he said to himself as he holds up the key. Then he notices the inscription on the key, *"If one were blind of nine that see, a mystery solved, to use the key."*

"If one were blind?" he repeats out loud. "One WHAT?"

He moves his chair farther back from the desk so he can see under it better. Reading the words on the key once more, *"One of nine; nine that see."* "See WHAT?" he says to himself as he repeats *"Nine that see"* over and over while studying the desk. Then his attention turns to one of the massive legs. There he sees three carved lion heads.

"Hmm, three carved heads per leg, times four -- no wait, there are only three legs. Why didn't I notice that before?" There are two legs on his side of the desk but only one centered in the front. *"Very strange design."*

"Three legs, multiplied by three heads, works out to be nine heads. The nine that see!"

Kneeling once again, he examines each leg and the nine lion heads.

"Now which one is blind?"

113

He carefully checks each face only to find all of them have their eyes open, and none appear to be different from the rest.

"How can only one be blind if they are all the same?" he exclaims.

Sitting there scratching his head, he asks himself, *"How did the inscription go? If one were blind of nine that see, something, something?"*

As he looks from face to face, he wonders out loud, "Of nine that SEE? How do you make one of these wooden faces not see? Poke it in the eye? Ha!"

He laughs at his own joke and suddenly stops. *"Can that be it? You need to push on an eye or something?"* Sensing he is on the right track, he moves from leg to leg, pushing on one eye after another, but to no avail. By now he is becoming more and more frustrated, yet at the same time more determined to find the answer and the secret safe.

"It must be something to do with lions' eyes," he says out loud. "Do you cover them up? No, I don't see any electric eyes in them. I tried pushing each eye, and it didn't work. Wait a minute...you can't make one blind by poking only ONE eye. You need to poke BOTH of them!"

With this new revelation, he returns to the faces and starts pushing both eyes on each lion's head. First he pushes the lion's eyes on the leg to the right-of-center, but nothing happens. Then he tries the left-of-center leg, with no response. Finally he tries the center leg. CLICK! The eyes retract into the leg at the same time that a panel opens up in the bottom of the desk. The opening reveals a small safe with a lock, which looks as if the key would fit. Upon trying the key, he finds it does indeed fit. He turns it slowly, and the safe opens.

Inside the safe he discovers a leather-covered journal. Randle opens it to find a note from his father. The note says,

Contained in this box are the clues to finding a secret. The journal tells of how it was found and lost many years ago when the secret was stolen from our forefathers. The records of the search for them and the many failures over the years have been written in this journal. I feel I am close to finding them after searching for more than 50 years. But now with my health

114

failing, I leave this ledger and journal to help in your search. Guard it well, for no one knows of it or the secret we seek. If you succeed in finding them, they will bring you fame and fortune.

"Secrets and lost fortunes! Now we're getting somewhere!"

He turns the journal over in his hands, checking out the designs engraved in the old book. On the outer cover, he recognizes the family crest. Inscribed under the crest is another rhyme: *"A secret lost, a tiny thing, when found again, will riches bring."*

He remembers his grandfather's tales of mystery and treasure and the stories of how their ancestors found and lost a great treasure. Down through the years, each new generation would take up the hunt, but they never found it again. Now that's what he wants to do, take up the hunt!

"The hunt for what?" he asks himself. *"I don't even know what Grandfather was talking about."*

He only knew that as a young lad, the stories had intrigued him and captured his imagination. He picks up the ledger and notices it has an iron cross on the front. He opens the ledger to find it is written in German, and he sees a date in the upper-right corner of the first page, it reads, "1917, 12, Marsch."

"In 1917?" He says to himself. *"Why, that's clear back in World War One."* As he tries to read more, he slams the journal shut. *"GERMAN! I wish I had paid attention in class. I need someone who can read this for me. No! Wait! I will do this myself. I don't want anyone else seeing this!"*

His attention turns to the ledger just as his private line rings. Still reading the ledger, he answers distractedly, "Yes?"

"Your aunt again, Sir; she insists she talk to you immediately," Miss Baryl announces.

"Very well," Randle says calmly; "Put her through." As the phone clicks, he says, "Aunt Matilda, it's good to hear from you. How are you feeling? Well, I hope."

"RANDLE!" she shouts. "What are you up to? I've been trying to get through to you for three days. I want some answers, and I mean NOW!"

Smiling to himself, Randle replies, "I'm so sorry we've been missing each other, but you know how busy it is around here. Oh, by the way, I found it!"

"Listen to me, Randle, if you ever..." She stops and then adds, "Found it. Found WHAT? Are you saying you found your father's ledger? Randle, do not play with me!"

"No, no! Aunty, you see I found it just now. I also found a journal from World War One, but it's in German."

"Don't say anything more over the phone." she demands. "I will be there as soon as I can!"

"Yes, Aunt Matilda. I look forward to seeing you," he lies.

* * * * *

At the station, the train comes to a halt. Parked nearby is a big black limo. Randle Hobart gets out and goes over to meet his aunt at her private railroad car.

"Good morning, Aunty! How was your trip?"

"Awful, just awful!" she replies grumpily as she slowly steps down from the rail car. "This thing sways and clanks so, a body can't even get a night's rest."

Randle, taking her hand to help her down, remarks, "Why don't you use one of our jets? They're much faster and a lot quieter."

She looks at him with a scowl. "Now, Randle, you know I hate airplanes! Ever since your grandfather was shot down and killed in 1939, I just don't trust them. No, not at all!"

The trip to Hobart headquarters is quiet, mostly because his aunt fell asleep on the way into town. Randle is anxious to show his aunt what he found, hoping that once she sees the journal, she would get off his back for a while.

In the meantime, Randle has been trying to figure out how to discover what the German ledger has to do with the treasure his father talked about in his notes.

When the private elevator arrives at Randle's outer office, Miss Baryl is busily typing away on her computer. She looks up as the elevator doors slide open, and Randle and an elderly woman enter the office, her chauffeur pushing her wheelchair. The older lady looks to be in her 80's and is dressed in fine clothes and jewelry. Upon seeing the aunt, she says to herself,

116

"Oh, no; not **her** again! I thought the kid was bad enough until SHE started coming around after Randle's father died."

As the two Hobarts approach, she stands and greets them.

"Good morning, Miss Hobart, Mr. Hobart."

Neither one even looks at her, or acknowledges her in the least.

As they enter his office, Randle announces, "We do not wish to be disturbed!" and abruptly shuts the door.

Once inside, Aunt Matilda starts asking questions. "Well, what have you learned so far? Did you translate the ledger? And what of the little ones your father talked about? I want to see a little one for myself!"

Randle sits down behind his large desk as her chauffeur parks her wheelchair nearby.

"I will try to answer all you questions, but what about HIM?" he says, nodding at the chauffeur.

She turns to look at her chauffeur. "Never mind him! Get on with it."

Randle hesitates. "But Aunty?"

"Oh! All right!" she concedes. "Jameson, wait outside." "Yes, Madam," he says as he leaves.

Now with just the two of them in the office, Randle continues, "I haven't had much time. You know those stories about the little ones are only stories, Aunty; just stories, that's all!"

"No, they are not just stories, and stop calling me Aunty. I HATE that! Do you hear me?"

"Yes, Aunt Matilda, but Father never found any real proof they exist."

"What about the German's ledger? What information did you find in it?"

"I don't know. I haven't been able to read it," he answers.

"And what are you doing about it? Are you going to translate the ledger yourself?" his aunt presses him.

"No! I had Miss Baryl buy a program to do it, and when she completes translating..."

"You did WHAT?" his aunt screams. "Are you OUT OF YOUR MIND? Now she will know all about our SECRET! You IDIOT!"

117

Hobart shrinks in his chair behind his desk and tries to calm her down. "But, Aunt Matilda, she has been with this company all these years and was very loyal to father."

"I don't trust her or anyone else! As soon as she finishes the translation, I want her gone! Do you understand me?"

"Yes, Aunt Matilda.

"Send Jameson back in."

The chauffeur comes in and starts pushing the wheelchair out of Randle's office. At the door, his aunt turns around and speaks a final warning. "Remember, Nephew, I hold the power! And YOU, just like your FATHER, are merely the PUPPET head of this company." With that she leaves.

Miss Baryl is listening to all this from her desk, as she had done many times before. No one knows that many years before, she had placed a secret microphone in the ceiling directly above the big desk. She had rigged it so the microphone would transmit to the same earphones she uses when typing the boss's dictations.

As she hears all this, she thinks to herself, *"Why in the world is this group of dwarfs so important to them? Somehow I must find out what this is all about. I must protect myself from HER,"* She quickly finishes interpreting the German ledger.

* * * * *

It has been weeks since Randle put in place a full worldwide search for the little ones and the treasure. In his office he is yelling on the phone at one of his operatives, "I want them FOUND. I will not explain how important this is to you again. If you don't find them for me, and SOON, I will see to it something HAPPENS to you, and it will be a PERMANENT SOMETHING. Do I make myself CLEAR?" He slams the phone down and curses.

Just then the door to his office flies open, and in rolls his aunt, unannounced. Her chauffeur pushes her to the front of Randle's big desk, locks the brakes on her wheelchair, tips his hat, and promptly leaves the office.

"Well, Randle, I see you're in a fine mood. Do we have any results yet?"

118

"I was about to call you," he lies. "We are making some progress, Aunt!"

His face pale, his voice is shaky.

"Randle, SOME PROGRESS is not what I want to hear. You are my nephew, and I love you, but if you do not find them in short order, all the power and wealth of Hobart enterprises will be STRIPPED from you. I will bring you down to NOTHING." Her voice filled with anger and distaste. "I will DESTROY you and see to it that the memory of your name is forgotten FOREVER!"

The last words she yells as she slams her fist down hard on the arm of her wheelchair. Her eyes are glaring red, and so is the tone of her voice! Then suddenly she softens, and continues, "Sweetheart, always remember that I am the real power behind the Hobart name. I am sure with more money and resources than most small countries at your disposal, you can find anyone in the world, let alone a clan of small people. Do not let your aunt down, Nephew. That would not be wise! Do you understand, Sweetie?" The last words she delivers with a smile.

"Yes, Aunt Matilda," he stutters. "Let me bring you up to date." He clears his throat and continues, "We have six agents. Here, let me show you." He reaches in one of the desk drawers and pushes a button. A panel on the wall across from his desk opens up to reveal a large monitor displaying a map. He gets up from his chair and goes over to the monitor and points at the map. "Two are in Florida and one is in Kentucky. We have narrowed the search in the U.S. to the southern states. Three of my best men are in Ireland, where they are following up on some very promising leads."

"Randle," his aunt interrupts, "I do not CARE how many people you use. I only want results and quickly, Dear." With that she pushes a button on her wheelchair. Her chauffeur returns, releases the brakes and turns her around, and they start for the private elevator.

Before the door closes, she adds, "Remember, Randle, if you don't find them, and I don't get to see them with my own eyes before I die, you lose everything. Everything!" Her last words send a chill down Randle's spine, as the door slides shut with a sinister hiss.

Miss Baryl hears Randle talking out loud to himself, "I'm a

119

PUPPET, am I? I'll show HER, the dried-up old windbag!"

She can hear him going through the drawers in his father's old desk. He is opening and closing them and then ruffling through papers. Then the office gets very quiet, and in a low voice, Randle says, "I must get rid of her, but how? She has things set up so that if she doesn't give the go-ahead to the board of directors before she dies, I lose it all! Curse her! If only I can find them and keep them from her, I could get her to give me the okay. Yeah, I can blackmail her by holding them back from her! I MUST find them!"

Just then Randle's private phone rings. He answers, "Yes! What do you have for me? Who? Wait tell me her name again… Katelyn O'Rourke? Okay, what about her? Yeah, you believe she is a descendant of whom? Oh! Elizabeth O'Rourke? How did you arrive at that? Oh, by tracing Elizabeth's family tree. You went to one of those websites and found her there. You blundering IDIOT, those things are phony! WHAT? Okay! She lives right here in London. Go ahead and look into it, but I need results FAST, and I mean NOW! Put a tail on her, and see where it leads.

Chapter 14
Trust

Miss Baryl, after hearing the discussion and the threats, decides it is time to get to the bottom of whatever is going on. "This is beginning to sound very serious and dangerous," she says to herself as she leaves work that evening. She must to try to contact this Katelyn O'Rourke. She needs find out what this is all about. Heather Baryl located Katelyn's phone number in the London Directory; she uses her cell phone to call her.

"Hello, is this Katelyn O'Rourke?"

"Yes. May I ask who is calling?"

"You don't know me, Miss O'Rourke, but I must see you in person. It's of vital importance!"

"I'm sorry... who is this?"

"My name is Heather Baryl, and I fear you are in grave danger!"

"Danger? Whatever from?"

"Please, Miss O'Rourke! I must talk to you in person. Can we meet?"

"I don't know what this is all about, but I suppose we can meet at my apartment. Here, I'll give you my address."

"No! We must not meet there. I suspect you're being followed!"

"FOLLOWED? By WHO?"

Now Katelyn is frightened, and she is pretty sure she knows what this is all about. But she must play dumb and try to get as much information as she can.

"We must meet in secret, and you must make sure you are not followed!" Heather warns.

"Wait! Is this a joke? Am I on the radio or something?" Katelyn asks, playing along.

"No! I assure you this is not a joke! Now, can we at least meet and let me explain?"

"This all sounds kind of mysterious, but, okay -- if I assume you are telling me the truth and this is not a joke, what is it you want from me?"

Heather, seeing this is not going to be as easy as she had assumed, tries to calm down so she can convince Katelyn she is telling the truth. "We can meet in a public place like a park or at the mall," she says. "Wherever you feel is best. But I want you to take precautions. Go there in a roundabout way, so as to lose anyone who might be following you. Do you understand?"

Katelyn asks, "Who are you? Do I know you?"

"No, you do not know me. We have never met, but I have knowledge of a secret others are trying to uncover, and I am afraid their search for the secret may put you in harm's way."

"Secret? What secret?"

"Please, Katelyn, I cannot say any more over the phone. Will you meet me?"

Katelyn, hearing the distress in the woman's voice, decides to meet her. "Yes, I will! When and where?"

"Okay! First you pick where, and then we can work out how to go about it."

They talk about meeting in a park about half way between Katelyn's house and where Heather lives. Then Heather gives her a few things to check for to see if anyone is following her. Next they plan a route with several stops at shops and a movie so Katelyn can be sure she isn't being followed. The last thing they set is the time to meet, 4:15 p.m. the following day.

In the morning, Heather calls the manager in charge of the secretaries at work saying she has forgotten a doctor's appointment and would be out all day. Randle Hobart is not going to be in the office, so she doesn't need for anyone to cover for her.

Heather also goes through a routine to make sure she isn't followed. She arrives at the park at 4:12 p.m. She drives around twice before deciding where to park. As she pulls in, she notices a young lady with flaming-red hair, sitting in the car two spaces over and assumes she must be Katelyn.

Heather is shaking with fright as she gets out of her car and walks over to Katelyn's car.

Katelyn sees her get out, and as she approaches her car, Katelyn rolls down the window a little. Not knowing what to expect, she is ready to drive off quickly.

Heather stops near the front of Katelyn's car. "Miss O'Rourke?"

"Yes! Are you Heather?"

122

"Yes! Please, can we walk in the park?"

Katelyn is relieved that this little lady in her mid-50s with graying hair pulled back in a bun doesn't look threatening at all. She decides it will be all right to go with her and gets out of the car. They start walking.

"What is this all about, Miss Baryl?"

As they walk together, Heather looks at Katelyn and thinks, *"Well, you've come this far -- you might as well tell her all you know!"* She takes a breath and begins, "What I'm about to tell you will most likely shock you. After years of loyal service, I am about to betray my employer. Even though I might lose everything just by contacting you, I must tell you what I found out."

As they walk a little further, they come to a bench located near the center of the park. Katelyn, noticing how the older woman is obviously under a lot of stress, suggests they sit down. "Why don't we sit here, and you can tell me what it is that's troubling you so."

"Yes, thank you," Heather says. When they sit down, Katelyn notices how pale and shaken Heather is. Hoping to relieve some of her fear, Katelyn began softly, "Please tell me what this is all about, and maybe I can help you?"

Heather starts to cry. "I've worked for the Hobarts for 29 years. I have known of some terrible things they did to get ahead in their business. However, I always looked the other way and did my job." She sniffs and reaches in her purse to get out a hanky. Dabbing at her nose, she continues, "But when I learned of what they are up to with the little ones, I couldn't stay quiet anymore!"

"The little ones?" Katelyn asks, trying to act like she didn't understand what Heather is talking about.

Now the look on Heather's face becomes harder as she adds, "Katelyn, I read the journal from the German officer in World War One. I know who you are and who your uncle is, as well! So don't play dumb! I will most likely lose my retirement over this, and I didn't come here to play silly games. I know of the little people in Ireland and of the treasure they hold."

Now Katelyn is sure this lady is telling the truth. "What is it you want from me?"

123

Heather looks up at her. "I don't want anything from you. What I want is to stop them from getting their grimy hands on those little ones and to help keep you and your uncle safe, if I can."

Chapter 15
Trouble in Ireland

A few days later, somewhere deep in a forest of Ireland, Michael is running full out when he trips over a tree root, sending his tiny frame sprawling. Slowly he gets up and carefully takes inventory, dusting himself off as he does. "Nothing broken," he says as he rubs his skinned knee. "Better slow down before I do break something!" he chides himself. "I must get back to the village fast, but I need to be in one piece."

It is nighttime and very dark in the forest, too dark to be running, and he knows it. But the news he carries is so bad he has forgotten about the danger in his haste to get back. He limps a little as he starts out again, slower this time, but still moving at a trot.

"Lord, guide my feet this night," is the small prayer he says aloud.

* * * * *

Back in the hills, Shawn Dugan is standing outside the entrance to the little cave they only recently had moved into and now call home. As the elder of the village, he is worried. It is both his nature and his job to worry. He can worry over the smallest things, but this night his concerns are of the larger size, the safety of his people!

Shawn, Mike, and the rest of the people are all Tinys!

It's been well over a month since his last contact with their benefactor, Thomas O'Rourke. Shawn and Thomas have been friends for many years. He knows Thomas to be the kind of person who is always on time, so when Thomas had failed to show up at the normal time and place for their monthly meeting a week ago, Shawn has started to worry.

Shawn sent Mike Flanagan, the village's best hunter, to find out what is wrong. Now Mike is late in returning, and of course Shawn is worried.

"Mike is our best, and if he doesn't return, I don't know what to do next," Shawn says to himself as he looks out into the darkness of the night, hoping to see Mike.

His thoughts are about the people in his care. "We must leave this place, for sure, but where to go?" he questions out loud.

"In out of the cool night, that's where you'll be going, Shawn Dugan, I'm thinking."

Shawn turns to see his wife standing in the entrance to the cave, hands on her hips.

* * * * *

In the forest, as Michael runs, his thoughts go back over the events of the last two days.

It had taken him at least 24 hours to reach the home of Thomas O'Rourke. When he finally arrives, it is growing dark. Knowing some of the Bigs has dogs for pets; Mike leaves the cover of the forest and approaches the back of their house with great caution and stealth.

He has to get past the house next to the O'Rourke's. As he gets about halfway, he hears a dog coming around to the backyard. Michael drops flat on the ground, hoping the dog doesn't see him.

The dog comes around the corner and goes to the center of the yard. All the while, Mike is trying to see if the dog is coming at him, but the grass is too high where he is lying. He decides to stay flat in hopes he isn't seen.

The dog sniffs the air, sits down, and scratches the back of his ear with his hind leg. Then he stands up and goes toward the house, stopping at a pan of water near the faucet.

Mike hears the dog drinking and takes advantage of the distraction to move quietly to the nearest tree. From behind the tree, he sneaks a peak and sees no dog. Mike panics.

"Did he see me move? Where is he? Is he coming after me?"

Mike tries to get a grip on himself and listens if he can hear the dog coming his way, but all he can hear is the slight breeze blowing through the tree.

"Where is the dog? I must find out. Must not freeze. Must move now!"

Forcing himself to move, he peeks around the side of the

126

tree. *"No dog?"*

Then he hears the dog barking from in front of the house.

Mike scrambles up the tree out of harm's way.

Resting safely up in the tree, Mike takes the time to scan the area and get his bearings. *"Now, the dog is in the front yard of the neighbor's house. The O'Rourke house is on the right."* With the eyes of a skilled hunter, he slowly takes in the terrain before him. He stops and watches after seeing a picture through the window of the neighbor's house; the picture is moving.

"Oh, yeah," he says to himself, remembering some of the hunters talking about how the Bigs have things they call TVs. He watches for a while and sees a scene where a man falls down and is hurt. Then a young boy picks up a phone, dials 999, and help arrives.

Mike looks around and -- seeing it's clear -- climbs down and moves toward the O'Rourke house.

He halts at the edge of the yard to remove a piece of paper from his small pocket. On it is written instructions on how to get inside the O'Rourke house. After reading them again, he folds up the paper and puts it away.

"Before I go in, I better have a look around!" Cautiously moving closer to the house, he heads around the right side to the front to check there first. But as he rounds the corner of the house, he stops short. Parked in front of the house, with three men sitting inside, is a large black vehicle.

Mike is well hidden behind a bush and knows they can't see him. He decides to wait in position for a few minutes to see if they are staying or leaving.

Mike hears one of the men talking: "He's not answering his phone. What do you want us to do now?"

"No, Sir!" The man talking turns his head to reveal the cell phone he is holding to his ear, and he continues to talk. "Yes, Sir. We talked to him yesterday and told him what you said we should say.... No, Sir, all the lights are out. We know he's in there, because Don saw him through a window, and he is asleep in his bed.... Mr. Hobart, are you sure he's the one you've been looking for? ... No, Sir, as far as we can find out, he lives alone. There is a niece who lives in London. All the information we have tells us she is his only living relative.... No, Sir, we haven't seen her. We got the information using the bugging device I told you we put on his window.... Sir, he sure doesn't live like a man with millions of dollars.... Yes, Sir, as soon as it gets dark, we will talk to him again. I will..."

A police patrol car comes around the corner.

The man quickly says, "Police! I'll call you back!" and hangs up. As the police go on down the street, Tim, who is on the phone, tells Don behind the wheel, "Get us out of here; start the car and drive away slowly!"

Mike watches them drive around the corner and out of sight. Meanwhile, the police car continues on down the street.

Mike carefully makes his way around to the other side of the house and finds the side door. As he gets nearer, he spots the doggy door.

He remembers Shawn telling him that Mr. O'Rourke doesn't own a dog, but he is still cautious when he sees the small door.

"Come on!" he tells himself. *"Get a grip on your nerves, and get in there before those guys decide to come back."*

Then he spots the dog dish sitting on the step. After a closer look, he realizes the dish is empty except for some dried-up old leaves and a lot of dust.

"Dust!" he thinks to himself. *"So he doesn't have a dog!"*

Now he feels it's safe to enter through the doggy door. Ever so carefully, he pushes on it to see if the door moves, and it does! Pushing harder, the doggy door opens wide, and he enters the house.

Inside he finds a whole different world than he is used to. All the things in the house are huge, built for Big people. To him, it looks like he has entered the home of a giant -- but this giant is their friend and benefactor.

After taking a few seconds to get his bearings, Mike heads for the room he assumes is the bedroom. Entering the room, he goes over to the bed where Thomas O'Rourke is lying.

"Looks like he's sleeping. I must warn him about the men I saw outside!" Mike whispers to himself.

He looks around for a way to get up on the bed. Not finding anything to climb on, Mike goes over to the bed, grabs hold of the bedcovers, and starts to pull himself up.

Mr. O'Rourke wakes with a start. "What? Who's there?" he

128

exclaims, and he tries to sit up. But he is very weak and can only get up on one elbow. Rubbing his eyes, he sees Mike as he finally gets upon the foot of his bed.

Mike removes his hat, saying, "I'm sorry I gave you a start, Mr. O'Rourke, but I had to warn you."

"Warn me? Of what?"

Mike comes a little closer so the elderly man can hear him better.

"When I was outside, I saw three men in a black car. One of them was talking to someone on the phone."

O'Rourke's eyes open wide, and Mike can see the look of fear on his face.

"Where are they? Are they here now?" Thomas asks as he starts looking around in a frantic way.

"No! They are gone for now, but I fear they will return soon. What is it they want?"

"They're some of Hobart's men," O'Rourke responds. "They've been trying to get me to tell them about your people!" O'Rourke answers, almost in tears.

"Katelyn tried to warn me about how she thought someone has been following her around, and I wouldn't listen."

"Who is Katelyn?"

"She is my niece and all I have left in this world. Except you dear little ones," he says as tears roll down his cheeks. "I'm afraid I cannot take care of you any longer," he says as he falls back on his pillows.

Getting weaker by the moment, he holds out his hand to Mike, and mutters, "Must let Katelyn...know...how...to...find...little...ones." Struggling to get the words out, he adds, "Help...them...leave...here!" He closes his eyes and passes out.

Mike sits on the bed, wondering what he can do to help. But, at the back door, he hears, "O'Rourke, OPEN UP! We want to talk to you."

Thomas wakes again and tries to answer them, but he has grown even weaker. "Hide quickly!" he whispers to Mike, pointing to the door that leads to the spare bedroom. "These are very bad men, and they mustn't find you here."

Mike jumps down to the floor and runs into the spare room. As he gets inside the door, he hears, "Open the door, Old Man.

129

We told you we would be back!"

O'Rourke tries again to sit up, but he is much too weak and falls back into bed just as the back door is forced open.

Mike, hidden behind the spare bedroom door, peeks through the crack between the door and the doorframe. He hears the back door swing open with a loud crash as wood splinters from the doorframe fly all over the room. Two of the men he had seen in the car come into the house. They are dressed all in black and look mean. When they reach Thomas's room, the bigger man goes over to the bed.

"Get out of my house," demands Thomas in a weak voice.

The man grabs hold of the front of Thomas's nightshirt and with only one hand lifts him nearly off the bed. "We told you if you didn't call Mr. Hobart and tell him what he wants to know, we would be back."

Thomas starts to say something. "You will never..." his eyes go wide, then slowly close for the last time.

The other man, seeing what just happened, yells, "Now look what you've done! Hobart will have our hides, he will."

Mike can hear everything the two men are talking about.

"Shut up, Fool! I'm trying to figure out what to do here," the big man says as he let go of O'Rourke and turns to leave the room. He snaps his fingers, "I've got it! We don't tell Hobart we talked to the old man. We just say he was dead when we came in. Yeah, that'll work! Now let's get out of here!"

They start to leave. "No, wait! We better call Hobart and find out what to do next," the other one says reluctantly, knowing that it is going to make Hobart angry when they call him, but realizing they have to call.

Hobart is livid and tells them, "Torch the place and get out!" They go to get the can of petrol in the SUV, but the can is empty. So they climb in the car and leave to find a gas station.

Mike hears the car drive away and waits a little while. Then, carefully, he comes out of hiding, goes to the front window, climbs up on a chair and looks out to see if they really are gone. Seeing they are, he returns to the man who was their only hope of finding a safe place to live.

Mike notices a phone on the nightstand. Remembering what he had seen through the window next door, he climbs up on the

130

bedside table, lifts the receiver off the phone, and dials 999.

"Nine-nine-nine operator. What is your emergency?"

Mike, not sure what to do, yells as loud as he can, "Help!"

"Hello? Do you require help? I can hardly hear you? Hello?" But the operator hears no answer.

Mike hears a car pull up outside. He jumps down, runs back to look out of the window, and sees Hobart's men getting out of the car. This time, one of them is holding a red can.

"Petrol!" Mike exclaims as he drops, runs, and hides behind a chair not far from the back door, saying to himself, "If they burn down the house, I will have a chance to get out through the doggy door."

The bad guys just get to the back door when they hear a police siren.

"Let's get outta here!" one of them half yells as they run and scramble back into their car and drive off.

As it turns out, a police car was not far away when the 999 operator called the police to report the strange call from Mr. O'Rourke's number. The officers arrive quickly and go to the front door; when no one answers, they try to open it, only to find it is locked. The police go around the house searching for another way in. When they find the broken back door, they quickly enter and search the house, finding only Mr. O'Rourke. A check shows that he is not breathing, so one of the officers calls for an ambulance as the other checks the rest of the house. However, Michael is able to remain hidden.

Mike watches as the medics arrive and try to revive Mr. O'Rourke. Unable to, they put him on a stretcher and take him away. Mike is in shock, trying to figure out what to do, when a young woman drives up and comes to the front door. Seeing police tape across it, she calls, "Uncle Thomas?" But there is no reply. She goes around to the back door and finds it had been broken in.

Hearing a car pull up in front of the house, she goes around to see whom it is. As the policemen get out of the car, she goes over and asks, "What is going on? Where's my uncle?"

"Sorry, Miss, but there's been a bit of trouble here. May I ask who you are?"

"I'm Katelyn O'Rourke, the niece of Mr. O'Rourke, who lives

131

here."

"Well, miss, we responded to a 999 call, and upon arriving, we found the back door had been forced open. We then entered the premises to find the resident in his bed, deceased. We searched the house but found no one. We had just pulled away when we saw your car stop here, so we returned."

Katelyn is crying as she asks, "What...happened? Was he murdered? Who did this?"

"We don't know, Miss. We suspect foul play. But we won't know what caused your uncle's death until we hear from the medical examiner."

"Is there anything I can do to help?" she asks.

"Would you mind having a look around the house to see what, if anything, has been taken?"

"Yes, of course I'll look," Katelyn answers and starts into the house just as the officer gets another call and needs to leave.

As they get in the police car, he announces, "We'll be back as soon as possible, Miss. If you don't mind remaining for a bit, we would like to talk more when we get back?"

"Of course. I'll stay and wait for you," Katelyn replies, and she enters the house.

Mike, having again returned to hide in the spare bedroom, watches as she enters the bedroom of her uncle and sees the mess made by the medics who had tried to revive her uncle.

Sitting down in the chair next to his bed, she starts to cry.

"Uncle! Uncle -- I tried to tell you I thought someone was following me. I was afraid they would find you and make you show them where the little ones are hiding. What am I to do now? You told me if anything happened to you, I was to go to them and help them. But how can I find them? Why didn't you tell me? I know you were so afraid I might be hurt if Hobart's men found out I knew about them, but now no one knows! How can I ever find them to warn them?"

132

After hearing this, Michael runs over to her from his hiding place and announces, "I think maybe I can help!"

Chapter 16
New Benefactor

Katelyn O'Rourke jumps with a start, then turns to see the little man standing next to her.

"Sorry, Miss! I didn't mean to give you a start! But I do believe I can help," he continues with a big grin on his face.

"I suppose you can, indeed!" Katelyn replies, wiping the tears from her eyes. Taking a tissue from the bedside table, she dabs at her eyes and nose, and looking at him over the tissue, she asks, "Where in the world did you come from?"

"I'm afraid I have been here all along," he answers, shaking his head sadly. "It was some thugs who work for a man named Hobart. They came in and tried to get Mr. O'Rourke to tell them where we were... I mean to say, where my people are."

"Did they see you? They didn't hurt you, did they?"

"No, Miss, they didn't see me because your uncle told me to hide."

Sitting there, still sniffling and looking down at the tissue in her hand, she asks, "Did Uncle Thomas say anything else?"

Michael walks over to stand next to her. "He said he never had a chance to tell you how to contact us. I suspect he thought you were in danger from those men."

Katelyn looks down at him and tries to smile. "Oh! I'm all right; he worried too much about me." Again the tears start to fall. "I tried to warn him, you know. He was so weak, and I was afraid they would hurt him!" – she sniffed -- "And now they have!"

Michael reaches up and touches her hand, "It will be okay Miss. We'll help you."

Now she smiles a little. "I thought I'm supposed to help you!"

Michael climbs up on the bed and sits down. "Well, I guess we'll just have to help each other."

With a questioning look on her face, she says, "I'm afraid I don't have any idea of where to start."

There is a knock on the front door. "Police -- open up, please!"

"Hide quickly!" she whispers as she starts for the door.

134

Looking back over her shoulder, she sees Mike running back into the spare bedroom. When she gets to the door, she looks through the peephole before opening it. Seeing a policeman and a police car outside, she opens up the door.

"Miss, did you find anything missing or out of place?" asks the policeman.

Katelyn indicates for him to come in and replies, "I'm sorry. I'm afraid I've been crying and haven't looked yet."

"That's all right, Miss. If I may, I would like to take a second and have a look for myself?"

"Oh, sure, go ahead," she answers the policeman, while saying to herself, *"I pray the little one is well hidden."*

As they both walk back to her uncle's bedroom, she asks, "What are we looking for?"

The officer takes out a notebook and writes in it as they walk. He looks up to say, "We presume that whoever broke in wanted to rob your uncle. But they were stopped when he managed to place a 999 call. We happened to be in the area, and I'm sure our siren must have chased them away."

Katelyn, not wanting to give away any information, says, "Yes, that must have been it. I can't imagine what they were after. My uncle never has had much in the way of money. The only thing I recall he had that might be worth anything would be his collection of comic books and a few old hardback books he loved."

While they slowly work their way through the house, Michael runs into the closet, quickly climbs up a coat, and gets up on the top shelf. He scrambles over a stack of old magazines and hides behind them.

"Do you know where he kept his collection?" the policeman questions, as they enter the room where Michael is hiding.

Katelyn goes over to the closet, opens the door, and points to the stack of comic books, not realizing that Michael might be hiding there.

The officer looks at them and starts to reach up but changes his mind. "Does it appear they're all there?"

Katelyn takes a long look. As she's checking the books, she notices a tiny shoe sticking out from behind one of the stacks. She turns around quickly and replies, "Yes! As far as I can see,

135

they are all here!"

The officer closes his notebook and turns to leave. "All right then, Miss. We've probably covered everything for now. Of course, you will need to come down to the station and file a report."

"Of course," Katelyn remarks. "I must call a repairman to fix the door, and then I'll be down."

"Good. Sorry for your loss, Miss," he says with a tip of his hat and is out the door.

After making sure that the police were gone, she hurries back into the room where Mike is. "You can come out now -- it's safe!"

Mike slowly climbs down the same coat he had used before. As he lands on the floor, Katelyn says with a sigh, "I almost blew it with the comic books! I never dreamed you'd be up there."

Mike smiles up at her, "And I thought it looked like a very good place to hide." He laughs, and then he turns serious. "Katelyn, I must go back now and report what has happened. Will you be safe here?"

Katelyn kneels down and takes his tiny hand in hers. "I will be alright, but I have a question."

"What is it you wish to know?"

She grins and asks, "What's your name, Sir?"

Michael laughs, "My apologies, Miss! Me names Michael Flanagan."

"Michael Flanagan it is then, and a lovely name at that." She giggles and then asks, "How am I to contact you? And what are we to do about finding a safe place for you and the rest of the Tinys?"

Taking off his tiny hat, he scratches his head. "I don't know what to do about how or where we are to go. I will have a talk with the elders and Lord willing, return here to this house one week from today."

She snaps her finger as if she just remembered something important. "I just remembered! Uncle told me a secret way you little ones can get into the house."

"And what might that be?" Michael asks.

"There is an old doghouse out in the backyard that has a secret door at the back. You must push on the left side of one of

136

the boards, and a door will open. Once inside, you just follow the instructions you will find on the wall, Uncle told me," Katelyn explains.

"I saw the doghouse earlier when I was in the backyard. So you just follow the instructions, is it?"

"Yes! And I will be here. You must come at night. I will be in the house with no lights on, just in case the house is being watched by those Hobart men," says Katelyn.

"Where does this secret passage open in the house, if you don't mind me asking? I wouldn't like to walk right into one of those men when I come in, you know."

"Oh! Here, I can show you. It's under the kitchen sink," she says as she gets up and heads to the kitchen. Going to the sink and opening up the cabinet door, she gets down on her knees and reaches behind all the cans and bottles of cleaning stuff. She shows him what looks like a place where the back wall was repaired with a panel of plywood.

"When you come in, you can stop under here. Listen to see if I am alone, or if those men are here, before you come out from under the sink. Okay?"

"Yes, that will work. And now I must go," he says. Starting for the broken back door, he stops and turns to ask, "What are you going to do about this?" He points to the door.

"I know a man who can replace it. I will call him now and get the door fixed and made more secure."

Mike nods his head, tips his hat, and turns again to go. Before he reaches the door, Katelyn hears him say, "The Lord keep you safe, Katelyn O'Rourke!"

She answers back, "And you as well, Michael Flanagan!"

Chapter 17
Call for Help

The run back home takes Michael all night and the next day to reach the caves where the others are waiting.

He tells Shawn Dugan and the elders all he had seen and heard at the O'Rourke house. They all say a prayer for their old benefactor they had grown to love, then tells Michael to go rest. They will let him know when they reach a decision.

Tired to the bone, Michael wants nothing more than a meal and a few hours' sleep. As he rounds the corner in the cave where his makeshift house is, he sees a light coming from his doorway and he wonders, "Now what? Who can this be? I told them all I know..."

Miss Drew Fitzpatrick pokes her head out of his door and announces, "I was thinkin' you would be hungry. So I made your breakfast for you, Michael Flanagan, and I'll have none of your sass about it!"

"Aye, and you'll get none from me, Lass, and thank you!" Michael gave a tired reply.

"Oh! Lass, is it now? Well it wasn't 'Lass' when you kissed me goodbye a week ago!"

Michael slumps down on the front step. "Now, Drew, you know it's the tiredness in me that's talking now. Don't be angry with me. I'm so tired, I don't know what I'm saying, except I love..." And he passes out.

Drew almost drops the skillet of food she is holding! She quickly put it on the fireplace, runs to sit down next to him, pulls his head up, and places it on her lap. "Oh, Michael, I was so worried about you. I almost lost my mind! I missed you so. Please be all right!"

Michael, without opening his eyes, in almost a whisper, says, "Tis true I do love you, Lass!"

Drew hugs him and cries, "And I love you, Michael!"

* * * * *

It has been almost a week since Michael's return. When he is asked to meet with the elders again, Shawn makes the

138

announcement. "Michael, we decided to send you back with the information Miss O'Rourke will require so she can contact the benefactor in America. Now, we've never done this before. Not in my lifetime or in any of the others' before us. This address was given to me at my last meeting with Thomas O'Rourke. He was feeling sick and concerned for us if something should happen to him. We now know something did! Do you feel up to another run back to town, Lad?"

"Yes, I'm okay now. I had a good rest and some fine meals," replies Mike.

They all laugh, knowing that Drew, finally declaring her love for him, is taking good care of him.

"Well, then -- off with you. Above all, don't let that piece of paper fall into the wrong hands!"

The trek through the woods back to the O'Rourke house is uneventful. Mike makes good time, arriving again just as the sun is setting the next day.

As he approaches the neighborhood, he notices the O'Rourke house is dark. No lights can be seen in any of the windows. As he did the last time he was at the house, he cautiously moves around to the front.

Again he spots the big black SUV parked down the block. This time he can't tell if anyone is in it. He stays in the underbrush, waiting to see if anyone is in the house or nearby. He doesn't hear or see anything, so he moves around back to try the secret way in through the dummy doghouse.

Katelyn has been hiding inside the house, having arrived about two hours ago and entering through the side door. When it started getting dark, she left the lights off so anyone looking at the place would never guess anyone was there. But waiting in the dark is becoming very spooky. About ready to give up and leave, she hears a noise coming from the kitchen.

She reaches over and grabs the golf club she had found in her uncle's closet earlier. Getting up, she moves quietly to one side of the kitchen doorway. She brings the club up, ready to strike whoever comes through the door.

When Mike opens the secret door, he knocks over a can of cleanser that is under the kitchen sink. He waits a few moments before opening the cabinet door and coming out from under the

139

sink. He stands there with the cabinet door open, ready to scamper back outside if anything goes wrong. He thought he heard movement just as he opened the cabinet door, but it stopped.

Then he hears a faint voice from the front room: "Michael, is that you?" Katelyn asks as she peeks around the doorway.

Seeing her face, he steps clear of the cabinet door and answers, "Would you be thinkin' there be pixies stumblin about in the dark? Would you now?" He laughs.

As she comes around the door and sees him, she sits down on the floor and holds out her hand for him to come to her. He runs over and sits beside her.

"I've been so frightened!" she says, pointing in the direction where the SUV is parked. "Those men arrived about an hour ago. They've been just sitting there, waiting."

"Aye! I saw the car as I took a wee look around before coming in. Do you know who they are or what they want?" he questions, looking up at her.

"Yes, yes, I do! Thanks to a lady who works for their boss, I know everything!"

"Are we safe here, Lass?"

"Well, I doubt they know I'm here. But they are dangerous and will stop at nothing to get their hands on you and your people!" Then she tells Michael, "The Hobart family have been trying to find you little ones for generations. "Do you know what that is all about?"

Mike knows but he doesn't want to be too free with information. "I'm not sure. Do we need to leave and go someplace else?"

"I'm afraid they might see us leave. How can we get them to go away?" she wonders.

After considering for a minute, Mike asks, "Is the phone still working?"

"I believe so," she answers as she gets up and starts to pick up the phone; suddenly she freezes in place. "What if they bugged the phone?"

"Bugged? What do you mean, Lass?"

"They might have put a device in it so they can hear when someone makes a call," she explains.

140

"Well, then -- that won't do, will it now?"

"Wait!" she almost shouts." I have my cell phone in my purse. We can use it."

"And what of those men? Won't they hear it too?" questions Mike.

"No, no! I've had it with me all along, so they couldn't have put anything in it," she tells him.

"Good; then you can call the police," Mike answers.

"But they will ask questions," she argues.

"Simply tell them you suspect these are the same men who broke in last week," Mike encourages.

Before she can make the call, however, they hear a commotion outside. Both of them go over to the front window. Mike climbs up on a chair so he can see outside. Two police cars had pulled up and were blocking the SUV. As the police officers approach the SUV with guns drawn, Mike and Katelyn wonder what's going on.

It turns out that an anonymous caller out walking his dog noticed the black SUV parked near the O'Rourke house. The caller had remembered that he seen this same SUV parked by the O'Rourke house on the night of the attempted robbery and Mr. O'Rourke's death.

Again, the police had been only a few blocks away, but this time they were able to have two units on the scene. They both respond quickly, approaching the SUV from two different directions and blocking it in.

While these dummies were supposed to be watching the O'Rourke house, one was busy listening to the radio, one was in the back seat cleaning his gun, and one was asleep with the wiretap earphones on his head. When the police officers arrest them and search the car, they find two cans of gasoline, burglary tools, telephone bugging and recording equipment, and all the tapes they had illegally recorded, including their phone calls to one Randle Hobart.

Back in the house, Mike and Katelyn watch as the three men are handcuffed and taken away.

"Well, now -- I wonder how that happened?" questions Katelyn. "I hope that takes care of those three for a while."

141

Michael is glad to see the danger has passed, at least for the time being. Still worried about what they are going to do to solve his little group's problem, he says, "I'm glad to see them gone. I wonder how long it will be before they or someone else like those thugs are back looking for us."

Katelyn turns away from the window and sits down on the floor next to the brave little man. "What did your council suggest we do?"

"They want you to try to contact the American Tinys' guardian. The Council thinks it best if we go to America." he answers.

"Do they know how or who to contact?"

"Yes -- I have it right here," he answers as he pulls the paper from inside his shirt.

As she reads the note, Michael tells her the council's instructions,

"Tell them to bring some of the Tinys with them so we can be sure who they are. Also, insist the Tinys meet me here using the secret way into the house. Tell them to meet us one week from today. They must bring only one big person with them. That way we can take every care not to be trapped or tricked."

"Yes, I'll tell them. I will be here as well, just as I am tonight," she announces.

Michael looks up at her and, seeing the deep concern on her face, says, "It will be all right now, Katelyn, Lass. Don't you be worrying none!"

Then he thinks to himself, *"Now what will she be doing with herself when the likes of us are gone off to America, I wonder."* He asks, "Katelyn, do you have family here?"

Looking at his, tired, worried face, she replies, "No, I have no one now that Uncle is gone! Why do you ask?"

"Well, I was wondering what you are going to do when we are gone."

"I don't know. I guess I will stay in London for now. There is the business to look after, you know."

"Why don't you come with us to America? You are our benefactor now, you know."

142

Chapter 18
Tiny Commandos

At Hawk Industries headquarters in Nashville, Janet is busy in her office with the daily running of the company. Her secretary comes in with a registered letter from Ireland. Janet immediately stops what she is doing and opens it. After reading the letter, she tells her secretary to cancel all her appointments for the rest of the day. The minute the secretary leaves, Janet's picks up the cell phone identical to the one she gave Conor and calls him. When he answers, she says, "Conor, this is Janet."

"Hi, Janet. What's up?"

"Are you at Grandpa's?"

"Yes."

"I need to meet with you, Grandpa, and the gentleman I met the last time I was at Grandpa's house."

"Okay. Is there a problem?"

Trying to disguise her message, she answers, "Just a little one, but I'm afraid it requires our immediate attention."

"Okay. Do you want us to come there?"

"No – that shouldn't be necessary," Janet, answers. "Just ask Grandpa if we can meet at the place where he and I met the last time."

"Okay. Just a minute," Conor says as he turns to his grandfather. "It sounds like there is a problem, and Janet can't tell me over the phone. She wants to meet at the last place you two met."

"Oh," Grandpa says, as he sits up in his easy chair. "That's a code word for big trouble and to be careful! Tell her that will be fine, and we'll be there at 7:15 tonight."

Conor frowns at the idea of Janet and Grandpa and their cryptic messages; after giving Janet his grandfather's answer, they both hang up. He looks at Grandpa and asks, "7:15 p.m.? How did you come up with that time?"

"It's another code, Scooter, to tell her where we're really going to meet!"

"Oh! Huh?"

"I'll explain in the car. Go get Graybeard, and tell him it's an emergency!"

After Conor goes to the Tinys' village and gets Graybeard, the three climb into the new silver Tesla Model S that Grandpa had bought Conor, and they head for Nashville. After a two-hour drive, they arrive at the Hawk Industries headquarters building a little east of the Nashville airport. The main building covers a city block and stands 20 stories tall.

Grandpa tells Conor to pull into the underground parking garage. Once they are inside, he directs him to head to the southwest corner, where Grandpa points to a group of three freight elevator doors. As they get closer, Grandpa pulls a remote-control unit out of his pocket and pushes a button. The left door opens.

"Drive into that one!"

"Drive in?" questions Conor.

"Go ahead -- it's okay," Grandpa says.

Once the car is inside the elevator, Grandpa pushes another button that shuts the door and they start to descend. They drop down a few floors before coming to a stop at sub-level five. When the door opens, Conor can see a well-lit tunnel appearing to run for at least a quarter of a mile. He drives in and Grandpa tells him to turn at the second left; as he does, he notices that it is a dead end, with four parking spaces. He pulls in, parks, turns off the car, and looks over at Grandpa.

"This is more like something you see in a spy movie than a corporate office. Why all this secrecy?"

As the three are getting out of the car, Grandpa explains, "Well, we do a lot of work for the government and military. Some of our own projects are secret, and this is necessary in order to keep them secret!"

He and Graybeard start toward a door. Grandpa stops and turns around to see Conor still standing by the car, looking around.

"What's wrong, Grandson?"

"Nothing. It's just so Hollywood-like and surreal!"

"Well, besides the need for secrecy, Grandson, I've always kind of liked those Double-Oh-Seven movies." He and Graybeard laugh.

Conor catches up with the two of them. They go through a door into an outer office. Ed Barns, who is waiting inside, gets up

144

from behind a desk, and comes around to greet them.

"Good evening, Mr. O'Brien," he directs at Grandpa. Looking down at Graybeard, he asks, "And how are you tonight, Mr. O'Doul?" Then he looks up at Conor. "And how's the new boss?" as he holds out his hand and shakes Conor's.

"Hey, you're the driver from the airport -- the one who drove Grandpa and me around?"

"That's right. Mrs. Cook hired me as your -- shall we say -- assistant." Ed is a very confident 57-year-old ex-CIA agent, 6-foot-2 with a muscular frame and a handsome smile. His piercing gray-blue eyes seem to see everything, and the dark brown hair he always wears short, military-style, is starting to gray around the temples. His dark-blue suit shows off his broad shoulders but conceals much. He discreetly opens his jacket to reveal a gun tucked neatly under his arm. "Welcome to your little home-away-from-home."

He turns and opens the door to the meeting room. After everyone is inside, Ed steps in, closes the door, and remains inside. Already there is Janet, sitting on one of the couches placed off to the side of the room. She gets up from the couch and walks over to greet them.

"Good evening, Guys," Janet, says, indicating they should join her on the couches.

As they all sit down, she smiles at Conor. "Well, what do you think of your grandfather's hideout? Kind of 'Spy Movie,' isn't it?"

"I would say so," Conor answers as he glances around with a worried look on his face.

"Something bothering you, Conor?" Janet asks, seeing his concern.

"I was just wondering what else I might find in this Double-Oh-Seven Land we call Hawk Industries," Conor remarks.

"I had planned to finish giving you the tour this week, but now we have this trouble in Ireland," she says, reading the letter from Katelyn O'Rourke to everyone. The letter, containing all the details about the Hobarts and their search for the Tinys, is information Hobart's secretary had given to Katelyn.

Conor, who has been writing in his ever-present notebook, looks up. "What can we do to help them?"

145

Janet answers, "The way I see it, we need to do three things. First and foremost is to ensure the safety of the Tinys in Ireland. Second is to come up with a way to remove all evidence of the Tinys' existence from the hands of the Hobarts. Third, find a way to discredit the Hobarts."

Ed Barns, who has been taking all this in, speaks up, "Well, since the aunt has such a fascination with the Tinys, you should have her make their acquaintance in a Halloween kind of way!"

"A what?" asks Janet, with a look of surprise!

Ed laughs and answers, "It's possible that with a **little** help, we could scare the Tinys right out of her -- in a way that would make her not want to see another Tiny, ever!"

Graybeard laughs. "Now that sounds like fun! Can I get in on this?"

"Me, too!" chimes in Grandpa. "I can come up with a few things the Tinys can do to her that will curl her hair!"

"Okay, then. You three put your heads together and decide on some ideas. Don't forget: You have very little time, but all the resources of the company," Janet says.

Checking his notes, Conor asks Janet, "Didn't Miss O'Rourke's letter say Hobart's secretary is willing to help us?"

Janet nods her head in agreement.

"Good. That's what I thought. Why don't we arrange a meeting in London?

-- With Miss Baryl, Miss O'Rourke, Ed, you, and me -- as soon as possible," Conor suggests.

"That's a good idea, Conor, but I'm not so sure you should be involved in this," Janet comments.

"Well, I need to start being involved sometime. What's your opinion, Grandpa?"

"He's right; you might as well take him with you," Grandpa said. "And besides, I want Conor to start coordinating anything having to do with the Tinys."

"Okay. I'll get right on it," Janet replies.

"I'd like to bring Scott Curtis, my dad's friend from Micro Technology Division, in on all this. Remember, you met him at my parents'… thing," Conor says, not wanting to say "funeral." "Scott is a brilliant engineer, and I know my dad trusted him completely. He will be a big help if we invite him into our little

Copyright 2015 Gary E. Reavis, Sr.

circle of friends. Besides, we need some things built for the Tinys. He is just the man to get the job done, quickly and quietly. Conor asks, "Does anyone have a problem with me letting him in on our secret?" He looks from face to face, and they all shake their heads, no.

"Okay! Janet, will you please arrange for him to fly in tomorrow? I'll go over what I want from him before we leave for London."

"Sure. I'll call him as soon as we finish," Janet replies, thinking, *"So, young Conor HAS decided to pick up the O'Brien torch and run with it. Good!"*

Ed asks Janet, "Correct me if I'm wrong, but didn't I just see our new, corporate jet prototype over at Hawk Aviation, getting ready to go through its final long-distance flight tests?"

"Why, yes -- you did. Why?"

"Good! Then that's how we will transport the Irish Tinys back here to Tennessee."

Janet, a bit puzzled, asks, "How can we pull that off? With all the heightened security and going through customs in both the U.S. and Ireland, it will be impossible!"

Ed explains, "I noticed the test plane is jammed full of test gear and equipment. We can simply replace some of it with dummy equipment. We'll then have room to build little seats and a place for our small friends. We will, of course, need to come up with a plan on how we will get them from where they are now to the airport in Dublin. Any ideas?"

When no one says anything, Ed takes a deep breath and decides it's time for him to put his expertise to use. Turning to Graybeard, he says, "Okay. I need you to pick four or five Tinys to come with us to Ireland, where they will work with the Irish scouts or whatever they call themselves.

"Once we arrive, there are two important tasks they'll be needed for. First, they will need to make contact with the Irish Tinys as per the instructions in the letter. Second, we'll use them to infiltrate both the home of Hobart's aunt and Hobart's office. Can you do that?"

Graybeard pulls on his beard and answers, "Yes – and I know just the scouts we'll need for the job. I do have one question."

"What is it?"

"Well, won't the Hobart building and offices be highly secured?"

"You're correct, but if our meeting with Miss Baryl goes as I suspect, we'll have no problem with access," Ed explains.

"Oh, yes; she can be a great help. I forgot for a moment she is willing to help us," Graybeard acknowledges.

Ed leans back in his chair, and announces, "If there are no more questions, I suggest we all get to work on getting the Tinys out of Ireland and home here to Tennessee!"

Conor looks up from his notes and says, "I suggest we call this **Operation Transport.**"

"Very good idea, Conor," Janet announces. **"Operation Transport,** it is."

In Ireland the next day, Katelyn O'Rourke receives an overnight registered letter from Janet, it reads:

To: Katelyn O'Rourke
Dublin, Ireland

Miss O'Rourke, we received your letter and understand you have a small problem requiring our attention.

Per your instructions, we put things in motion here, and the interested parties should arrive there at the appointed date and time.

We understand the item mentioned will need to be moved to another location, and we are making preparations to do so.

We hear a third party is also interested in the item, and we are going to make them a separate offer.

Should the matter require immediate attention, please go to the Hawk building in London at 446 Main Street and see Mr. John Harold. He will have additional instructions and a secure phone for you to use to get in touch with me.

Sincerely
Janet Cook
CEO Hawk Industries.

148

Copyright 2015 Gary E. Reavis, Sr.

Janet also sent an overnight registered letter to Heather Baryl that said:

To: Heather Baryl
London, England

Miss Baryl, your name has reached my desk in our search for quality personnel.

I believe we have a friend in common. We are aware of the assistance you gave to her with her little problem.

We would like to meet with you to discuss a similar problem we have here in the U.S.

We also understand you will be retiring from your present position soon. We feel you would be a valuable member of our team.

We would like to extend to you an offer for a position as a special consultant. Please reply.

Sincerely,

Janet Cook
CEO Hawk Industries.

That night Heather calls Katelyn. "Katelyn, this is Heather."

"Hi, Heather."

"Did you get a letter today?" Heather asks.

"Why, yes I did! Did you?"

"Yes, and I don't know what to make of it. Can we meet and talk this over?"

"I'm still in Ireland, but I'll take a plane and be in London around 2 p.m.

"Let's meet at the same spot at 3 p.m.," Katelyn says, and hangs up.

They meet in the park. Heather seems a bit nervous and tells Katelyn, "I've been worried that Mr. Hobart might find out about my talking to you. Now I get an offer from a company in America. I really don't know what to make of this." She hands the letter to Katelyn.

Katelyn reads it, and when she sees the signature at the bottom, she smiles. "This is from the people in America who are going to help my little ones. So it appears they want you to come to America and work for them. This is a reward for your helping me."

Heather giggles. "You mean I don't have to worry anymore about losing my job?"

Katelyn gives her a hug. "That's the way I see it." Heather breaks down and cries.

The next morning:

Scott arrives in Nashville after a 10-minute limo ride from the airport to Hawk Industries headquarters. Conor's secretary meets him and takes him to Conor's offices, where he finds young Conor busy working at a modeling computer.

Conor looks up as Scott comes in. "Hi, Scott -- how was your flight?"

"Okay -- kind of early at 4:30 a.m., but other than that, just great!"

"Yeah! Sorry for the short notice and the early hour, but we have a special problem, an extremely tight schedule, and a lot that needs to be done."

Scott sets down his briefcase and coat and then approaches the computer. "Okay! What's up?"

"First, I need to ask you a question," Conor says.

"Okay, shoot. What's on your mind?"

Conor tries to hold back a grin. "Do you believe in little people?"

"Huh? Little people? You mean like dwarfs and the like?"

"No -- more like leprechauns and fairies."

"Leprechauns? No, I don't believe in fairy tales. Why do you ask?"

Just then Janet opens the door to one of Conor's other rooms. "Hi, Scott," she says with a smile. He returns her smile, "Hi, Janet; nice to see you again."

Scott and Janet had met before. They had both liked each other right from the start. Afterwards, when Scott had asked a few of his friends about her, he learned she had been a widow for the past five years and had a teenage daughter.

"Nice to see you, too," she adds. Now she is grinning from ear to ear.

150

Scott gets a funny feeling and looks back and forth between the two smiling faces. "Hey, what's going on here? What's this all about?"

Janet, who is still standing in the doorway, moves a little to her right, and Graybeard steps out from behind her pant leg.

Scott looks from Janet to Graybeard, to Conor, to Graybeard, to Janet, back to Graybeard, and back to Janet, and finally at Graybeard.

"Wow!" is all he can say.

Graybeard walks right up to him and holds out his hand. "Glad to meet you, Scott. I've heard good things about you."

Scott looks like he is going to faint. "Wow! What? I can't... How in the...Where did...Wow!"

"Sounds just like what I said when I first met him," Conor adds.

They all laugh.

Janet walks over and takes Scott's hand, pulling it down to meet Graybeard's. Taking Scott's thumb and finger, she closes it on Graybeard's hand and shakes it.

"See, he won't bite!" she laughs. "Oh! By the way, he's not a leprechaun or a fairy, for that matter."

"Oh! That's good to know!" Scott manages to get out.

Janet leads him over to the couch and sits down with him. He is still staring at Graybeard when Conor starts telling him all about the Tinys and how he and his family, and now a few friends, have become the Tinys' protectors and benefactors. He continues to tell him all about their history, the trouble Hobart and his aunt are causing the Irish Tinys, and what Conor and his little group plan to do about it.

He is explaining all this to Scott when he notices that Janet is still holding Scott's hand. He grins and keeps on with the where, what, and who of their plan to rescue the Tinys in Ireland.

After he finishes, he asks, "Any questions?"

Scott answers, "I don't know where to start. You really expect to just go over there and take on Hobart and his tough guys and pick up how many tiny people? And then bring them back here, and nobody is going to say or do anything?"

Graybeard asks, "Conor, may I say something?"

"Of course; go right ahead."

151

"Scott, I'm glad you see the difficulties we must overcome. This is one of the reasons Conor wanted you on the team. We came up with a plan we think will work. But I would like for you to go over it with Conor and Janet, to see if you can find anything that might cause our plan to fail. Isn't this what you both want?" he questions, nodding to Janet and Conor.

"Yes, of course," Janet says.

Conor agrees, "Yes, and when we finish here, I have some designs for things we will need to take with us. I would like for you to look them over and if you approve, get the shops working on them right away. We leave for Ireland a week from tomorrow. And oh! By the way, you're now the new Chief Engineer of Hawk Industries!"

Scott shakes his head. "Go to Ireland. Beat up bad guys. Break into a man's office and steal documents. Rescue little people. Smuggle them out of Ireland and into the U.S. We leave in less then a week. Should be a piece of cake!"

Everyone is silent for a moment, and then Janet says, "Lord, help us!"

Everyone says, "Amen!"

152

Chapter 19
New Revelations

The next morning, Scott calls Conor on the secure phone he had been given. "Conor, I need to talk to a few of the Little People and get some idea of what they can do physically and mentally. Can you arrange it?"

"I can do better than that. I'm tied up over here working on the jet with Ed, but I'm sure Janet won't mind taking you to my grandpa's house,"

"Grandpa's house?"

"You will understand better once you get there," Conor says.

"Okay! You're the boss," Scott remarks.

"Ah, cut it out, Scott. You know I'm not the boss, yet! Oh, and by the way, they like to be addressed as Tinys, not Little People," Conor adds.

"Tinys," Scott answers. "Okay. Got it. Oh, and you did say you are going to ask Janet to take me, right?"

"You kind of like her, don't you?" teases Conor.

"Yes, Conor, I do!"

"Good. I'll give her a call and set up a meeting with the Tinys."

"Okay. See you later, and Conor..."

"Yeah?"

"Thanks for the new job, Boss."

"Will you stop that?" They both laugh.

It's about five minutes later when Janet walks into Scott's new office -- just two doors down from hers.

"Good morning, Scott."

"Good morning. Did Conor call you just now?" Scott asks as he gets up from his desk and comes around to greet her.

"Yes, he did, and I would be glad to take you to Grandpa's house. I called the airport, and the helicopter will be here in 30 minutes. I assume you're in a hurry, so I cleared my calendar for the day."

"Thank you! I'm glad you can show me around. I'm still trying to catch up on all of this. I can use all the help I can get."

They talk for a few minutes, and then it's time to go up to the roof and catch the helicopter. Coming out of the door to the helicopter pad, Scott sees Ed Barns waiting by the chopper. "Good morning, Mrs. Cook, Mr. Curtis." After seeing the puzzled look on their faces, he adds, "Conor asked me to be in on this little adventure."

"Good!" Janet says. "Let's go!"

They all climb in and take off for Jamestown. After they put on their headsets, Janet tells Ed, "I called Grandpa, and he's arranged for us to meet them at his house. I have a company car waiting at the airport." She turns to Scott. "Is there anything else you need?"

"Yeah -- can you hold my hand? I'm afraid of flying!"

Janet quickly takes his hand and holds on tight. She doesn't notice Ed's face, as he turns away to look out the window in time to hide a grin. He knows from doing the background checks that Scott is a licensed pilot with hundreds of hours logged in the air. Ed says to himself, *"Nice move buddy!"*

Once they arrive at Grandpa's house, Scott and Ed are introduced to a few of the Tinys that Grandpa and Graybeard thought could help with Operation Transport.

Graybeard clears his throat and announces, "Let me introduce everyone. Our little group consists of my son Gary, our blacksmith and handyman. He can make almost anything out of very little. Mr. Vaughn is our teacher and the keeper of knowledge. You might call him a historian. Our best scouts are Eric and his brother Bryan. And then there's me -- I'm the leader of the Tinys. Now, what can we do for you?"

"Well, I need to test all of you to determine what you can do physically and mentally -- if you don't mind?" Scott says questioningly.

"What are these tests for?" asks Vaughn.

"Are you all familiar with Operation Transport?"

Graybeard speaks up: "Yes; they have all been briefed."

"Good! What I need to do is to construct some gadgets for the team of Tinys who are going to Ireland. In order to make things that will help and not hurt you, I need to know your limitations."

The Tinys all look at one another, and Graybeard nods his head to give the okay.

154

Gary steps forward and says, "I have a few ideas and drawings that might help."

Vaughn speaks next. "Scott, we know this is all new to you, so maybe I can help out. First, the IQ of every Tiny is tested at the age of 13, and we have found that all test above average; a few of us score much higher. Some of us, like Eric and Bryan, also have above-average physical abilities."

"What kind of physical abilities?"

Again the Tinys look to Graybeard for the okay and again he nods in agreement. Vaughn turns to Eric. "Show him."

Eric goes over to one side of the room, takes out his knife, and tosses it up in an arc almost to the ceiling and across the room. Everyone's eyes are on the knife as it flies through the air. When the knife reaches the other side of the room, Eric is standing there to catch it.

Scott stares in wonder. He then exclaims, "That is AMAZING! Can all of you move that fast?"

"No, only a few are born with his gift. Some of us can communicate with birds and animals. Others receive the knowledge to heal," Vaughn answers.

Scott is grinning from ear to ear while typing notes on his laptop. "Anything else?"

Gary walks over to Bryan and asks him to turn around so that Scott can see his backpack. When he does, the first thing Scott notices is he has it on upside-down. Gary takes a red rock from his pocket and puts it in Bryan's pack, leaving the flap open upside-down. Each of the other Tinys come over and take a red rock out of their pockets and place them in Bryan's backpack as Scott looks on, with a confused look on his face. After all of the Tinys have placed a red rock in Bryan's pack, Scott notices Bryan is now hovering about 6 inches off the ground. Gary closes the backpack, and gently gives Bryan a shove -- sending him sailing across the room as he floats in the air!

Scott goes over to Bryan still floating around and asks, "May I?"

Bryan grins. "Sure, go ahead." Scott gives him a slight push, and Bryan flies across the room again.

"It can't be the rocks -- how do they do that?" Scott asks.

Graybeard speaks up. "These stones were found many years

155

ago in a cave in England. A few of them came with us when we were brought here in 1919. They possess this lifting property we have learned how to use, as you can see. But as to how they work this way, that remains a mystery."

Gary remarks, "As you can imagine, they are not easy to work with. If you drop one, the rock will simply fly up and away. We have come to believe it has something to do with the earth's magnetic fields."

Scott is shaking his head. "I've never seen or heard of anything like this!"

Vaughn says, "I hope we demonstrated what we can do to your satisfaction."

"You've done that and more. Is there anything else I should know?"

Bryan replies, "Well, I can show you how high some of us can jump, if that would help?"

"It would help a lot. Go ahead."

As Bryan and the others all head for the door, Scott calls out, "Wait! Where are you going? I thought you were going to show me how high you can jump?"

Bryan calls back over his shoulder, "We need to go outside to show you."

Scott picks up his laptop and follows them outside to the front of Grandpa's house. Once everyone is out, Eric and Gary help Bryan take off his backpack and tie it to the porch railing so it won't fly away. Bryan goes over to one side of the porch and bends down. Scott blinks, and just that fast, Bryan jumps up, landing on the edge of the roof.

Scott is dumbfounded. "I can hardly trust my own eyes -- you just jumped 10 feet in the air in the blink of an eye!" he shouts as Bryan jumps quickly back to the ground with the same ease.

Vaughn comments, "He is one of our best jumpers, and a bit of a show-off at times."

Bryan walks up to Scott, takes out two red rocks from his pockets, and winks. They all laugh.

"So you tricked me!"

Bryan pats his pockets to show Scott he doesn't have any more rocks in them.

156

"Stand still," Bryan, says, as he jumps up and lands on Scott's shoulder. He jumps up again, does a flip over Scott's head, and lands on the other shoulder. Bryan jumps back down to the ground, lands, spins around once, and takes a bow. "Ta da!"

Scott is typing furiously on his laptop and mumbling to himself, "AMAZING! Simply amazing!"

As they all walk back inside the house, Grandpa announces, "Let's all go into the dining room where Grandma and Janet have some lunch ready."

As the blacksmith and handyman, Gary is very interested in what things and projects Scott is planning. Accordingly, he sits near him and asks, "Scott, I was wondering if I might see your lab and learn more about what you're going to be working on."

Scott swallows the last bite of ham and eggs, looks down at the little man sitting on the table, and thinks, *"I would love to have him in my lab, where I can find out how intelligent they really are!"* Then he says, "I would like that very much! Janet, can we arrange for Gary and anyone else who wants, to get access to my lab?"

Before Janet can answer him, Vaughn speaks up, "I would like to see your lab, also."

"Yes! We built a safe place for them to stay right at Hawk Headquarters," Grandpa butts in, looking up from his stack of pancakes. "We added a few rooms and things not on the recorded blueprints."

"Are they close to the lab?" questions Scott.

"Yes!" Grandpa answers with a smile, "We put in an apartment complex; a network of passageways; and shops, labs, and some supply rooms. All are constructed in between the floors, right under your offices and labs. They have access to all the floors by way of tunnels, stairs, and the neatest little elevators built right inside the walls."

Scott shakes his head. "The more I learn about this operation around here, the less I think I know!"

And they all laugh.

"But wait!" Scott exclaims suddenly. "How will they travel from here to there without taking the chance of being seen?"

Vaughn replies, "Let's go to Grandpa's den. Gary and I might have a few ideas." The three of them leave the others. Once there, Vaughn continues, "Gary and a few others have been watching NASCAR on TV with Grandpa, and Gary has come up with something that may help. Gary, you tell him."

"I will be glad to, but it would be much easier to simply show him my designs on Grandpa's laptop!"

"Laptop!" Scott exclaims. "I didn't know Grandpa has a computer."

"Oh, he does. Conor got one for him; but Grandpa mostly plays games on it," Vaughn comments. "But Conor showed us how to use it and, of course, Gary found a drawing program he likes. He's been up here using the computer as much as he can," Vaughn adds, "I find the Internet to be a very good way to do research."

Scott announces, "I'm still finding it hard to understand how you Tinys are able to get along so well in our big world. I mean, you all adapt so quickly to so many different situations."

Vaughn asks, "Scott, did you know that back in the 1600s AD, our forefathers thought we were the normal people and you all were giants and there were only a few of you?"

"Wow! When did your people find out they were the exception?"

"It was around 1650 AD, when Count William Hawks of England discovered them living in the woods in northern England. He was the one who brought them out into the real world."

"I wonder how I would feel if I suddenly found out I was among a very small minority, and the rest of the world was inhabited by giants," Scott says.

Gary interrupts, "Scott, I have some plans drawn up on the computer; would you like to see them?"

"Yes, very much. What are you working on?"

"Now, don't laugh, but like Vaughn said -- I have been watching NASCAR on TV with Grandpa."

"Okay?" Scott says questioningly, wondering where Gary is going with this.

Gary continues, "Anyway, I came up with an idea for a safety seat that one of us can ride in while being carried by a Big. It's designed like the ones being used in the racecars. Here, take a

158

look," he says as he brings up the design on the computer screen.

Scott studies Gary's drawings for a while and then says, "That's a good idea, and I like the design, Gary. This would protect you even if the container you're in is dropped."

Suddenly Scott has a light of inspiration. "Hey! You have helped solve our first problem!"

"How is that?" asks Gary.

"Well, I needed to figure out how to infiltrate Hobart's office without being detected, and after seeing this seat design, here's what we should be able to do..."

Working together over the next few hours, the three men -- two Tinys and one Big -- become not only friends but also colleagues.

* * * * *

Operation Transport quickly gets underway. The first step in the plan was for Janet to locate a place in Ireland where the team could load the Tinys onto the Hawk 500 jet. She came through with flying colors, finding an empty hangar for lease -- with living quarters upstairs -- that is located on a private airstrip only a few miles from the O'Rourke house just outside of Dublin.

The second part of the plan was for Ed -- with Conor tagging along and the two U.S. Tinys Eric and Bryan -- to fly the jet to Ireland. After they get through customs in Dublin, they would hop over, land at the small airstrip, and park the Hawk 500 jet in the rented hangar. Conor then would drive a rental van to Katelyn O'Rourke's uncle's house, where Eric and Bryan would make contact with Michael, the Irish Tiny who had contacted Mr. O'Rourke just before he died. The final point of this step was for Michael to arrange for all the Tinys to go to a location where Conor could meet them with the van and transport them to the hangar.

The third part of Operation Transport has Eric and Michael forming teams to take on Randle Hobart and his aunt. They would travel to England and there divide into two groups, one group to visit the aunt and another to infiltrate Hobart's office with the help of his secretary, Miss Baryl.

159

* * * * *

Conor, flying Hawk Industries' brand new jet, brings the nose of the Hawk 500 jet around to line up with the centerline of the runway, and announces, "Nashville tower, Hawk jet HJ500 on final approach for runway 36."

"Copy, HJ500, clear to land," is the reply from the tower.

Conor has had his private pilot's license for a year now, logging about 300 hours of flying time. Most of his training was with his dad two years before. Conor has flown several different types of airplanes, but this is his first jet, and he likes it. *"The Hawk 500 is a dream to fly,"* he thinks.

Ed Barns sits in the pilot's seat, watching Conor fly from the co-pilot's seat. He is very pleased with the young man's flying skills.

As the wheels touch down and the jet slows, Conor turns off the runway and stops short of the taxiway.

"Nashville Ground, Hawk 500 taxi to hangar."

"Hawk 500, you're clear to taxi."

"Hawk 500" is all Conor says as he advances the throttles and taxis across the field to the Hawk Industries hangar, where Scott and Janet are waiting. As the jet comes to a stop in front of the hangar and the engines shut down, the door behind the wing opens to reveal a young aviator smiling from ear to ear,

"Ta da!" he says as he steps down and comes over to greet them. Then he adds, "Well, I don't know how, but I got checked out in this baby in just three days!"

"Does this mean you can fly this thing all by yourself?" Scott asks as he points at the jet.

"No, I'm not old enough to fly a jet all by myself, so Ed will be the pilot in command, but I can fly her from the co-pilot's seat. Right, Ed? "

"Yes, you can, Conor. Now we are ready start Operation Transport."

160

Chapter 20
Nightmare in Hobart Mansion

A few days later in England:

Under a cloudy sky with no moon, the night is pitch-black. A slight drizzle falls on Eric and his team of Tinys, who wait in the woods for Bryan. Who has been sent ahead to make sure the coast is clear and give the signal that the mission can precede. A tiny pin of light comes from under the bushes near the back of the Hobart mansion -- all clear!

Eric speaks into his mic, "Okay. Move out, and take your positions."

It doesn't take as long as Eric had thought to put together this team made up of Tinys from both the American and Irish groups. He quickly finds the men he needs to do the job, and after only one day of rehearsals, he is confident they can pull this off with no problems. Now, of course, the moment they have been waiting for...**revenge**!

Scott, Gary, Vaughn, and Conor provide them with all the tools they need to do the job, including complete blueprints of the Hobart mansion and all its secret passageways -- thanks in part to Miss Baryl and an angry building contractor, who the Hobarts had refused to pay after he finished all of his work on the place. The Hobarts claimed his work was not up to specs and he used cheap materials. The fact that he had been in business for 15 years and was well known for the quality of his work did not count. His case didn't hold up under the pressure brought on by the Hobarts' high-priced lawyers, and the courts ruled in the Hobarts' favor. Conor and Scott were still baffled at how Ed had found out about this guy and had gotten him to cooperate.

Scott and Gary had assembled a number of items for the Tinys to carry in their backpacks, including:

1. A spool of nylon thread, a winch, and AA batteries. Using a bow and arrow, a Tiny can shoot a line from the floor clear into the ceiling of a Big's house and winch himself up to the ceiling or across a room.

2. A bottle of Quick Glue and a spray gun.

3. A container that can be filled with spray paint or knockout

161

spray.

4. Small, marble-sized balls that, when thrown on the ground, will break and fill the area with a very dense smoke.

5. Two tubes filled with ball bearings.

6. Two containers filled with chemicals and a spray gun. When the two are combined and sprayed out together, they make a spider-web effect.

7. Special arrows containing knockout medication. When the arrow hits a Big, the knockout meds go into the skin but the arrow drops out. It takes three arrow hits to put a full-sized man out!

8. A few dozen G.I. Joe 12-inch action figures dressed up to look like the Tinys to be used as decoys.

Now it's up to the team to get inside the mansion and scare the heck out of Hobart's aunt!

Using GPS and the diagram of the estate, they find it is child's-play to circumvent the security system; then enter the house through a secret door and tunnel under the garden. Once inside, they split up into three groups. One goes straight to the aunt's bedroom. Another hurries to make sure the servants are asleep and stay that way. The third group goes to the security room to ensure there isn't any evidence of them ever having been there.

Inside the bedroom, they find the layout just as the contractor had described. A very large four-poster canopy bed dominates the area; it sits in the center of the room, not touching any walls. On the far wall is an ornate dressing table and in the corner is a lounge chair. In the opposite corner is a writing desk and chair. A larger dresser with a huge mirror on the back hugs the remaining wall.

Everything is exactly as he told them, including the fact that the aunt has a phobia about crawly things like bugs. Boy, are they going to use that fear against her!

Of course, Aunt Matilda is fast asleep in her bed – until a loud cry for help wakes her with a start. She opens her eyes and looks around to see who or what made the noise. She starts to sit up in bed, but for some reason she can't move. Her arms feel like they are tied down, and suddenly she feels something jumping on

162

the foot of her bed. She raises her head enough to look down toward her feet. She spots him! But this can't be... a leprechaun dressed all in green with his little hat and a red beard is jumping up and down on her bed.

Matilda passes out.

Sometime later, she wakes again; slowly she opens her eyes, and looks at the foot of her bed, but no one is there. She sits up and shakes her head.

"I must have been dreaming," she says. She lays back down and just starts to go back to sleep, when she feels the bed move. Her eyes pop open! She sits up again, staring at the upper-right corner of the canopy, where she sees a giant spider web and a big hairy spider! She screams, jumps out of bed, and runs to the door. BAM! She hits the wall. *Wall? Where is the door? There should be a door here,"* she thinks. She is now very confused, and to make matters worse, when she looks back at the bed, the spider moves. She screams again, and tries to find the light switch by the door, but the door is gone! *"Where is the door?"* she wonders.

Then she sees him standing next to her dresser...a leprechaun!

Matilda is shaking so badly she can hardly speak, but she squeaks out a question: "What do you want?"

He slowly raises his arm and points his finger at her, and in a ghostly voice answers, "You are the one who wanted to see us. You want us as your pets. You and your nephew are the ones who have been trying to find us. Now you have!" And, poof! He disappears.

She faints on the floor.

The next time she wakes up, it's to music. A soft little tune is coming from somewhere in her room. She opens her eyes and sits up to find she is back in bed. Remembering the spider, she quickly looks to her right. No spider and no web. Where is that music coming from?

Getting out of bed, she slips on her robe, put her feet into her slippers, grabs her cane, stands, and starts to take a step, but she can't move her feet.

"What's wrong with my legs?" she wonders. "I can't even lift my foot."

163

Sitting back down on the bed, she tries to lift her legs up, but they won't move. She strains and strains to lift her legs. Suddenly her feet pop out of her slippers, which have been glued to the floor. The momentum sends her falling backward on the bed to land on her back. Now she is looking up, right at a leprechaun sitting suspended in midair, playing a flute!

She yells and rolls out of bed; still believing she can't walk, she crawls over to where the door should be, but it isn't there. The Tinys had moved all the furniture around so now the door is on the other side of the room.

While she is sitting on the floor trying to figure out what happened to the door and how she can get away from these things, in the dim light she notices one of them sitting on her dresser. Then she spots another over on her desk.

No wait! There are three more of them! There's another standing in the doorway to her closet. Now one is on her bed jumping up and down! She is going out of her mind! She sees them everywhere she looks!

"Why are you here?" she asks.

"Your family has hunted us for hundreds of years. Now it's our turn to **hunt _you_**!"

"No, no! Go away! I don't want to see you anymore."

"But don't you want to play?"

"No! No! Have mercy on an old woman," Matilda cries.

"Mercy? You and your family have never shown mercy to anyone. Now you must pay! _**You must pay!**_"

_"No!"_ she screams and faints again.

Quickly the Tinys put everything back the way it was. Leaving the mean and wicked old woman lying on the floor, they disappear into the night.

That is exactly where her maid found her the next morning, sobbing and blubbering on the floor about spiders and leprechauns -- how they are after her and out to get her.

The servant calls her nephew and tells him it looks as if his aunt has gone completely mad. By the time he arrives with a doctor, she is comatose and needing to be put in a sanitarium. They search her room, but everything looks like it always had. There are no signs that anyone or anything had been there the night before.

164

Chapter 21
The Deal

Later in London...

It has been two days since Randle Hobart had put his aunt into the sanitarium. He is on cloud nine because everything is going his way. With her out of the picture, he gains full control of Hobart Industries and he is busy making plans.

The search for the little ones and the treasure is not going well. Three of his operatives had been arrested in Ireland. But right now, he has other fish to fry. Randle is at his desk, looking over some proposals, when his secretary buzzes him.

"Sir, a Ms. Cook is here to see you," she announces over the intercom.

He looks up from his work, frowns, and pushes a button on his desk. "Ms. Cook? I don't recall an appointment with a Ms. Cook? What does she want?"

"She is here from America with a proposal from Hawk Industries," Miss Baryl answers, as she smiles at Janet.

"A proposal, from Hawk? Send her in."

Miss Baryl opens the door to his office and escorts Janet to a chair in front of Hobart's massive, three-legged desk. Hobart doesn't even rise to greet her or come around to shake her hand.

"So what sort of proposal do you have for me?"

Janet puts down her new, specially built briefcase, and sits back in the chair. She replies, "We are interested in purchasing all of Hobart Industries' holdings in America and Ireland."

Hobart almost falls out of his chair. He stands up. "You WHAT?" he shouts.

Janet calmly picks up the briefcase and places it on her lap, opening it so he can't see what's inside. She takes out a very thick package of legal papers and places them on his desk. She purposely has put together a very large amount of legal jargon, knowing Hobart is the type who would be too lazy to read everything.

"I trust you will find our offer to your liking," she says. After carefully closing and locking her briefcase, she gently places it on the floor next to her chair and gets up to leave.

She is halfway to the door when he looks up from starting to read the proposal, "Wait! What do you want me to do?"

She smiles, "Simply to accept it! I will be in touch tomorrow, and by the way, this offer goes away at midday tomorrow!" And she leaves.

Hobart sits there and stares at the big stack of papers. He opens the proposal and starts to read through all the "party of the first part," etc. After about a minute, he thumbs through most of the rest.

When he gets to the last page, where all the numbers appear, he reads the bottom line, whistles, and exclaims out loud, "I'm rich! With Aunty out of the picture for now, I can pull this off. I'll take my share of this deal and forget all about this lousy business and go have some fun! By the time Aunty comes back around, if she ever does, it will be too late! Ha, ha, ha, ha!"

Meanwhile, inside the briefcase Janet "forgot," the two Tinys -- Michael and Eric -- are sitting in their protective seats, listening and recording everything. They are wearing black, tight-fitting, one-piece jumpsuits and what looks like fighter pilot helmets.

Scott had used Gary's design to construct their seats to be like those used by NASCAR, but on a much-smaller scale. The seats hold them in tight and protect them in case they are dropped or knocked over. Using his and Conor's ideas, Scott had put together this one-of-a-kind briefcase. Although it looks like a regular briefcase, the high-tech device was built for one job: to get them into Hobart's office. The occupants, who are snug inside, can see through the one-way siding and hear everything said in Hobart's office.

Earlier, when Janet had been waiting in Hobart's outer office, Miss Baryl had passed her the key to the safe. Miss Baryl had removed it from Hobart's desk earlier and Janet had slipped the key into the briefcase before she left. Now all the two Tiny men need to do is wait for Hobart to leave his office.

Hobart finally gets up from his desk and comes around to leave. When he spots the briefcase, he starts to reach down to pick it up. Both Tinys freeze, holding their breaths as the shadow of the huge hand falls over them. Then Hobart stops...looks at the

166

briefcase for a second, shrugs and leaves it there. He walks over to his private elevator and leaves.

After the elevator door closes, Michael looks at Eric who is looking at him, and they both silently mouth, "Whew!"

Once Hobart gets in his car, he punches in his office number on his dashboard computer screen. When Miss Baryl answers, he announces, "I have left for the day. When Ms. Cook calls tomorrow, tell her she has a deal! Oh, and tell her she forgot her briefcase in my office." The line goes dead with a click.

Miss Baryl smiles, then goes to his office and turns off the lights. She then closes the door, leaving the two hidden Tinys in the dark.

Eric is the first to act. He flips open the cover on his arm-mounted computer. With the cover open, he can view the display screen, which is located inside the cover. The screen comes on, and he silently types, "How long should we wait?"

Michael, who is seated in front of Eric, feels his device vibrate, reaches over, opens it, and reads Eric's message. He types his reply, "Another hour should be enough."

Not wanting their voices to be picked up by any hidden microphones, the two had prearranged this silent mode of communication before they got into their hideaway briefcase.

Even though Heather had assured everyone that the office would be clear, with the exception of her little secret microphone above Hobart's desk, no one is taking any chances. To the members of Operation Transport, she is still somewhat on probation -- so they are taking extra precautions.

Eric types in a few more commands, sets his alarm to vibrate in one hour, and settles in for a short nap.

At the end of an hour, they wake up and undo their seat belts. Michael opens a little door on the side of the briefcase. Both Tinys exit and look around. Seeing it's clear, they go to work.

First, the two of them open a side panel on the briefcase to reveal an array of tools, which include a fold-up extension ladder. They place it under the desk, in the center.

Michael goes back to get some gear and straps on a small tool belt full of gadgets. He goes around the desk until he finds the leg he is looking for and starts climbing it. Meanwhile, Eric is extending the ladder so that it reaches the bottom of the desk. By

167

that point, Michael has climbed up to the lion's head, and he checks to see if Eric is ready. Eric is already up the ladder, waiting at the top. He gives Mike the thumbs-up signal, Mike pushes on the lion's two eyes, and for his efforts gets a click.

Eric ducks just as the trapdoor under the desk drops open and barely misses his head. From his backpack, he removes the key and inserts it into the lock. With a swift turn, the hidden safe opens to reveal the wooden box Heather had told them was there.

The box is much too big for Eric to lug down by himself, so he rigs a string-and-pulley system he had brought to the top of the ladder and lowers the box down to the floor. He locks the safe, shuts the trapdoor, and climbs down. With Mike's help, the two carry the box over to the briefcase and secure it in place.

Next, they go around to the front of the desk, where Mike again climbs one of the legs and makes his way up to the top of the massive desk. Once there, he lowers a string down to Eric, who ties on the key and Mike pulls it up.

Using a letter opener he finds on the desk, he manages to pry open the drawer Heather had told them to put the key in.

Mike tosses the key at the slightly open drawer. It misses, bounces off the edge, and falls right at Eric! However, Eric's quick reflexes save him from being hit. But now the key and the string are both down on the floor.

Eric gets up from where he lands and motions to Mike to wait. He goes to the equipment compartment in the briefcase and comes back with a bow and arrow. He ties the end of the string to the arrow and shoots it up past Mike. As the arrow passes Mike, he grabs the string and lets the arrow fall on the desk.

This time, when Mike pulls the key up, he is extra careful as he lowers it into the drawer.

Now he has to figure out how to untie the string from the key. He removes the arrow and takes his end of the string and wraps it around the desk lamp stand. Holding onto the string end coming up from the key and the one coming from around the lamp, Mike lowers himself into the drawer. Untying the key, he takes the two ends of the string wrapped around the lamp, and lowers the ends down to the floor. Eric grabs them and holds them tight so Mike can use them to climb down.

Before he climbs down, however, Mike remembers Janet's instructions about Hobart's computer. He goes over to the desktop computer, moves the mouse, and sure enough the computer screen comes to life, just as Janet had said it would.

"How does she know this guy so well?" he thinks to himself. *"She said he would not read the document, and he didn't. Then she told us he would leave his computer on, and he did. Wow, she's good at her job!"*

Mike turns to see Eric climbing up the string and onto the desk. He points to the computer screen, and Eric nods in approval. Eric quickly pulls a data stick out of his backpack, looks around the computer, and finds the USB port. After plugging in the data stick, he goes around to the mouse, moves the curser on the screen over the top of the icon that looks like a hawk and pushes the left mouse button. The screen blinks; they can hear the disk drive whirling around at a high speed, and then everything stops.

Eric retrieves the data stick. The two of them go over to the string and use it to descend to the floor. Once they are safely

169

down, they both grab the string; by pulling it back against the drawer and under the desk, they manage to shut the drawer containing the key.

Mike pulls on one side of the string, and it comes down. They pack everything back into their special briefcase. Eric uses hand signals to indicate they should eat the sandwiches they had brought and get ready to wait out the night.

The next morning, Randle Hobart is a man on a mission. "This is the best day of my life," he says to himself. "I can feel the money in my pocket already!" He calls his office to tell Heather he has some things to do and she is to call him as soon as Ms. Cook calls or comes in.

He then goes to the car dealer and orders a new, very expensive Aston Martin. That done, he drives down to the yacht sales office and signs the contract on the boat he has been wanting for a long time -- the one he had blackmailed the president of Simms Shipping into selling him.

From the yacht sales office, he goes back uptown to the office of Jamaica Properties and writes them a check for the house in Jamaica he has always wanted. The salesman takes the check to his manager to get his okay. The manager, seeing the name on the check, picks up the phone and makes a call. "I have a check from Randle Hobart for $22 million," he says to the party on the other end of the phone. "I see. What should I do? Yes, I understand, and thank you."

The manager hangs up the phone and goes to the office where Hobart is waiting. Hobart, seeing the check in the manager's hand, asks, "Is there a problem?"

"No, not at all, Sir!" the manager assures Hobart as he hands the check to the sales clerk.

"Merely a formality. After all, it is a rather large amount. You understand, of course?"

"Of course. As I told your man here, the funds will be available by the end of the week."

"Very good, Sir. I hope you enjoy your beautiful house in Jamaica."

Hobart is going over all the legal papers and signing the contract for the house when he gets a call from his office.

170

"Sir, Ms. Cook will be here in half an hour," Miss Baryl tells him.

"Very good. I'll be there straight away," he informs her, rushing to get through the signing of all the paper work without reading it.

After she hangs up, Heather quickly goes into Hobart's office, picks up the briefcase, carries it out, and sets it down close to her desk; she then closes Hobart's office door, returns to her desk, and sits down.

"Are you two all right in there?" she whispers.

From the briefcase, Michael replies, "Top of the morning to you. We are fine and ready to get out of this contraption, we are."

"They will be arriving soon, so be patient," she says.

Eric says, "Good morning, Miss Baryl. Would you mind turning this thing around and placing it right next to your desk? Then we can get out and stretch our legs under your desk, and if anyone comes, we can quickly jump back in."

"Oh! Of course, there -- How's that?"

"Just fine. Thank you." Eric answers as they get out and stretch.

Although Hobart tries to hurry through the contract signing, it seems to be taking too long. He checks his watch, which reads 11:32 a.m. He has 28 minutes to get back to his office and sign the biggest deal of his life.

"Let's see now; it will take about 15 minutes from here to get to the office," he thinks to himself. *"Good! Plenty of time!"*

He signs the last of the contracts for his Jamaica house and rushes out to his car, only to find it being picked up by a tow truck.

"What are you doing!" he yells at the driver.

The tow truck driver is a very large, burly man with no sense of humor. "I'm towing this here vehicle, I am," he answers.

"No! You can't -- this is my car!" Hobart yells again.

By now the car has been lifted up and secured to the back of the tow truck. The driver tears off a copy of the paper work he filled out and hands it to Hobart. As he does, he points to the NO PARKING sign where Hobart's vehicle had been parked.

Hobart looks in amazement at the sign and says, "That wasn't there when I parked here!"

171

The driver just shrugs, gets into his truck, and drives off with Hobart's car.

Hobart stands in amazement for a minute and watches his car go down the street. Then he looks at his watch --11:46 a.m.--"I'll be late!" he says as he frantically tries to hail a cab as he takes out his phone and dials his office.

"Mr. Hobart's office," Miss Baryl answers.

"It's me," he says. "I'm having trouble getting back to the office. Is she there?"

"Yes, Sir. She's been here for about half an hour. Where are you?"

"I have to take a cab, but I will be there in 15 minutes. Please get her to wait!" Hobart pleads.

"I will do my best, Sir."

She put down the phone, and winks at Janet, who's been listening in on the conversation.

"He will never make it in time."

Before the two women go into Hobart's office, Janet reaches down and picks up the briefcase. Once inside with the door closed, Janet announces, "Okay, guys, you can come out, and make yourselves at home."

They both come out slowly, stretching and yawning. Eric asks, "What happens next?"

Janet explains, "The taxi driver will take the long way here. It will take about 20 minutes. When Mr. Hobart arrives, he will find..."

* * * * *

The cab ride is a nightmare. Hobart can't get the driver to understand his directions. The fool goes the wrong way and then has to retrace their route. They finally pull up in front of the corporate offices. Hobart throws some money at the driver and runs inside.

As the cab pulls away from the curb, the driver speaks into a hidden microphone.

"He's just now entering the building, and boy, he is mad!" Ed Barns reports as he removes his fake beard and laughs.

When the elevator doors open to Hobart's office, he finds

172

Miss Baryl is not at her desk. He figures that she must be in his office with Ms. Cook. Crossing the room, he enters his office -- only to find it empty! He goes to his desk and dials the receptionist.

"This is Randle. Do you know where Ms. Cook is?"

"Yes, Sir, Ms. Cook left at 12:01 p.m.," she tells him.

"What? She left? No!" He checks his watch to find that the time is 12:16 p.m. "Where is Miss Baryl?" he asks the receptionist.

"Miss Baryl left the building, Sir."

"What? She left, too? Where did she go?"

"I'm afraid I don't know, Sir."

"Well, do you know when she plans to return?"

"It's not likely she will be returning, sir. She informed me she is retiring and would not be back."

"She what? Retired? No, she can't retire! Didn't she have another month to go?"

"That's all the information I have, Sir. Will there be anything else?"

He doesn't answer because he has just looked at his desk and has noticed that the contract is missing! Randle Hobart suddenly realizes he has failed, again. He slumps down in his chair. The phone slowly slips out of his hand and falls to the floor.

His mind is spinning, and his brain won't work! He must do something, but what? How can he get the Hawk people to come back with the deal and the contract?

Why did all these things go wrong right when he was about to pull off the biggest deal in the company's history? Why? He gets up and starts pacing the floor.

"I must think," he tells himself. "I need a plan."

He stops in his tracks. "Oh, no!" he wails. The check! I have to cover the check by Friday, but how? How can I get $22 million by Friday?"

He sits back down, but his head is still spinning from the realization that he has lost the big deal. In desperation, he goes over and over what has happened, trying to come up with something… anything. Finally, an idea hits him. He jumps out of his chair and starts pacing again, and then he says, "That's it! I'll do it!"

He goes back to his desk and pushes the button for the receptionist.

"Yes, Sir?"

"Do you have a number for Ms. Cook, from Hawk Industries?"

"Yes, Sir, She left her card with Miss Baryl."

"Good. Get her on the phone, and tell her I would like to talk to her straight away. Tell her I have a much better deal for her!"

"Yes, Sir. I'll get right on it."

Janet Cook is already at the airport, waiting on Scott and Conor to arrive with the jet, when she receives the call from Hobart's receptionist.

"Hello. Yes, this is Janet Cook. Who's calling, please?"

"Ms. Cook, this is Mr. Hobart's receptionist, and he would like to talk to you about the offer you made."

"I'm afraid that offer is no longer on the table," Janet informs her.

"Yes, we understand, but Mr. Hobart would like you to entertain a much better offer."

"What sort of offer are we talking about?"

"I'm not at liberty to say. But if you would call Mr. Hobart at his office, I'm sure he will explain."

"Very well," Janet says. "I have a few minutes before my plane gets here. What is his private number?"

After the receptionist gives her the number, Janet calls Conor in the jet. "Hi, Conor. Well, he called with a better offer, just like we thought. He is expecting me to call him back. Do you still want to do this? It will take a lot to pull it off!"

"I know, Janet, and I trust you know how to proceed. So go ahead and do it the way you believe is best for us -- and remember, he's very sneaky and slimy. So don't let him wiggle off the hook!"

"Okay, Conor. I'm on it! See you in a few."

She punches in a phone number on her cell, and when the phone is answered, she announces, "We are ready to proceed. What is your answer? Very well, I have the contracts with me now and can be in your office in about 30 minutes."

Janet hangs up in time to see the Hawk jet pulling into a spot

174

at the private jet terminal. She walks outside to meet Scott and Conor as they open the door and come down the steps.

"Well, how did it go?" Conor asks.

"Just as we thought it would. We have everything we wanted, including our little surprise!"

"Great!" Conor says. "Now we can move to the final stage and get those Tinys out of Ireland and home to Tennessee."

"Hi, Mom," Brittany says as she pokes her head out of the jet's door.

"Brittany! What are you doing here? You're supposed to be at home."

"Hey, if Conor gets to play 007, so do I," she teases her mother.

"I asked her to fly over and join us. I thought our meeting later with Miss O'Rourke might go smoother if Brittany is there. You know, if she sees another young lady and not just me," Conor explains.

"I see. Good idea."

After they talk for a few minutes, Janet looks at her watch. "I need to get to the Hobart office building right away."

Conor smiles and points past her shoulder at the bright blue helicopter sitting nearby. "I thought you might need a flying carpet, so I arranged one."

"Why, thank you, kind sir; you're adapting to your new lifestyle very nicely!" She laughs and heads for the helicopter.

Hobart arrives back at his office after lunch to find a new secretary sitting at Miss Baryl's old desk.

"Good afternoon, Sir."

He looks her over and asks, "Is Ms. Cook in there?" as he points to the door of his office.

"No, Sir."

He seems disturbed as he says, "Well, when she arrives, send her right in."

"Yes, Sir!"

Just then the door to the conference room across the hall opens, and the board of directors and Ms. Cook come out. They all shake her hand and go their separate ways except for Ms. Cook and the chairman of the board.

175

Dumbstruck, Hobart stands outside his office with his mouth open.

Finally, the chairman comes over to him and announces, "Well, Randle, you finally did it! I want your resignation on my desk within the hour. I must say, you will not be missed!" He laughs and then turns and remarks to Ms. Cook, "Thank you again. Have a pleasant trip back to the States."

"You are most welcome, and thank you!" she replies as she goes over and pushes the up elevator button.

Hobart is still standing there, wondering what just happened. "I thought we had a deal."

Janet turns to face him. "You and I never did have a deal! The board of directors and I did. After they learned of the things you've been involved with, it's clear they feel you will no longer be needed at Hobart Industries."

Then she moves in toward him, looks him in the face, and leans in close; whispering so that the secretary can't hear, she warns: "And if you ever endanger my little friends again, we will destroy you completely! Do you understand?"

Hobart is so shocked by what he just heard, he can't even answer.

Janet, seeing the elevator has arrived, walks in and is gone.

* * * * *

Later in his office, Hobart is cleaning out his desk and getting ready to leave the company job he really didn't want in the first place. He is still in a state of confusion as to what went wrong. He keeps going over and over the past few days' events, trying to sort out all that has happened.

Opening the desk drawer where he keeps the safe key and seeing it still there, he picks it up. To open the hidden trapdoor under the bottom of his desk, he again pushes the lion's eyes, and crawls under his desk. Once the trapdoor is open, he quickly unlocks the safe. Fully expecting to just reach in and remove the box, he is again thoroughly confused when he realizes the safe is empty!

"WHAT? HOW?" he yells. "I've been robbed, but how? How did they know?"

176

Then it dawns on him. "Miss Baryl! She is the only one who knew about the safe. She took the journal. I will call the police and have her picked up!"

He calls his secretary, but there is no answer. He then calls the receptionist desk.

"Yes, Sir?" A new voice answers.

"Get the police over here straight away; I've been robbed!"

"Robbed? Good heavens! Are you all right, Sir?"

"No, I'm not all right; just call them <u>NOW</u>!" he screams.

"Yes, Sir. Right away, Sir!"

Only a minute later the receptionist buzzes the intercom. "Sir, the police are here to see you."

"Here already? Very good, send them in."

As the police lieutenant and another officer enter his office, Hobart gets up and comes around his desk to meet them. "Good, you're here..." he starts to say when the officer grabs him by the arm. Before he knows what is going on, both of his arms are behind him and in handcuffs.

"What is all this?"

"You're under arrest!"

"Arrest for what?"

The lieutenant pulls out his pad and opens it up to check his notes. "Let's see what we have here: accessory to assault, involuntary manslaughter, invasion of privacy, writing bad checks, and attempted extortion. Now come along quietly. That's a good boy!"

Back at the airport, the guys have the corporate jet fueled and ready to go. Janet arrives and climbs aboard.

Conor asks, "So what about Randle Hobart? Is he all taken care of?"

"Yes! He is all wrapped up and tied with a bow, or better still, handcuffs!"

With her last comment, they all laugh and Conor announces, "Well, then -- let's go finish Operation Transport!"

Chapter 22
Bring Them Home

In Ireland, the van driven by Conor is on its way to a very important meeting. They're on their way to make first contact with the Irish Tinys' benefactor, Katelyn O'Rourke.

Sitting beside Conor as they drive through the Irish streets are the two Tinys from Tennessee, Eric, and Bryan. Wondering about meeting the Irish Tinys, Eric is especially concerned about he and Bryan making their first contact with the Irish Big, Katelyn O'Rourke, so he is glad Michael will be there. In the back seat, Brittany is anxious about meeting the girl from Ireland.

Conor pulls over to the curb and stops the van, parking about a block away and on the opposite side of the street from Thomas O'Rourke's house. Eric stands up in the passenger seat and looks out the window to see a misty rain falling and the fog getting thicker. They have a few minutes to wait until the pre-arranged time.

As Eric and Bryan get out of the van, the two Tinys take a long look around to see if any Bigs are about. They doubt anyone would be out on a night like this, with the fog and the drizzling rain. The streetlights glowing dimly through the fog make the area look and feel gloomy. Seeing it's clear, Eric gives a thumbs-up to Conor, who is looking down at them from the driver's side window.

The two Tinys start out. Eric turns to Bryan. "Stay close and alert. I don't like being this close to so many Bigs!"

Bryan, who has been looking forward to the adventure, is about to burst with excitement. "I've got your back, Bro!"

Working their way down the street toward the O'Rourke house, they can hear the big people in their homes, getting ready for the evening meal. They hear children running and giggling as parents call them to come and eat.

Thinking of his home back in Tennessee, some 3,000 miles away, Eric says to himself, *"I hope I didn't bite off more than I can chew by taking on this assignment."*

They are right across from the O'Rourke house, when Eric stops. He knows they must cross the street and go behind the

178

house as per their instructions. But neither of them has crossed this large of a paved street on foot before. To them, the street looks like a mile of wide-open ground – an area where some big person could easily see them. Maybe a car might come along, which would not be good, either!

Conor had driven around the area a few times to make sure no one was watching the house. So right now, Eric's only concern is with this wide-open space, the street.

"Are you ready for a run?" he asks his brother.

"I'm ready. Let's go," answers Bryan, and they begin running. About halfway across, they hear the barking of a dog!

Eric and Bryan both freeze, until they realize the bark had come from further down the street. They continue on, this time even faster. Reaching the curb, Eric announces, "Dogs... I don't like dogs!" He pants.

Bryan, catching his breath, remarks, "The dog we met on our trip back from the lake was nice, and he really liked Dina!" They both remember the big lick the dog gave Dina and laugh.

"Okay. Let's get around to the back and find the doghouse," Eric directs.

They move out one at a time, first Eric and then Bryan, covering each other as they move from one bush to another. They work their way closer to the doghouse when, from somewhere nearby, a small voice announces, "You lads look like you've done this before." It is Michael hiding in a bush not far from the doghouse. "It's a joy to see two strapping young fellows like you!" he continues, as he steps out to greet them.

Eric comes over, holds out his hand, and shakes Michael's. "Boy, are we glad to see you!"

Michael beams a smile, and you can hear the relief in his voice, "Suren, it's a joy to see the likes of you two lads." They shake hands. "If you'll follow me, I'll take you in to meet Miss O'Rourke, who is waiting for us inside."

They follow Michael around to the back of the phony doghouse, through the false door, and inside -- where they find a toy train sitting on its track.

Michael walks over to the train and climbs onto one of the empty flatbed cars. As he sits down, he tells the guys, "Climb aboard, Lads. It's only a short ride into the house from here."

179

Both look at each other, shrug, and climb aboard.

Michael pushes a button, and the train starts down the track into a dark tunnel. As they enter the pitch-black tunnel, the train's headlight automatically comes on. They drop down a steep slope that takes them under and across the yard, up another slope, and into the house.

As they come to a stop, Eric notices they are now inside a false wall. Michael jumps off the train, and the guys follow. He walks about 5 feet inside this false wall until he comes to a small door. Michael opens it and steps through, with the American Tinys following behind him. The first thing they notice is they are under a kitchen sink inside the sink cabinet.

Bryan looks around, "Now, that's a clever way to get inside."

Michael smiles, "The first time I rode that contraption into the tunnel, I was a wee bit frightened until the light turned on!"

Katelyn O'Rourke is sitting at the kitchen table, waiting, when she hears, from under the sink, the Tinys talking.

Michael opens the cabinet door and the three of them step out onto the kitchen floor.

Michael is the first to speak. "Katelyn, may I present Eric and Bryan from America."

Katelyn kneels down on the floor and holds out her hands to greet them. The two Tiny men, seeing the bright smile on her face and the tears in her eyes, know right away they have found another friend! They both come over to her, each taking hold of a hand.

Eric announces, "Miss O'Rourke, it is indeed a pleasure to meet you. We have heard so many good things about you."

Bryan pipes in, "Yeah, but they didn't tell us you were so pretty!"

They all laugh.

Michael announces, "We better go now. It doesn't look like the house is being watched, but I don't want to take any chances. Katelyn, if you will go out the side door and come around to the backyard, we will go back the way we came and meet you by the doghouse."

"Okay!" Katelyn grabs her purse, and starts for the door. The three Tinys hurry back under the sink through the secret door and along the false wall to the train. Once they are all onboard,

Michael pushes another button, and they head back to the doghouse.

When they get outside, they find Katelyn waiting for them.

Eric tells everyone, "Please wait here while I go around to the front and make sure it's all clear."

He disappears, but is back a few moments later. "It looks okay," he says. "Let's go!"

Once they reach the van, Eric suggests that Katelyn get in the front passenger seat, and that the three Tinys ride in the back with Brittany.

With that, they all get in the van. After they close the doors, Eric says, "Katelyn and Michael, may I introduce you to our benefactor, Mr. Conor O'Brien, and our friend Miss Brittany Cook."

Grinning like a monkey at this strikingly beautiful, redheaded young woman, Conor says, "Nice to meet you!" as he shakes her hand vigorously.

From the back seat, Brittany says, "Hi, Katelyn. Did you get my email?"

"Yes, I did, and thank you for coming with Mr. O'Brien."

Brittany thinks, "She sure looks older then 17 in that dress and high heals. Look at Conor, all dreamy eyed and flustered. He never looks at me like that?"

"Nice to finally meet you, Mr. O'Brien," Katelyn adds, smiling back at Conor.

With the handshaking continuing for some time, Bryan interrupts with, "Isn't she pretty, Conor?"

"Uh, huh!" Conor replies dreamily.

But when the four in the back seat all start laughing, the spell is broken, and the two in the front seat stop shaking hands.

"We need to get going," Michael comments. "I don't like being out in the open like this."

Conor turns back to the steering wheel, starts the van, and asks Katelyn, "Do you mind if we take you to where the plane and the rest of our team are?"

"No, not at all! I'm excited to meet the others so I may thank all of you for what you are doing."

"Good -- fasten your seat belts. Here we go," Conor says as he speeds away from the O'Rourke house and back to the hangar

181

where the other members of the Transport team are waiting.

From the shadows of a house across the street, a man has been waiting and watching. After a few minutes, the dark figure moves quietly from shadow to shadow, working his way down the street and around the corner to where his car awaits. Once inside, he picks up his cell phone, dialing as he starts the car before he drives off. When the phone is answered, he announces, "The package has been picked up and is on the move."

"Any problems?" asks the person on the other end of the line.

"None," is the reply.

"Okay; then I'll see you at the hangar," Scott says.

"I'll be around, but you won't see me," laughs Ed.

While they're driving along, Conor says, "I'm so sorry we couldn't get here sooner, before your uncle..."

Before he can finish, Katelyn reaches over and touches his arm. "It's all right, Mr. O'Brien. You came as soon as you knew what was going on, and I'm most grateful!"

"Thank you, but please call me Conor. My father was Mr. O'Brien."

"All right, but you must call me Katelyn or Kate, if you please."

Most of the trip back to the airport and the rented hangar is quiet. Everyone is deep in thought, with concerns about what needs to be done the next day -- everyone except Conor, who can't stop thinking about what a beautiful woman Katelyn is. He keeps trying to get another look at her, but it's too hard to see in the dark van. The van drifts toward the right side of the road. *"Oops! I better concentrate on my driving,"* he says to himself. *"It's the left lane over here, isn't it?"*

Katelyn is also doing some thinking. *"He's very young to be the head of such a large, important company, and the benefactor of the little ones, as well. I'll bet he's about the same age as me. I didn't expect him to be so cute!"*

In the back seat, Bryan has been wondering, *"How many more Tinys are here in Ireland?"* Eric's mind is on the same track. *"When will we meet the rest of the Tinys? I hope there are lots of pretty girls!"*

Arriving at the hangar and approaching the side door, they see someone dressed in black near the entrance, but they can't make out who it is.

Conor pulls up closer, and when he turns the van toward the side of the hangar, the headlights shows them it's Scott. He's been keeping an eye open for them. After they park, Scott comes over to the van and helps Katelyn with her door. "You must be Katelyn," he says, as he holds open the van door and offers his hand to help her step down. "Hi; I'm Scott."

"Pleased to meet you, Scott."

Once out of the van, Scott leads the group through the side door of the hangar and inside, where the others are waiting. Katelyn sees Heather and runs over to give her a big hug. Stepping back, she says, "I'm so glad to see you!"

Heather can hardly contain her tears. "I'm glad to see you, too!"

Conor takes Katelyn's hand and brings her over to meet Janet. "Janet Cook, meet Katelyn O'Rourke."

"I'm pleased to meet you, Miss O'Rourke. Would you and Miss Baryl join Brittany and me upstairs in the living quarters while the men get the jet ready for tomorrow?"

"Katelyn, I would like to show you around later," Conor says softly to her. "We can talk then, if you don't mind?"

As the ladies walk up the stairs, Katelyn stops to reply, "I would like that very much, Conor."

Turning, she continues on up to the living quarters. Conor watches her with a silly grin on his face until Bryan jumps in with "I don't know about the rest of you, but I'm hungry, and I sure can use a bathroom break!"

Conor snaps out of his trance. "That's a good idea, Bryan, let's all go up and join the ladies for some refreshments. We can check the plane after we get something to eat."

They all agree and follow the women.

Later, after Conor and Scott have come down and gone over the complete checklist on the jet to make sure everything is ready for the next day's getaway, Conor joins Katelyn and asks, "Would you like to join me for a tour of the airplane?"

"Yes -- I am interested in seeing this new jet."

Conor is showing her the plane with all the instrument panels and test equipment in it, when Katelyn questions, "How are you going to have room for the little ones in here with all this?"

Conor takes her over to one of the instrument panels in the middle of the plane. Reaches under one of the panel corners and hits a button. With a click, the panel opens to reveal rows of little seats that look like they came from an airliner, except these are quite a bit smaller and just the right size for a Tiny.

When she sees this, she looks back at him and asks, "How in the world did you arrange to do this?"

"I have my resources," he grins. "We were also able to install two functioning bathrooms, the appropriate size for our little friends. Scott even added some drink dispensers and, oh yeah, each seat has a pillow and blanket."

"How did you manage to make all these wonderful little things?"

"One of the companies we own is a toy manufacturer," he explains.

After closing the panel, he takes her hand and leads her back out of the plane and over to an office at the back of the hangar, where there is a small waiting room. As they enter, Conor says, "You and I have a lot to discuss, don't we? I know it's late, but there's so much I want to know about you, and I want to tell you about us. Do you mind if we talk for a while?"

"I don't mind at all, but how will I get back to the house?"

"Oh, I forgot to tell you, or show you -- this place has plenty of bedrooms, and the ladies made one up for you. That is, if you wish to stay. I don't want you worried that we're holding you here or anything!"

"Oh, no! I don't feel you are, not in the least! You all have been so nice to me. I don't know how to start to thank you for what you're doing for the little ones."

"So you will stay?" Conor asks.

"Yes. I would like that very much. I want to know all about the Tinys in America, and you and your family," she adds as she settles back in her chair.

Conor and Katelyn talk for hours. They find out they both feel a great need to care for the Tinys. The two of them love the ones they consider wonderful little gifts from God, and they

184

marvel at how much their lives have changed since meeting them.

They both like a lot of the same things, and neither one cares too much for the rich life but, instead, like things a bit simpler.

She tells Conor she is worried about not being able to see the Tinys anymore. He assures her she can come and visit anytime. He tells her all about his grandparents and how and where they live. "Tennessee sounds like a nice place," she says.

After talking for a while, Conor realizes for the first time that Katelyn's last name, O'Rourke, is the same as his great-great-great grandmother's. The realization hits him like a brick! He is beginning to like her, and now it occurs to him they might be related!

He has to ask her, but how to do it without letting her know how much he is starting to like her? After worrying about it for some time, he finally just comes out with it.

"Kate, I have been wondering about something."

"Oh! What is it?"

"It's your family name, O'Rourke. My great-great-great grandmother was an O'Rourke, and I just thought..."

She laughs out loud and remarks, "If you're concerned that we're related, you can stop worrying!"

"Huh! How?"

"I'm not an O'Rourke!"

"You're not an O'Rourke? But you told everyone you were."

"What I mean to say is, I'm adopted. I took my adoptive parents' name. I'm a Kelly by birth."

"Kelly? You mean you're not an O'Rourke?"

"Yes! I mean, no! I'm not!"

He jumps up and starts dancing around, yelling, "Kelly, Kelly, Kelly ...what a wonderful name!"

She is laughing, and he is dancing when Scott and Janet come in to see what all the fuss is about. "What is going on?" Janet asks.

Kate is laughing so hard at Conor dancing that she can't answer her. Finally, Conor stops dancing, comes over, and shakes Scott's hand, "She's not really an O'Rourke!" he says as he plops down beside Katelyn.

Scott looks at the two of them grinning and blushing and

185

back at Janet. "What in the world are you talking about?"

"You don't get it, do you? I thought she was an O'Rourke. But she's a Kelly, not an O'Rourke."

Conor explains how he was worried about Kate and him being related through his great-great-great grandmother.

After they all have a good laugh, Janet and Scott stay for a while, and the four of them go over their plans for getting the Tinys out of Ireland.

It must have been around 4 in the morning, when everyone else had long since gone to bed, that Conor finally gets up enough nerve to ask her to come to America with them.

"That way you can see for yourself how they'll live -- how we all take care of them. You would get to meet my grandparents and see Tennessee. So what do you say?" he blurts out all at once.

She is beginning to like this O'Brien fellow more than she thought was possible in such a short time. She doesn't want any of them to go. *"Maybe going with them is not such a bad idea. After all, with Mom and Dad O'Rourke and now uncle Thomas all gone, I am alone here."*

"I need to think it over and get some sleep. Can I let you know in the morning?" she asks with a yawn.

He hasn't realized how late it is until she yawns. He yawns, too, and they both laugh.

"You're probably right. Let's get some rest, and we can talk some more tomorrow, or should I say today?"

Conor shows her to her room. As they say good night, he looks at her and says, "I know we only just met and hardly know each other, Katelyn, but I would like the opportunity to get to know you better."

"Me, too," she says, giving him a big sleepy smile. "Good night!" they both say at the same time.

After breakfast the next morning, they all go downstairs to the hangar. The guys are getting the van ready to go pick up all of the Tinys and bring them back to the hangar. The ladies are making sure the secret compartment in the airplane for the Tinys has plenty of water and prepared food for the trip.

When it looks like everything is in order, Katelyn goes over

186

to Conor and asks, "How many trips will you need to make in the van to get all of the Tinys and their things?"

Conor wipes off his hands, after checking the engines for the fourth time, puts the rag in his back pocket, and answers, "Well, after talking to Michael, we estimate it will take four to five trips -- three to bring most of the people and at least two loads for their belongings."

"What are you going to do about their belongings? It doesn't look like there is enough room in the plane for the people and their things," Kate notes.

"You're right! We had planned to ship their belongings as airfreight. But I must admit I hadn't given that part of the move much thought. We still have to get some crates or boxes for packing," answers Conor.

Katelyn considers possible options and then says, "I can make a call and have a truck full of crates here in about an hour."

"You can? Oh, yeah; I forgot we have a shipping company right near here. What a great idea. Thanks!"

So when Conor and the three Tinys leave in the van, Katelyn makes her call, and starts things rolling.

Michael had arranged for the Irish Tinys to meet them on a back road in the woods near the caves where they lived. The old dirt road is still a little muddy from the rain the night before. To keep from slipping and sliding, Conor has to drive slower than he would like.

Nearing the spot he had picked, Michael tells Conor where to stop. "There, after the big oak tree on the right," he points.

"Okay!" Conor answers, and he pulls over to stop a little past the big oak tree. Conor opens the side door and Michael jumps down to the ground. He looks around carefully, but doesn't see anyone. He is beginning to worry. "What can have gone wrong for them not to be here?" he asks. Suddenly, from up in the oak tree, he hears, "Well, if it isn't Michael Flanagan himself! Top of the morning, Michael!"

Michael looks up to see Shawn Dugan, the leader of their little group, smiling down at him from one of the branches.

Michael remarks, "And to you as well, Shawn Dugan. Are the others here with you?"

"Aye! They are, Lad; that they are!"

187

He puts his fingers to his lips and whistles, and the Irish Tinys begin appearing from behind every tree and bush. Men, women, and children -- all 200-plus of them -- are carrying as much as they can. As they all gather around the old oak tree, Conor gets out of the van, along with Eric and Bryan.

Eric comes around the front of the van, and as he sees all of them, he stops, and with tears in his eyes, lowers his head to say a soft prayer. "Thank You, Lord God, for these special gifts You now place in our care. I ask for Your help this day as we bring them to a new home in Tennessee. Amen!"

All the Tinys say, "Amen!"

When Shawn climbs down from the tree, Michael introduces him to Conor, Eric, and Bryan. Then Conor announces, "We must hurry and get them into the van!"

Chapter 23
Flight Home

Once everyone is on board, the plane takes off for Dublin. After landing at the Dublin airport, Ed and Conor park the HK500 as near to the customs office as possible. Ed had ordered an auxiliary power and air-conditioning unit to be attached to the plane. The test equipment needs to be kept running and must not overheat.

They have to wait about an hour before the customs and security personnel come out to go over the aircraft so they can get their clearance to depart Ireland. Finally a customs official arrives and comes aboard.

Ed spots him approaching, and takes out his checklist and is going over each item with Conor when the customs official enters the plane.

"Customs," is all the man says, and starts looking around at all the test equipment. He goes up to the front of the plane, where there are seats for six passengers right behind the cockpit and a built-in storage compartment stacked full of cables and spare parts for the test equipment.

The custom official looks around and asks Ed, "How many people?"

"Six, plus the pilot," Ed answers nonchalantly.

"Names, please," the customs official asks, just as the security officer arrives. As the officer boards, he brings along a large German shepherd. The officer looks at the customs official and then at Ed. Ed nods to the security officer, giving him the okay to start their search for drugs or weapons. Ed turns his attention back to the customs official, and he points to each person as he identifies them: "Scott Curtis, our chief engineer; Janet Cook, the corporation's CEO, and her daughter, Brittany; Heather Baryl, one of our employees; and Katelyn O'Rourke, our Ireland division CEO. This is Conor O'Brien, the owner, and myself, I'm--"

The man holds up his hand and announces, "We know who you are, Mr. Barns." He looks past Ed to the security officer who finishes his sweep of the plane and gives him the thumbs-up sign. "If you will sign here please, that will be all we need."

189

Ed signs the paper work. The security officer and the German shepherd leave the plane, followed shortly by the customs official. Ed closes the door and lets out a sigh. "Well, that was fast!" As he walks up to the cockpit, he tells everyone to get in his or her seats and buckle up. Ed gets in the pilot's seat, fires up the engines, and puts on his earphones. When he receives permission from the tower, he announces, "Hang on everyone; we're outta here!"

Ed pushes the throttles forward, and the jet moves down the runway like it was shot out of a cannon. At 150 knots, Ed rotates the nose, and they begin climbing into the clear blue sky. Once they reach cruising altitude, he sets the autopilot, turns to Conor in the co-pilot seat, and offers, "Why don't you take the controls for a while so I can have a break." Conor climbs into the pilot's seat and announces over the intercom, "Okay, Folks. You can get out of your seats if you want to and move around. Katelyn, if you would like to see the view from up here, please join me in the cockpit."

After Katelyn, Brittany, and Janet help show some of the Tinys where they can get refreshments and where the bathrooms are, Katelyn joins Conor up front.

When she enters, Conor points to the co-pilot's seat, and she very carefully climbs into it and sits down. She looks at the array of instruments in the cockpit, then out the window and down at the ocean. "How high are we?"

Conor points to the flat panel where the airspeed, altitude, and heading are displayed and tells her, "27,000 feet right now. Air Traffic Control will keep us at this altitude for about three more hours before we will start our descent into U.S. airspace."

Katelyn follows Conor when he points to the instruments and is still studying the flat panel. After a bit, she remarks, "We are traveling at 630 miles per hour on a heading of 265 degrees, and we are 2,659 miles from our destination, correct?"

Conor looks at her and beams! "You know how to fly?"

"No, but I have read about airplanes, and flying has been one of my interests since I was old enough to remember."

Conor turns in his seat to face her and with a big grin, "Wow, will you marry me?"

She throws her head back and laughs.

190

Back in the cabin, most of the Tinys are getting used to the plane. Some of them get out of their seats, move around, and talk to each other. For a while, Eric and Bryan help direct those who ask how to use the drink dispenser or where to find the restrooms.

Things settle down and Bryan is busy talking to some of the teenagers gathered around him. Eric is standing off to one side daydreaming when a young lady comes up to him. "I was wondering if one of you lads would mind showing me the rest of the plane?"

Eric, realizing this pretty young lady is talking to him, snaps out of his daydream, says, "I would be glad to show you around if you like. My name is Eric."

"I know, and he is your younger brother Bryan," she says. "I'm Andrea."

Just then Michael's younger sister runs up, "Can I come with you?"

"Eric, this is Michael's sister," Andrea says grudgingly, muttering to herself, "I found **this** one; go find your **own**."

"No! You can't come with us," she responds. "Go over there and find out what Bryan is doing with the other kids." She takes Eric's hand and heads for the open test panel leading out into the rest of the aircraft.

As Eric is taking Andrea around to see the different areas of the plane, they meet Shawn, who has been looking around by himself. Stopping next to Shawn, Andrea says as she points to the cockpit door, "Father, why don't you go look in there?"

Eric thinks to himself, *"So that's who she is -- the daughter of the Irish leader. Hmmm."*

Shawn reaches up to scratch his beard, nods, and heads for the front of the plane.

Andrea again takes Eric's hand and heads for the back of the plane, where they run into Michael and Drew, who also have been looking around. Michael introduces Drew to Eric. "Drew, I would like you to meet Eric, from America. He is the head scout. Eric, this is Drew, my intended."

"Intended?" questions Eric.

"I believe in America you would say fiancée," Andrea adds.

"Oh! Glad to meet you! Are you enjoying the flight?"

"Yes, very much!" Drew answers. "This is the first time I

have flown. As a matter of fact, this is the first time for all of us from Ireland. Is it not?" she questions as she looks at Michael.

"Yes, it is, and a very exciting thing, this flying!" comments Michael.

"Have you flown much before?" Drew asks Eric.

"No, the trip over here was my first time."

Andrea asks, "How long will it take for us to get there?"

After contemplating the question for a moment, Eris says, "I'm not sure, but it did take about six hours when we flew over here. So, I would assume it'd be about the same time for the return trip."

Turning to Michael and Drew, Eric adds, "Would you two like to join us in the back?" He points at the place where the test equipment cabinets end right before the aft bulkhead of the aircraft, leaving an open area of floor about 3 feet by 4 feet. "I saw a blanket up front not being used. I'll go get it and make a soft place to sit," he says as he runs off to get the blanket. While he is gone, Drew looks at Andrea.

"Eric is very nice, isn't he, Andrea?"

"Yes, he is -- and cute too!" and they laugh.

Eric returns with the blanket, and they all help fold it into a soft sitting area. The four of them sit down and start getting acquainted.

Meanwhile, Shawn Dugan has gone up to the front of the plane to see the cockpit. Entering, he sees all the instruments and switches, and exclaims, "How in the world do you know where to look or what to push?"

Conor looks around to see Shawn standing slightly behind and in-between the pilot and co-pilot seats. "Why don't you come on in and climb up in the co-pilot's seat with Katelyn and take a look around?"

"Yes! Come on up here with me and see this wonderful view."

"Now I don't want to be botheren ya, Lad, while you're driven this thing!" Shawn says.

"It's okay. You're not bothering me, and besides, I'm not driving right now anyway," Conor adds.

"You're not? Then who in blazes is?" questions Shawn.

"The auto pilot is doing all the flying right now. I'm just

192

keeping an eye on things," Conor answers.

"Auto pilot, you say, and just what is this auto pilot you be talking about? All I see is you two sitting here and neither one of you has hold of those steering things?" Shawn asks as he climbs up into the seat with Katelyn, turns around, and looks out the windshield just as a little cloud passes by. He looks out the side window and down at the sea below, then back at Conor and smiles. "Tis a wonder, this flying machine, is it not?"

"Aye, it is that," Katelyn says almost in a whisper.

Back in the seating area for the Tinys, Bryan has become the hero of the children, having shown them the goodies Conor, Scott, and the ladies had put onboard for all to enjoy. What the kids like most are the soft drinks. Root beer and orange turn out to be at the top of the request list, with candy coming in a close second. Their parents all choose sandwiches and milk or tea.

After filling the kids with goodies, he takes them to the back where he shows them a flat, box-like machine. When he pushes the button in the front, it opens up. What the children see inside are squares with letters and numbers on them. A few seconds later, pictures start appearing on the inside of the lid. All that can be heard from the kids are "Oohs" and "Aahs." Bryan is smiling from ear to ear. Next he pushes a few buttons and using the mouse pad, moves the cursor on top of a picture on the screen, and when he pushes another button, magic happens.

On the computer screen is a video of the Tinys' village near Jamestown, Tennessee, and greetings from the Tennessee Tinys. Bryan spends the next hour or so answering all their questions.

Soon it is time to start their approach into the Nashville airport.

Conor announces over the intercom, "Well, it's time to get ready to land. So, will you all please return to your seats? Scott, make sure we are all buttoned up and ready for Customs. Let's pray things go as smooth as they did in Ireland. Now, once we stop, everyone must be very quiet and still until I say it's okay." After his announcement, Ed takes over the controls and becomes very busy talking to traffic control and the airport tower for landing instructions.

The landing is smooth, and they are given permission to park

193

outside the Hawk Industries hangar to wait for Customs. Once the customs official boards, he looks over the paperwork from Ireland, checks the inside of the plane and everyone's ID, asks Ed to sign a form. Saying "Good evening," he is gone.

Janet had called ahead and arranged to have a motorhome waiting for them in the hangar. The plane is towed into the hangar and the hangar doors shut. By the time the ground crew secures the aircraft, it's getting late. Ed tells the ground crew they can go on home for the evening and that they will download all the results of the aircraft tests the next morning. Once the last of the crew leaves, it is dark outside, and the only ones left in the hangar are the seven Bigs and all the Tinys who are still waiting in the jet.

Scott, Brittany, and Janet check all offices to make sure they are empty. Conor and Katelyn start helping the Tinys transfer from the plane to the RV. Once they are all inside the RV, Scott, Janet, Brittany and Heather say their goodbyes. Ed, Conor and Katelyn drive the RV the 96 miles to Grandpa's house a few miles outside of Jamestown.

Pulling up to the house, Conor can see Grandpa and Grandma waiting on the front porch. When they come to a stop, Conor reaches up and turns on the interior lights and announces, "We are finally at your new home. Welcome to America!"

The Tinys are all whooping and hollering, and some are dancing with joy.

As they climb out of the RV, Graybeard is waiting for them with about 20 of the Tennessee Tinys ready to greet them and guide them to their new homes in the woods of Tennessee. Conor, seeing Graybeard and crew have everything under control, takes Katelyn by the hand and leads her up to the porch.

"Grandpa, Grandma -- I would like you to meet Katelyn O'Rourke from Ireland.

When they start in from the porch, Conor looks back over his shoulder as he and Katelyn head for the kitchen, "Oh, and by the way, she isn't really an O'Rourke; she's a Kelly!" And the two teens giggle.

194

Chapter 24
Ed Barns

The next morning all of the members of the Operation Transport team are at Conor's grandparents' house. Grandma has made a big breakfast for everyone. They all find a seat at the table, and before they dig in, Grandpa bows his head, and the others do the same -- all, that is, except for Ed, who has always felt uncomfortable when grace is said. But when Grandpa starts saying grace, Ed respectfully bows his head. Grandfather prays, "Heavenly Father, we give You thanks for Your bounty and ask You to bless the hands that prepared it. We thank You for Janet, Brittany, Scott and Ed, and our newest members, Katelyn and Heather, who You sent to help us in taking care of our little friends. We ask for Your guidance as we try to do each task set before us the best we can, remembering always that Your grace is sufficient! Amen!"

All through the meal, Ed keeps going over those words in his head. Although he has heard Grandpa pray before, he is a little curious and confused about what was meant by "Your grace is sufficient."

He usually feels uncomfortable and uneasy around religious nuts -- what he used to call people like this, the ones who read the Bible, pray, and things like that. But here, it's different. Here he feels a kind of peacefulness and a sense of being right at home.

Ed had realized after only a few days that Conor, Scott, and Janet were Christians. Strangely, he hadn't been put off by it. Despite what he had been led to believe in his upbringing, no one here shoved a Bible in his face or called him a sinner! On the contrary, they had accepted him from the beginning, treating him like family, and he liked that. He liked it a lot!

Later, after everyone had pitched in and helped Grandma with cleaning up the kitchen, Ed finds Grandpa out on the front porch all by himself, sitting in his favorite chair. Ed joins him and, after sitting down in one of the rockers, asks, "Can I ask you a question about what you said at the table?"

Grandpa looks over at him with that smile of his that set people at ease. "Sure, Ed -- shoot."

Ed looks down at his hands in his lap, "I don't know much

about the Bible, and I wasn't taught about God and such..." He hesitates.

"Go on, Son, what's on your mind?"

"Well, when you said, 'Your grace is sufficient,' what did you mean by that?"

"The scriptures tell us we're saved by the grace of God. When Jesus died on the cross for all our sins -- past, present, and future -- that was enough. The debt of our sins was paid for. We only need to confess that we have sinned, accept God's gift of forgiveness, and ask the Lord to come into our hearts! In other words, through God's grace, the work on the cross is sufficient! We are forgiven!" Grandpa proclaims.

Deep in thought for some time, Ed finally says, "Thank you for explaining. I never heard it put like that before."

Grandpa continues, "Let me paraphrase it this way: He knows where you've been, and He knows what you've done, and He still loves you and wants you to come home!"

Ed sits on the porch with a tear in his eye.

Grandpa gets up. "When you're ready, Son, just talk to Him. He knows your heart!"

Grandpa starts to go in the house but stops when Ed tells him, "I don't believe God can forgive me!"

Grandpa comes back over and places a hand on Ed's shoulder, "Son, He already has! You just need to accept His forgiveness."

"But I've done terrible things!" Ed confesses to Grandpa. "How can He forgive me? I'm afraid He won't forgive what I've had to do!"

Sitting back down and after a short, silent prayer, Grandpa tells him, "Fear of God is a good thing. It shows that you respect God as being the almighty. But He is also a loving God, the One who created us and wants our fellowship with Him. You see, Ed, God is able to forgive and to forget our sins. We try to forget things, but we cannot, but God can! Whatever you did, God will forgive!"

Grandpa reaches over and picks up his Bible and opens it, and after searching through a few verses, "Ah! Here it is in Isaiah. Here's what God has to say about your sins, Isaiah 1:18.

"'Come now, let us reason together,' said the Lord. 'Though

your sins are like scarlet, they shall be white as snow; though they are red as crimson, they shall be like wool.'"

Ed considers what Grandpa had said for a while. Grandpa just sits and waits for him. Finally, Ed asks, "What do I need to do or say?"

Grandpa answers, "That's the easy part, Son. It's called the sinner's prayer, and it goes something like this, "Lord, I have sinned. Please forgive me and come into my heart!'"

Ed lowers his head and quietly asks God to forgive him and to let him find the peace he sees in these wonderful people.

197

Chapter 25
Free-Dome

Three months later in Tennessee...

The siren blares, and it can be heard all over town. People are running everywhere, trying to get to the safety of the buildings. Once inside, window shutters are being slammed and locks are being thrown on the heavy doors. On the outskirts of town is what looks like a military compound with four buildings and a sign over the gate that reads "Rangers." The sign on the first building reads "Barracks" and the second, "Headquarters." The third building is the "Dining Hall" and the fourth is the "Command Center."

About 30 young men all dressed alike come running from different parts of the compound to fall into formation in front of the barracks. The men all wear form-fitting camouflage uniforms with knee-high, lace-up moccasins. Around each waist is a belt that holds two pouches and a large knife. On their backs each has a bow and a quiver of arrows. Each man wears his hair differently – some have long hair tied back in ponytails, others have shoulder- length hair, and some have their heads shaved. Every ranger has a communications headset with a microphone.

The door to the headquarters building flies open. Standing in the doorway is the captain dressed the same as the others, except a knife, two pouches, and four smoke grenades hang from his belt. His long hair is dark red and tied back in a ponytail.

"Squads four and five secure the town. No one on the streets until we sound the all-clear!" he commands as he descends the stairs. Ranger squads four and five break formation and head for three vehicles parked next to the main gate, and quickly they are on their way

"Communications, give me an update," the captain speaks into his headset.

"Communications, here, Cap. We have three high-flying intruders coming in from the east of town, flying fast and erratic. Over."

"Copy that. Keep me advised if there's any change in direction, Ranger 1 out,"

"Will do, Cap; out" is the reply.

198

"Remaining squads mount up!" the captain orders.

The rangers climb onto a large truck with a flatbed. The driver is already behind the wheel as the captain jumps in, "Head to the east of town!"

The rangers drive around the outside of town, take a right, and head due east past a row of homes. They haven't gone far when the captain orders, "Stop!" He jumps out of the truck and over his shoulder commands, "Rangers, dismount!" The men seem to move as one, jumping down and forming into squads.

"Squad leaders front and center!"

Three men step forward in responses to his command. "The three of you are the only ones to fire and only on my signal, is that clear? I want everyone else notched and ready in case this thing goes sour."

"Yes, Sir" they reply.

"We don't have much time. Second squad: Take the left of the field. Third squad: Go to the right. First: Spread out in the center. Everyone at 20-foot intervals and stay alert! Move out!" the captain orders.

Moments later, the captain hears in his ear peace, "All squads in position, Sir!"

"Copy that," he replies.

His eyes are watching the sky to the east. Then he sees them. Three dots getting bigger and bigger the closer they get. It takes him only a few seconds to determine what they are. Wasps! With at least 3-inch wingspans, the wasps are a quarter the size of his Tiny rangers.

"Here they come. Stand by!" the captain says as he pulls two grenades from his belt. These are not ordinary smoke grenades; they are filled with a chemical that attracts insects.

"I hope the chemical works on wasps like Conor said it would!" he says as he pulls the pins and tosses the two canisters as close to the center of the field as he can. After two loud pops, green smoke begins to stream out from both of the canisters. The reactions from the wasps take only moments. It is so fast it seems unreal. Sensing the chemical, they zero in on the field and dive with lightning speed, landing softly in the smoke.

The captain whispers into his mic, "Squad leaders, target the nearest wasp to your position. On my mark."

199

He watches as the wasps search the ground for whatever the chemical made them think is there. "Fire!" Three arrows shoot into the field, with two of them striking their targets. Instantly the creatures go stiff and collapse where they are. At the last moment, the third wasp changes position, and the arrow glances off the remaining insect's hard head! The wasp spreads its wings and launches into the air, but its speed is no match for the fourth arrow.

The captain, sighting along his arrow's shaft, fires the instant he realized the other arrow missed its target. His arrow flashes across the field and is embedded with a thud into the body of the wasp. The insect doesn't get more than 6 feet off the ground. The captain moves his thumb to the back of the bow and presses a button. Instantly the wasp goes stiff as the electric shock arches through its body. The wasp drops to the ground with a loud thump, and a cloud of dust swirls into the air.

There is silence for a moment, then, "Ranger 1 to second squad -- advance and confirm the kills!"

With its arrows at the ready, the second squad approaches the center of the field. "Kills confirmed, Cap."

"Ranger 1 to Ranger team -- great job, Guys! Fall out, and get this mess cleaned up."

A shout of joy goes up from all the rangers!

"Ranger 1 to command center. Sound the all-clear!"

"Yes, Sir" is the reply. A moment later, the siren can be heard once more in the distance.

It doesn't take long for the rangers to pile the dead wasps onto the flatbed truck and strap them down.

"Ranger 1 to squad leaders two and four -- meet me by the truck!"

In a few moments, the squad leaders report to the captain.

"Eric, I need you to take second squad to the outer perimeter and find the breech! Bryan, you do the same with the fourth squad on the inner perimeter! We must find out how they got in. I want 30-minute COM checks with the control center, and as soon as the opening is located, we will send out a repair crew. Stay on station until the repairs are complete."

"Yes, Sir."

With their new orders, the leaders are off to gather their squads and head out.

Over the COM link the captain announces, "Everybody on your toes and remember this is a big day. We have a very special guest coming this afternoon, so look sharp. We don't want any more intruders today!"

Later that day...

Eric reports the breach repaired, and the squad is returning to the compound. Bryan reports in with the captain, and his team goes to the dining hall to get some lunch. The truck with second squad pulls into the compound. Eric jumps out and comes over to the captain.

"Well, did you find where the wasps got in?" asks the captain.

"Yes, Sir! One of the double-door hatches came loose, and they managed to pry a hatch open. I have the maintenance team, along with my squad, going over every one of the hatches now, and so far everything is okay!" answers Eric.

"How long will it take to complete their inspection?"

"They will be done way before our guests arrive," Eric assures, and continues, "So there's plenty of time for me to polish your brass, clean your boots, and press your pants, Your Lordship!"

"Now cut that out, Eric; you know I still believe you should be the captain, not me!

Eric is doubled over as he laughs so hard at Michael's red face.

"Not me!" Eric exclaims. "You're older than me, remember. Besides, now you get to worry about inspections, intruders, and all that. I only have my squad to worry about."

"Well, next year when you take over, I get to sit back and watch you worry!" Michael says.

Mike and Eric have become the best of friends after working together in Ireland and now here in Tennessee.

The responsibility of keeping the town and its residences safe and secure has fallen on the two of them. Once the Irish Tinys arrived and the additional housing was built, their quaint little village soon became a thriving settlement. Working together, they combined the scouts from America and the hunters from Ireland into a unit patterned after the old Texas Rangers. With a captain as the leader of the group, squads, and squad leaders, Michael was voted in as their first captain.

"Okay, go ahead and get something to eat and get back to getting ready for our guest."

"Yes, My Captain." Eric smirks with a deep bow, and as he turns to leave, he jumps to one side just in time to make Mike miss his kick to Eric's behind.

"Ha, ha! Missed again," Eric taunts as he runs off to the dining hall.

Later that same day, the guests begin arriving at Grandpa's house for the special celebration.

Conor, Brittany, and Katelyn had driven in the night before. Scott and Janet are due anytime. Ed and Heather are just pulling in to park, near the front of the house, when Conor's cell phone rings. He and Grandpa are sitting at the kitchen table having coffee. He pulls his phone out of his pocket and sees a text message. Touching the screen, he reads, "Just turned into the driveway."

Grandpa looks at him with concern, "Anything wrong, Grandson?"

"Nope, it's from Scott; they're on the driveway. Should be

202

here in about three minutes if they don't fall into one of those ruts and disappear!" Conor remarks, and they both laugh.

"Grandpa, are you ever going to get those ruts repaired and the driveway paved?"

"Nope! Those ruts are a great deterrent to looky-loos and nosy people. They stay! And besides, Grandma and I only go to town about once a month. We're never in a big hurry like you younguns are."

Just then Ed and Heather come in. "Good morning, everyone!" they say as they come over and sit down at the table with Conor and Grandpa. "How's everyone today?"

Grandpa smiles and answers, "If we were any more blessed, we'd have to be in Heaven! And how are you two?"

"Good and looking forward to today's gathering," Ed replies and then stops for a minute before saying, "You know, I've never seen the Tinys' village."

"Well, we can fix that just as soon as the rest of the guests arrive."

Grandma and Katelyn come into the kitchen. When they see Ed and Heather, they both come over and give them hugs.

"Would you like some coffee or tea?" Katelyn asks, even before Grandma can get her mouth open.

"Coffee would be great," Ed answers.

Heather asks, "I don't want to be a bother, but might I have a spot of tea?"

Grandma watches as Katelyn goes over to the cabinet, gets cups, removes the pot from the coffee maker, pours Ed a cup, and hands it to him. Then she puts on a pot of water for tea. Grandma smiles and is pleased that Katelyn feels so comfortable in their home. *"That's a good sign,"* she thinks to herself.

Finally, Scott and Janet arrive and are greeted with hugs and handshakes all around.

Scott announces, "Well, is everyone ready to go see our handiwork?"

"Yes!" everyone responds.

All of them head out the back door and into the woods. They travel the same path Conor, Brittany, and Janet had taken so many months ago when they first met the Tennessee Tinys. Now they are going to see all the Tinys together, at last!

After they travel a little more than a quarter of a mile, they come to the same rocks Grandpa used to open the sticker bushes before. He does the honors again, and they all enter.

Conor steps forward and calls out in the direction of the line of trees. "Okay, Michael, show yourselves."

With that, suddenly around the largest of the trees appears what looks like a glass dome. Conor turns to the group and announces, "Welcome to *Free-Dome*!"

Inside the dome, everyone can see the Tinys smiling and waving up at their friends. The dome completely encloses the Tinys' village.

This time it is Ed who says, "Wow! That is impressive, Scott -- nice work!" Graybeard, Eric, and Michael, along with Shawn Dugan, come out of the dome to greet the group. They all go over to the far side of the clearing where Grandpa had placed a picnic table and benches so the Big people would have a place to sit when they visited. The Tinys are all sitting on the table with the group of Bigs on the benches at either side.

After all had exchanges their greetings, Janet asks, "Well, Mr. Dugan, what do you and our Irish friends make of all this?"

Shawn looks over at Janet and answers, "Me name's Shawn, Lass -- not Mr. Dugan." He adds, with a big grin on his face, "And we thank the Lord for all of you and this marvelous contraption Scott and Conor made to keep us all safe here in beautiful Tennessee!"

Grandpa and Grandma look at each other and then around at this group, made up of big and little people, all gathered together. Finally, they feel their Tiny friends will be well cared for and safe.

Copyright 2015 Gary E. Reavis, Sr.

Names of American little people:

There are many legions, tales and stories told among the Native American Indians of little people. Here is a list of some of the Native American Nations and their names for the little people.

Little People Names - Nations:

Ircinraq - Yup'ik
Ishigaq - Inuit
Jogahoh - Iroquois
Mannegishi - Cree
Memegwesi - Anishinaabe
Memegawensi - Anishinaabe
Memengweshii - Anishinaabe
Pa'iins - Anishinaabe
Nimerigar - Shoshone
Nirumbee or Awwakkulé - Crow
Nunnupi - Comanche
Pukwudgie - Wampanoag
Yehasuri - Catawba
Yunwi Tsundi - Cherokee

The Tennessee Tinys series of books:
Book #1 - Tinys
Book #2 - Giants - release date - 2016
Book #3 - Troubles - release date - 2016